Justin stepped outside, the others following. They stared in awe.

The ruined tower stood at the centre of a plain of glazed, ruby-red rock, as smooth as marble. In the night sky, feathery clouds were lit by moonshine. The moon itself was a pale body streaked with scarlet veins: it seemed to stare at them like a bloodshot eye.

Had there been any lingering doubts that they were no longer on Earth, these were dispelled by the sight of the moon. They had stepped through the mirror into another world entirely.

# THE TWILIGHT REALM

*Christopher Carpenter*

ARROW BOOKS

Arrow Books Limited
17–21 Conway Street, London W1P 6JD

An imprint of the Hutchinson Publishing Group

London Melbourne Sydney Auckland
Johannesburg and agencies throughout
the world

First published in Great Britain by Arrow Books 1985

© Christopher Carpenter 1985

Set in Baskerville by
Photobooks (Bristol) Ltd

Made and printed in Great Britain by
Anchor Brendon Limited, Tiptree, Essex

ISBN 0 09 938560 0

*To Faith*
*Instigator & Inspiration*

# Contents

# Prologue

Friday night was games night.

Downstairs in the cellar, Teresa and Willie had already arrived. Paul Kinnersley was in the kitchen above his uncle's shop, making coffee for his friends. It was approaching seven o'clock, and soon Kate and Justin would arrive and their numbers would be complete. Every week the five of them gathered in the cellar to fight wizards and witches and weird creatures of every description.

It was a bright July evening, but across the landing a light was burning inside his uncle's bedroom, as if he had drawn the curtains against the sun. Paul went to the door and tapped on it. There was no response. He tapped again.

'Yes?' Ivor Kinnersley said in a distracted tone.

'I'm making coffee,' Paul said. 'Do you want any?'

'No. Not now.'

Paul retreated back to the kitchen, knowing from his uncle's tone of voice that he did not want to be disturbed. Over the past year his uncle Ivor had become increasingly solitary and eccentric, locking himself inside his room for hours at a time. Paul knew that he had become interested in spiritualism and

9

often conducted one-man seances in the hope of contacting his dead wife; sometimes Paul could hear him mumbling unintelligibly to himself behind his locked door. At other times a distant look would appear on his face, almost as if he was seeing the world for the first time. Paul had begun to wonder if his uncle was going senile, and he didn't know what to do.

He put the coffees on a tray with a plate of biscuits and carried them down the narrow stairway. His uncle's shop, which was called Enigma Variations, sold everything from jigsaw puzzles and sets of Monopoly to Rubik cubes and the latest computer video games. It lay in a Soho sidestreet, sandwiched between a kebab house and a seedy bookshop. His uncle had owned the place for over twenty years, and had doggedly resisted lucrative offers from developers who wanted to buy up the shop and turn it into a sex club or a massage parlour. The Kinnersley family had lived in that part of London for generations, and they had no desire to move elsewhere.

A wide-angle mirror high in one corner of the shop gave Paul's reflection a swollen-headed appearance; he wore Levis and a dark blue shirt. Today was actually his twenty-first birthday, though he had told no one about it and his uncle had evidently forgotten. Paul hadn't liked to remember any of his birthdays since the death of his cousin Brian.

Paul descended a second flight of stairs to the cellar. Willie and Teresa were already sitting at the table, discussing the progress of the latest adventure in which they were engaged. Willie, tall and hugely built, was still wearing his donkey jacket, while Teresa, short and plump, was dressed in denim dungarees over an army-surplus shirt. They were

10

studying their character sheets and comparing notes: when they had adjourned the previous week, Justin had succeeded in trapping both of them in a labyrinth where they were under threat from a fire-breathing minotaur.

'Coffee's up,' Paul said, putting the tray down on the table. He had made five cups in anticipation of Kate and Justin's arrival.

Teresa took hers, putting three spoonfuls of sugar into it.

'How's work?' Paul asked her.

'Hectic as usual,' she told him. 'I spent most of the afternoon dyeing a seventeen-year-old boy's hair all the colours of the rainbow. He's an apprentice with a firm of accountants.'

'That should go down well in the office.'

'That's just the idea. He hates the job and wants to give his boss the excuse to sack him. How's business?'

'Slow but steady. I think my uncle's grooming me *in absentia* to take over the shop full time. He hasn't emerged from his room all day.'

'*In absentia*. Sounds like you've been boning up on your Hindustani again.'

Paul smiled and reddened a little; the others often teased him for his academic leanings. They were all old classmates, and none of them had been able to understand why he had not gone on to university but had left school after passing his 'A' Levels to work in his uncle's shop. He had a very good reason, in fact, but it was not something he felt he could explain to anyone.

'Help yourself to the biscuits,' he said to Teresa.

'Not for me,' she replied, patting her midriff. 'I'm stuffed.'

Teresa had come directly from her parents' house

11

after polishing off a large plate of fish and chips followed by a jam doughnut and a choux bun. She was squat and freckled, with a cheerful disposition and a sweet tooth that was irresistible. She ate with gusto because she knew there was no point in doing anything else; even if she dieted and took up regular exercise she could never become one of those beautiful, willowy creatures who adorned shampoo advertisements or modelled designer jeans. She could never be beautiful, no matter what she did, because she was broad and large-boned and had a nose which spread too far over her face and ears which jutted out just a little bit too much for comfort. But she tried to be philosophical about her shortcomings, and usually maintained an air of bluff good humour. At the salon she was popular with the customers, who generally preferred her relaxed line in chatter to the more aloof elegance of the other two assistants.

'You sure I can't tempt you?' Paul asked.

'You could. But I just don't have the room. Besides, I think Willie's cornered the market.'

Willie was cramming chocolate digestives into his mouth, but he immediately stopped, looking guilty, and made to push the plate across the table to them. In his haste he fumbled, and the plate was knocked to the floor.

Willie sprang up, wanting to recover the spilled biscuits. There was a crunch and a cracking sound: he had trod on the plate and broken it.

He stared glumly and helplessly at Paul.

'Don't worry,' Paul said. 'These things happen.'

He fetched a dustpan and brush from upstairs. Willie insisted on clearing up the mess himself; the broken plate and biscuits were dumped into a waste-paper bin under the table. Willie still looked abashed.

12

'It was only a plate,' Teresa told him. 'It's not the end of the world.'

Willie simply shrugged awkwardly.

Paul, always uncomfortable with other people's embarrassment, said, 'How's your mum?' He wanted to take Willie's mind off the incident.

'She's all right,' Willie said.

'Any luck on the job front?'

'Yeah. I've got an audition with the Royal Ballet.'

It was one of his few jokes, and it reflected a certain sense of desperation. Willie had been unemployed for most of the time since leaving school at seventeen, managing to get only temporary menial jobs, none of which had lasted more than a few months. It was almost a year since he had last worked, but every week he doggedly visited the Job Centre and was tireless in attending interviews in the hope that someone would take him on.

Willie knew what the problem was: he was big and looked dumb and couldn't always get his words out as quickly as he'd like. Jobs were at a premium for people of his age, and if you were quick-thinking and smooth-talking you stood a better chance at interviews. But he had always taken his time over what he had to say, with the result that most people took him for an idiot. Sometimes when he told them that he had five 'O' levels they'd give him a look of disbelief and at that moment he'd know there was no chance of him getting the job. He'd never claim to be a genius; but he wasn't exactly stupid either.

Willie was tall enough to have hit his head on many lintels, and he habitually ducked when entering a room. He had reached six feet at the age of fourteen and had continued growing – and broadening – until he had attained the proportions of a boxer or

13

wrestler. He always walked with a slight stoop, as if to deny his height.

At school Willie had been a star rugby player, the ball nestling easily in his large hands, his powerful body making him an asset in any scrum. He had played prop forward for London Schools in several regional tournaments and had acquitted himself well. He'd often reflected that if he'd been born in America he probably would have got a football scholarship and would now be at university, with lots of girls cheering him on every time he stepped out on the field. Instead he was stuck in a poky flat in the middle of London, with no job and a bedridden mother to look after. The only way of making ends meet was by not doing anything that cost money. His weekly visits to Paul's were the sum total of his social life.

But Willie wasn't bitter; he didn't blame anyone. Times were tough and there were a lot of people worse off than him. At least he had real friends in Paul and Teresa and Kate and Justin. The five of them had all been close at school, and they'd stuck together afterwards. He also had his mother, who hadn't been well for years and who depended on him to look after her. He prepared her meals, did the washing, kept the house clean, and so on; it made him feel useful.

The doorbell rang at that moment. Paul went to answer it.

Through the glass he could see that it was Kate, wearing a summer dress of buttercup yellow. When he opened the door he saw that she was breathless and a little flustered.

'Is Justin here?' she asked.

'Not yet,' Paul said.

'Have you heard from him?'

14

Paul shook his head. 'Is something wrong?'

'No, nothing. It's just that I was supposed to meet him at six outside the Swiss Centre in Leicester Square. I waited over half an hour, but he didn't show up. I thought he might have come straight here.'

'You know Justin – he's always late.'

Kate nodded, trying to appear unconcerned. But her words belied her expression: 'I haven't seen him for three days.'

'Perhaps he's been busy. Hasn't he got exams?'

'Not until September. He hardly ever rings me.'

Justin was studying economics at Kingston Polytechnic, having given up his job as a computer programmer a year previously. Kate and Justin had been going out together ever since their last year at school, but it hadn't been plain sailing. He was often late for their dates and on occasions had not shown up at all. With his handsome looks and his fast line in patter, Justin had always been popular with women, and it was Kate's secret fear that he was dating other girls when she wasn't around.

Privately she felt that she was as much to blame for Justin's offhand attitude towards her as was Justin himself. Her trouble was that if she was concerned or anxious she couldn't help showing it. And Justin took advantage of this, playing on her insecurity and her faithfulness towards him. Paul had often counselled her that she should try to cultivate more independence and detachment in order to whet Justin's appetite for her; he would tell her that she was attractive and personable and ought to have more confidence in herself. She knew he was right and she tried her best; but where Justin was concerned she simply couldn't keep her feelings in check.

Kate Hastings was a slim and pretty young woman

with a head of long, honey-blonde hair. She worked as a staff nurse at the Charing Cross Hospital in Hammersmith, and in her professional duties she was an efficient and able worker, showing none of the self-doubts which she exhibited in her private life. She had dealt single-handed with cardiac arrests and epileptic attacks, and was not averse to disputing a doctor's diagnosis or arguing her case with a sister. She enjoyed her work, was quietly confident of her abilities and determined to make a success of her career. It was a source of some irritation to her that she was not able to display the same confidence in her relationship with Justin.

'Teresa and Willie are here,' Paul said. 'I'm sure Justin won't be long.'

Directly overhead, Paul could hear his uncle shuffling around like an old man. Ivor Kinnersley was in his late forties, but he looked twenty years older; the loss of his son Brian and then his wife had taken its toll on him. His hair had turned almost white and his face was haggard. Paul could scarcely look at him without feeling a pang of guilt. He blamed himself.

Paul and Kate went downstairs. The cellar was bare and unfurnished apart from the table and five chairs; its plastered walls were cracked and grimy with neglect. It was windowless, lit by a single bare electric bulb which hung from the ceiling. The place had once been used as a storeroom for old furniture, but now all that remained was a large and ancient gilt-edged mirror which was propped up against a wall. The mirror had once stood in Ivor Kinnersley's bedroom, but he had banished it there after his wife's death. The cellar's air of abandonment provided just the right kind of atmosphere for their games, making

16

it seem as if they were huddled in some secret chamber.

While they waited for Justin to arrive, they chatted about the current adventure – a quest to recover the Wand of the Worldmage which had been stolen by a villainous hobgoblin. The game had been devised by Justin, and they called it Axes and Enchanters, reflecting the brutal and sorcerous dangers which they faced on their quest. Justin was the guiding force behind the adventure, planning the campaign and constantly presenting the others with threats and dilemmas on which the very lives of their fantasy characters might depend.

The five of them had become interested in role-playing games during their final year at school. At first they had played games which were already on the market; but later Justin had begun to adapt their formats to create his own versions of them. At the outset of each game they threw dice to establish what abilities their particular characters would possess – how much strength, dexterity, weapons proficiency, magical power and so on – and then set off on their quest across Justin's fantasy domain, which had its own rules and laws that had to be obeyed. Justin would confront them with situations, and they would have to choose which strategy to adopt. Should they enter a closed room or bypass it? Accept the advice of a stranger met along the way, or treat him with suspicion? Attack a dragon or make a prudent retreat? The wrong decision might deplete them of vital stamina points or drain their magical abilities to the extent where they would be defenceless against the next threat. And if that happened, their characters would 'die', and they would be eliminated from the game.

17

Paul's character in the current campaign was a cleric whom he suspected would not last long in the savage and mystical realm through which he was travelling. And yet Paul was fond of the cleric, whom he had managed to instil with a certain shrewdness and a wry sense of humour. These were qualities which Paul would have liked to have possessed in real life; part of the fun in role-playing games was that you could become the kind of character you were too timid or hidebound to be in the ordinary world. The others were warriors, assassins and thieves – much better equipped to survive the quest. But Justin, as the Domain Master, liked to keep them constantly under threat; he was especially fond of nine-foot trolls who were immune to magic and would not hesitate to cleave human heads from their shoulders.

Though he enjoyed the games, Paul often felt hurt and even resentful whenever one of his characters was killed off. It was as if someone almost real had died, and it always made him feel that Justin had done him a positive injury. Then he would begin to brood, thinking that since he provided the location for their games, he should also have the chance to develop a fantasy world and act as its master. But Justin wouldn't have allowed that; he liked to be in charge, and everyone was accustomed to letting him have his way.

Paul could see that Kate still looked anxious, though she was pretending otherwise. There were times when he felt like hitting Justin for treating her with such indifference. But Paul would have given anything to be in Justin's position: he had admired Kate from afar ever since the fourth form at school, and his longing for her had not lessened one whit since then. Of course he had never mustered the courage to tell her as much; she had always been surrounded by admiring boys with far more confidence and personality than he had; and when Justin had finally got her in his clutches he knew that there was no hope for him.

'It's half past seven,' Teresa said. 'I don't think Justin's coming.'

'How are we going to play without him?' asked Kate, though the game was in fact the last thing on her mind at that monent.

'He'll be here,' said Willie. 'Justin never misses.'

'Well,' said Teresa. 'He'll just have to miss out on our little celebration.'

'What celebration?' asked Paul.

Teresa reached into her canvas shoulder-bag and withdrew a squat box.

'Your twenty-first birthday, of course,' she said.

The box contained a small cake covered with white icing, with 21 TODAY! inscribed on it in red and a single candle at its centre.

'I didn't think anyone knew,' Paul said.

'Kate remembered,' Teresa told him, 'so you can blame her.'

Kate was smiling faintly. 'I remembered you told me it was the day after American Independence Day.'

Paul recalled the occasion. He had been consoling Kate when Justin had failed to remember her birthday one year and had suggested that she tie her birthday to a well-known calendar date so that Justin would have no excuse for forgetting in future.

He fetched a knife from the kitchen upstairs, and the cake was promptly cut into five segments. Teresa, Willie and Kate then gave a cracked but hearty rendition of 'Happy Birthday to You' while Paul did his best to hide his embarrassment with a smile. He had never liked being the centre of attention, but he was pleased that Kate had remembered the date.

They had just finished singing when the doorbell rang again.

'I'll get it,' Kate said immediately.

She climbed the stairs, telling herself that she was going to be calm and composed and relaxed and offhand. But as soon as she saw that it was indeed Justin, she felt only a profound relief.

Justin was standing outside the door with his hands tucked into a brown leather jacket, a document wallet under his arm; the wallet contained the rules of the game and a list of spells which could be used by the players. Justin was a slim young man, no taller than she, with blond hair and striking blue eyes.

'What happened?' Kate said immediately. 'I waited for you for over half an hour.'

'The bus was late,' Justin replied, stepping into the shop. 'Then three came along together. It's bloody typical.'

There was no hint of apology in his tone, nor did he do any more than glance at her. Kate felt the familiar stirrings of anxiety that he might have been seeing some other woman.

'Are the others here?' Justin asked.

She nodded, looking somewhat doleful.

'What's up?' Justin asked.

'I was hoping we might have had some time to ourselves,' she said. 'I've hardly seen anything of you in the last few weeks.'

She hated the faintly whining note which she heard in her voice, but she couldn't help herself.

'The bus was late,' Justin said again. 'I can't be

held responsible for the inefficiencies of London Transport.'

'So nothing's wrong?'

'Wrong? What's supposed to be wrong?' He studied her. 'Do you think maybe I've been sneaking off to see someone else?'

'Have you?'

He grinned. 'I'm having this mad passionate affair with a bus conductress. Pink toenails and hands all dirty with the money.'

Kate did not smile. It was impossible to get him to take her anxiety seriously. He either laughed it off or complained that she was being neurotic. But for the past month or so she'd been feeling that Justin would prefer to do anything but spend time alone with her.

'Come on,' Justin said, moving towards the stairway. 'I want to see if I can kill off a few of you this evening.'

Kate watched him descend the stairs before following him. As he reached the bottom, something fell out of his jacket pocket. Kate knelt to retrieve it as Justin entered the cellar, unaware that he had lost anything.

It was a small black-and-white passport photograph of a pretty, dark-haired young woman. On the back was written: *To Justin. Lots of love and kisses. Lucy.*

Kate stared at the photograph for several seconds, her face growing hot. She could scarcely believe that her worst fears had been confirmed. She was tempted to snatch at the notion that Justin had simply been sent the photograph by some secret admirer whom he had not met or was not attracted to. But the photograph was crumpled at its edges, as if it had been in his pocket for some time. As if he could not bear to be parted from it. And the message on its back was final proof that he was seeing someone else.

Kate's immediate instinct was to follow him into the cellar, confront him with the photograph and demand an explanation. But she managed to stop herself, and instead stood at the bottom of the shadowy stairway until the blush had faded from her face. She couldn't bear to risk a scene in front of the others; she would have to bide her time until she and Justin were alone. Closing her left hand around the photograph, she entered the cellar.

'What's the cake in aid of?' Justin was asking Teresa. There was one piece left on the plate.

'It's Paul's twenty-first birthday,' Teresa said. 'That piece is yours.'

'Key of the door, eh?' Justin said to Paul. 'Think your uncle'll let you stay out after midnight now?'

'That's eighteen,' Paul said. 'You're behind the times.'

'So's your uncle. Didn't he keep you in short trousers until you were fourteen?'

Paul smiled diffidently. 'I'm just grateful he didn't make me wear a blazer with padded shoulders as well.'

Justin was stung. A blazer with padded shoulders was precisely what his own father had made him wear in his first few years at secondary school. His father was a strapping man and he liked to think that Justin would develop into a colossus as well. But he had remained lean and short for his age, so his father had made him wear built-up shoes, thick sweaters and all the rest of it. It was not something Justin liked to be reminded of.

'At least I had the backbone to hang it on,' he said to Paul.

There was a note of real bitterness in his voice, and Paul did not react.

Justin's anger quickly evaporated; he felt that he had won on points. He was invariably tempted to bait Paul because he knew that Paul, for all his shyness, was capable of the snappy comeback on occasions. But Justin was always determined to have the final word, even if it meant resorting to a direct insult. He wasn't going to let anyone get the better of him.

Paul looked uncomfortable, while the others were pretending to ignore the whiff of malice in the air.

'I think it's time we got started,' Teresa said.

'We already have,' Justin remarked with heavy irony.

Just then they heard footsteps descending the stairs, followed by a tapping on the door.

'It's open,' Paul called.

There was a further knock.

Paul shrugged and went to open the door, wondering if his uncle was becoming a little deaf in his premature old age. When he opened the door he saw that his uncle had a strange, remote expression on his face. It was an expression which Paul had seen on other occasions, as if he was not fully in touch with the real world.

Ivor Kinnersley moved slowly into the room, clutching a white plastic carrier-bag to his midriff.

'Good evening everyone,' he said without actually looking at anyone direct.

Paul felt uneasy. It was his uncle's voice, but somehow it didn't sound like him at all.

Ivor Kinnersley sat down in Paul's chair and studied the others without speaking, a vague smile on his face. Paul's embarrassment was growing by the second, and he said, 'Is there something you want?'

His uncle shook his head. 'I've brought something for you.' He put the carrier-bag on the table. 'Every week you gather down here to play your games. I know you enjoy yourselves, so I decided to give you something to increase your pleasure. I've made some characters for you.'

He rummaged in the carrier-bag and produced, one by one, five figurines carved in wood which he stood on the table. They were about nine inches high and very life-like; each had been painted so that the smallest detail of its clothing and weaponry was revealed.

Paul and the others stared at the figurines in wonderment. Paul himself had never known his uncle to possess any interest in let alone talent for wood-carving, and yet he must have spent the last several months sculpting the incredibly intricate figures and then painting them while closeted in his bedroom. Only the heads were devoid of detail: they had merely the crude outlines of features, as though awaiting the imprint of a real face.

The room was silent and everyone's eyes were on the figurines. Ivor Kinnersley picked up the largest of the five, a huge, muscle-bound man who held a large hammer of grey stone or metal. He wore a brown leather jerkin over tan breeches with studded black leather boots which matched the belt at his waist. The hammer was large, with a long thonged handle, but he seemed to wield it easily and radiated an air of immense physical strength and power.

'This one is a warrior,' Ivor Kinnersley said, his eyes on Justin. 'He carries an iron hammer which glows hot when battle-lust overtakes him. He has the muscle-power of three ordinary men and has never been defeated in combat.'

24

He put the figurine down and picked up another, of a woman dressed in a greyish-white tunic with a long hooded cloak which seemed to shimmer like hoarfrost; she wore white boots to match.

'This is an ice maiden.' His gaze was now on Kate. 'She wears a cloak woven out of a mystic material which enables her to generate an intense cold through her fingertips. She can freeze a river or turn molten metal stone-cold in a matter of seconds.'

Next he picked up the figure who carried a long black whip. He was dressed in a tunic of cucumber green over an ochre shirt and leggings. There was a leather belt at his waist, holding an array of knives and daggers and various pouches. He looked lean and agile.

Ivor Kinnersley turned to Willie.

'Here is a character who would be an invaluable asset in close-quarters fighting,' he said. 'Limber and swift-moving, he is adept with knives and is a lethal opponent in the cut and thrust of battle. But his main weapon is his black whip, which can cut an attacker to ribbons in seconds.'

The fourth figurine was a slim and dainty female dressed in a translucent robe of aquamarine over a tight-fitting tunic of midnight blue. The sleeves and skirts of the robe were voluminous, and the woman's raised arms made her resemble a large and delicate dragonfly. On each wrist she wore a bracelet of pale gold.

Teresa was already intent on the figure before Ivor Kinnersley looked at her.

'A character of subtle but remarkable power,' he said. 'In her normal guise she can sometimes sense the thoughts and emotions of other creatures. She is also able to fill their minds with illusions, so that she could protect herself by conjuring up the vision of a beast to frighten off an attacker. But this is not the end of her abilities. The golden bracelets which she wears can, when struck together, make her incorporeal, capable of flight and able to pass through solid matter. However, she loses her other mind-powers while in this form.'

The final figurine was a man who wore a plain bloused scarlet shirt over black leggings tucked into grey suede boots. Around his neck, on a thin golden chain, was a circular pendant with a milk-white stone like a large hemispherical pearl at its centre.

'Here we have a man who carries no obvious weapons and wears only a talisman. Yet that talisman is the source of his considerable powers, for through it he can harness the power of his mind to move inanimate objects, conjure up protective shields of mental force or stun attackers with concentrated bursts of psychic energy.'

Paul knew that his uncle was addressing him, and he could not take his eyes off the figurine. Though he told himself that it was only a well-carved and delicately painted piece of wood, it seemed far more than that: it seemed to radiate an aura of assurance, wisdom and forcefulness which Paul immediately responded to. He would have loved to be, to really be, such a character.

It was the same for the other four, each of whom had been drawn to the particular figurine which Ivor Kinnersley had held while addressing them, as if he knew that each one exemplified the particular qualities which they admired. Justin, for all his confidence and aggressiveness, had always wanted to be stronger and more powerfully built; the warrior was the epitome of physical power, the fantasy character of his dreams. And Teresa saw in the beautiful, elf-like woman all the beauty and grace of movement which she knew she lacked herself; she would have loved to exchange her plain, squat body for that of an ethereal creature who could fly. Willie was in no doubt that the nimble whipmaster possessed both the physical and mental dexterity which he secretly desired himself. And when Kate stared at the ice maiden she saw all the aloofness and absolute confidence in her own powers which would make her immune to the kind of emotional insecurity which Kate had suffered with Justin.

'Pick them up,' Ivor Kinnersley said.

Paul was now more convinced than ever that the man who was speaking was not the uncle who had raised him. His uncle was a diffident man of only moderate intelligence, and yet he had used words like 'incorporeal' and 'limber' – words which had never been part of his ordinary vocabulary. He was a man transformed into a stranger, and there was a sense of threat about him. Yet Paul was compelled to pick up the figurine, as were the other four.

It was a moment of some drama and strangeness. But then the real world briefly intervened when Willie, in picking up his figurine, hit the dangling light bulb with his head. It flickered, went out.

The incident, so typical of Willie, might have been sufficient to bring them all back to earth in other circumstances. But in plunging the room into darkness, Willie had inadvertently revealed that the figurines had begun to glow.

They radiated not only light but also a greater sense of their individual abilities and characters. Paul felt resolution and courage in his figurine, Justin experienced boldness and huge reserves of stamina,

27

Kate was instilled with a strong sense of independence, Teresa with an alluring feeling of her own gracefulness, and Willie with an awareness of his character's deftness both of body and mind.

Ivor Kinnersley rose from the table and went over to the old mirror which stood against the wall. They saw that the mirror's frame was lambent in the dimness of the room, and its silver surface began to shimmer like stirred water as they stared at it. Then it abruptly went dark, becoming something which did not seem to be a mirror any more but a doorway, a portal, into somewhere else. They could see nothing beyond it but a blackness, yet there was a sense of space, of a world opening up beyond its confines.

'Step through,' Ivor Kinnersley said in a quiet but commanding voice.

Paul knew that it was not his uncle at all who was speaking. He tried to draw back, to resist the command, to call out to the others that they should wait. But he could do nothing except move forward.

One by one the others were stepping into the mirror, the glowing figurines lighting their way like candles. As they passed through into the darkness beyond the mirror they vanished as if they had plunged into a wall of black water.

Paul was the last to enter. Just before he took the final step he managed to turn his head and look at his uncle, who was still standing at the head of the table. His uncle was smiling at him, but it was the kind of smile Paul had never seen on his face before. It was a smile of considerable pleasure, but there was no mistaking the sinister undertone in it. Then Paul was compelled to turn again and face the wall of darkness. He stepped forward and it embraced him.

# 1

# *The Ruined Tower*

Justin was the first to pass through the mirror. There was an instant of darkness, and suddenly he found himself standing in a circular room built of stone.

He was holding a heavy object in his right hand, and he saw that the figurine had become the iron hammer. He wielded it effortlessly and had a sense of great physical strength and stamina. Staring down at himself, he saw that his body had been transformed into the muscular warrior the figurine had been.

Behind him the dark portal was shimmering, and one by one the others stepped through. They, too, had become the characters of the figurines which they had held, their faces changed to varying degrees but still recognizable as their former selves. Kate's hair was now a frosty white, Paul appeared somehow older, and Willie's whole physique was altered so that he looked dapper; the usual expression of guileless-ness in his face had been replaced by something more knowing.

But it was in Teresa that the transformation was most striking. She was taller and slimmer, and her translucent robe gleamed on her graceful body. The familiar contours of her face had somehow been altered from plainness into prettiness without losing their essential qualities – she was still Teresa Lambert, but now she was beautiful, radiant.

For long moments all five of them simply stared at one another in wonderment and disbelief. Kate now held a long white cloak in her right hand, Paul a talisman on a golden chain, Teresa a pair of bracelets and Willie a black whip and a belt of daggers.

Teresa was the first to speak.

'This isn't happening,' she said. 'Tell me I'm dreaming.'

Her voice was utterly changed. It was light and melodious and quite unlike her usual gruff tone. It finally convinced her that somehow she had been transformed into the character of her figurine.

Willie did not need to speak to convince himself. The moment he had stepped into the stone chamber his mind had started racing, his familiar sluggish thoughts replaced by a consciousness that was far more incisive and quick-acting. He could feel the suppleness of his limbs and torso, and he knew that he was no longer a shambling hulk but a deft and agile whipmaster. He slipped the belt of daggers around his waist and buckled it up while continuing to stare at Teresa, the beautiful Teresa.

Kate, too, had no doubts that the transformation had taken place, even though she still held the photograph which had fallen from Justin's pocket in her left hand. Just before they had stepped through the mirror she had been on the point of despair at Justin's betrayal of her; but now, as she stared at the huge, muscular creature he had become, she felt nothing for him but disdain. The insensitivity with which he had always treated her in their relationship now seemed manifest in the bulging lines of his body, emotional hardheadedness translated into sheer brute force. There was something repellent about him, and the fact that she could feel such an abrupt sense of detachment from Justin convinced her that a profound change had taken place in her. Unseen by the others, she slipped the photograph up the sleeve of her tunic.

Paul was peering down at himself, at the scarlet shirt and black leggings which he now wore. In his hand he held the golden talisman with the pearl-white stone at its centre. He was conscious that he had become a man who possessed the instincts of leadership, but it was not a realization he welcomed. Much of the caution and diffidence which had marked his behaviour since Brian's death remained, and he felt ridiculous in his uniform, like a fool in fancy dress. Somehow he had taken on the guise of a warrior, but he still knew himself to be a coward.

The shimmering portal flickered out, and all that remained was a tall mirror similar to the one through which they had passed in the cellar room. But it was not the same mirror, nor were they in the same room. The stale air of the room had an indefinable quality of strangeness about it, and the stonework had a greenish hue.

With the fading of the portal's light, the room grew dim but not entirely dark. Looking up, they saw the night sky overhead, a sky dotted with stars. They were standing in the bottom of some ruined tower, a tower which had clearly not been inhabited for many years. Debris littered the edges of the room, and there was a thin coating of dust over everything. Directly opposite the mirror was a large arched door of dark wood, its handle like an ornate ship's wheel.

Suddenly the mirror began to shimmer once more.

They saw a glowing word slowly forming in its glass:

## MADRIMAR

The word meant nothing to them, yet they all sensed that it was the name of a place, a destination and a summons combined. As they stared at the glowing letters the word slowly faded, leaving a plain mirror once more.

They looked at one another, still not quite able to fully accept what had happened to them. In their gaudy uniforms and transformed bodies they were like strangers to one another.

Justin was keen to grasp the nettle of their new situation, to overcome their bewilderment with positive action. He made to say, 'Let's get out of here,' but to his surprise the words would not come as quickly and as easily as he wanted them to. He tried again, and all that emerged was a series of grunts. Embarrassed, he strode quickly over to the door and wrenched the wheel. It did not budge. He tried twisting it, and felt the mechanism engage. He tugged on the door, and it swung inwards.

Justin stepped outside, the others following. They stared in awe.

The ruined tower stood at the centre of a plain of glazed, ruby-red rock, as smooth as marble. In the night sky, feathery clouds were lit by moonshine. The moon itself was a pale body streaked wth scarlet veins: it seemed to stare at them like a bloodshot eye.

Had there been any lingering doubts that they were no longer on Earth, these were dispelled by the sight of the moon. They had stepped through the mirror into another world entirely.

Before anyone could speak, there came a faint snorting sound from behind the tower. Justin immediately gripped his hammer in both hands and cautiously moved around the base of the tower, prepared for any eventuality.

Five horses were tethered to metal hooks embedded in the tower's walls. At least, they were creatures resembling horses, though they were like no species found on Earth. Their skins had a reptilian sheen, and each mount was a different colour: one a reddish-brown, another a dark green, the third tawny, the fourth cream, the fifth gunmetal blue. They were tailless, with cloven hoofs and small white eyes, across which silvery nictitating membranes flashed. No earthly horses, then, but clearly meant for riding: each bore a bridle and a simple saddle of mottled hide.

As far as the eye could see, nothing living moved on the featureless plain around the tower. Willie and Kate approached the horses, Willie offering his palm to the snout of the tawny mount, Kate touching the sleek flank of the green. The skin was cool, sweatless: the horses were fresh.

'They were left here for us,' Kate said.

It was as much a query as a statement, but no one disputed it. The horses were docile, even friendly, the green nuzzling Kate as she stroked the plated ridge which was its substitute for a mane, the tawny horse trying to poke its nose into one of Willie's pouches, presumably in the hope of finding a titbit. Five saddled horses for five riders.

For a moment none of them moved. Then Justin smiled broadly and began to swing his hammer as though preparing himself for combat. Willie, too, felt a sudden desire to embrace the roles which had been thrust upon them. He switched his whip. It was long and made of some material which was at once

33

rubbery yet semi-metallic like graphite. Near the base of the ruined tower lay a small piece of rubble. Almost without thinking, Willie flicked the whip at it and saw the fragment fly up into the air as if hit by a bullet. His aim had been unerring. The belt of knives about his waist also felt like a natural part of his armoury which he would be able to use to good effect.

Meanwhile Teresa was slipping the golden bracelets over her wrists. They fitted snugly, as if they had always belonged there. She was immediately able to sense the mingling of excitement and unease in her companions, and she felt a great thrill at the potential of her power. But she made no move to strike her bracelets together. She wasn't ready for that, yet; she needed to get used to being a new person before she could think of trying to fly.

The roan horse was regarding her with its tiny white eyes, and she felt as if it belonged to her. A saddle-bag hung on each of the horses. She approached the roan and lifted the flap of its bag.

Inside she found a smoky flask filled with a colourless sparkling liquid; it was accompanied by several greenish carrot-like vegetables, a hunk of grey bread, a square of something resembling white cheese, two bell-shaped fruits with purple skins spotted with crimson, and finally an unclassifiable object which looked like a bunch of grapes that had been dipped in tar.

'Provisions,' she said to the others. 'For the journey.'

'Journey,' Justin managed to say; he had been determined to speak, but had only got the word out with some difficulty. It had emerged harsh and thick.

'To Madrimar,' Teresa said. 'We have to go there.'

She spoke as if she was addressing an idiot. Justin wanted to say that he had also deduced as much, but the words would not come and he abandoned the attempt for fear of sounding ridiculous. What had happened to him? His brain felt as active as ever, but there seemed to be some obstruction in his speech centres.

Kate was aware of Justin's difficulty. In the past his embarrassment would have been enough to make her blush herself, but now she felt nothing whatsoever. She turned away, holding out the shimmering white cloak in front of her. She was aware that both Paul and Justin were watching her as she slipped the cloak over her shoulders.

A creeping coldness began to envelop her body, and yet it was a pleasurable sensation, like taking a cool shower on a hot summer's day; it made her feel alert and invigorated and very conscious of her capabilities. She stood straight-backed and knew that she was an imposing figure.

She stretched out a hand and pointed it at the tower. For a moment nothing happened; then a coldness darted through her veins like iced water, and as she concentrated harder, jets of white fire spurted from her fingertips and splashed against the stone wall. They immediately crystallized into a patch of frosty white ice.

Paul studied the effect, finding it at once impressive and a little forbidding. He was still holding the talisman in his hand. The pearly stone in its golden mounting seemed to him at that moment like a blind eye whose sight would be restored if he donned it. But he made no move to do so. He was very conscious that around him the others had all embraced their new personas to varying degrees, and he felt out of place.

35

Something told him that, fitting to their new roles, they would soon be required to display valour and heroism, to fight for their very lives. The prospect daunted him and he felt like an impostor, as if someone else should have been chosen instead of him.

'Aren't you going to put it on?' asked Kate.

It was recognizably her old voice, and yet there was a stillness and a distance in her tone which he had never heard before. The question had been asked, but her tone implied that it was a matter of complete indifference to her whether he put it on or not.

'No,' said Paul. 'I don't think I will.'

They wandered over to join the others at the horses.

'I think we ought to mount up and get out of here,' Willie was saying.

He glanced at Justin as he spoke, a habit engendered by the fact that Justin had always been the one who took the important decisions amongst their group. Justin merely nodded his bullet-shaped head. His skin had always been suntanned even in winter – he owned an ultra-violet lamp – but now it was deeply bronzed. His fair hair had wilted on his skull so that he looked almost bald. He had immediately decided that the dark blue mount was to be his, and he proceeded to remove the flask from its saddle-bag and take a swig of the clear liquid.

'Water,' he managed to say to the expectant faces of the others.

'You'd better save that,' Paul said. 'It might be a long ride.'

'I think we're meant to head for Madrimar,' Teresa repeated.

The rest of them agreed, but as they stared around

36

the featureless plain, each of them had the same unspoken question: to ride to Madrimar was all very well, but which direction should they take?

At that precise moment a shooting star flared brightly across the sky, leaving a vivid white streak like a chalk mark on a speckled blackboard. All five of them followed it with their eyes as it vanished over the horizon, pointing the way they would ride.

# 2

# *A Rain of Fire*

The bloodshot moon hung overhead, casting a pinkish light over the plain. They had been riding for over an hour, and few words had been exchanged in that time, as if none of them had yet got used to the fact that they were in another world in new identities and were still wrapped up in wonderment, still wrestling with their profoundly changed circumstances.

This is certainly not Earth, Paul told himself again, and yet the air was breathable and the gravity was not noticeably different from normal. He had hooked the talisman chain around his belt, and he felt the jewel bump against his thigh as they rode along. He had been forced to take the cream mount, and felt like an unwilling knight on a white charger. He would have preferred a less ostentatious horse, but it had been Hobson's choice for him, the others having already selected their mounts. He also continued to feel self-conscious in his scarlet shirt and black leggings.

Kate rode just ahead of him on the green horse, her sparkling white cloak draped over its haunches. Her slipstream was cool, as if the cloak was chilling the air around it. She rode expertly, as they all did, and yet

Paul knew that none of them had been familiar with horses in the past. Riding skills were clearly part of the abilities which they had inherited on assuming their new identities.

Paul's instincts had been to remain at the ruined tower rather than immediately ride off in the direction indicated by the shooting star, but he had said nothing when it was clear that the others wanted to move on. They seemed eager to come to grips with their situation, as if this was the start of some new, extra-realistic role-playing game. But Paul remembered the smile on his uncle's face just before he had stepped through the mirror; it had left him feeling that this was certainly not a game.

As ever, Justin took the lead, riding ahead on the dark blue horse, one hand on the reins, the other gripping his iron hammer. He relished the sense of being an adventurer in a strange land, alert and eager to defend himself against any danger which might threaten them. Willie followed on the tawny horse, his whip coiled in his hand, his eyes scanning the horizon. They were still on a flat featureless plain, though it was hard to say whether the dark mass looming in the distance was a mountain range or a bank of clouds. Behind them came Teresa, who gripped the reins of her roan with both hands. The bracelets at her wrists struck lightly together as the horse trotted along, and she knew that she was teasing herself with the prospect of transformation into a being who could fly. In the past, in her old identity, she had often had dreams about flying, about soaring high over hills and fields like a bird. Now she was confident that she could achieve this by striking the bracelets together, but she still preferred to delay the moment.

Kate sat erect on her horse, enveloped by her cloak and completely content to ride in silence. Normally she always felt the need to be surrounded by people and diverted by conversation, but now the company of her placid thoughts was sufficient for her. She stared at the swollen, muscular figure of Justin on his horse and felt nothing. She was aware of the photograph which was still tucked into her sleeve, but she no longer had the urge to confront Justin with it because it no longer seemed a threat to her; it was hard to care about Justin or his infidelities. But the photograph would be worth keeping in reserve should he attempt to press his old demands on her.

It soon became clear that they were riding towards a bank of dark clouds rather than a mountain range. As though driven by a sudden wind, the clouds advanced rapidly over the plain, blotting out the bloodshot moon. Their horses began to snort and shuffle nervously – they made sounds just like ordinary horses – as the sky darkened to a deep purple and the clouds started to roil in an unnatural way.

All five of them instinctively drew together on their horses. But before any of them could speak, a blood-red glow filled the clouds directly overhead. Then a fiery rain descended on them.

It was a multi-coloured rain, as if comprised of tiny, luminous meteors which glowed all the colours of the spectrum. Yet these were no solid bodies, for as they hit the plain they splashed like liquid. Within seconds the riders were inundated with a hail of burning light which hit the flanks of the horses, sending them rearing up. Both Justin and Willie had to cling on hard to the reins to prevent themselves from being thrown, but Kate was hurled from her saddle onto the glassy surface of the plain.

She gasped as she landed awkwardly on her elbow, but she quickly realized that it was no serious injury. Bright droplets sizzled on the frosty material of her cloak, then struck her face like hot oil. She knew that she had to protect herself immediately.

Concentrating hard, she swept her hand over her head and a wide arch of ice formed in the air. She repeated the gesture several times until she was cocooned in an igloo of ice. She could hear the impact of the hot rain against its outer wall, but it could not touch her here.

Teresa struck her bracelets together in panic as soon as the rain began to fall. But nothing happened. She tried again, but still no transformation took place. She realized that she was not concentrating properly, and did everything she could to conjure up an image of herself as an ethereal creature before striking the bracelets together for a third time. The fiery rain was searing her face and her horse had started to panic, but as the bracelets collided with a metallic ring, she suddenly felt nothing. . .

. . .she was rising up, as light as air. Her horse fell away from her, the ground dwindled, and she knew she was flying. Sweeping her arms up, she soared higher, feeling wonderfully insubstantial. Flecks of lilac and gold and rose flashed through her, streaks of lime green and powder blue and orange which she could not feel at all as they sped through her body. She had become as transparent as a ghost.

Meanwhile Paul was tugging hard on the reins of his horse to prevent it from throwing him. He had seen Kate cocoon herself in ice, seen Teresa shimmer and then take to the air like some beautiful flying insect whom nothing could touch. But Justin's hammer and Willie's whip were no defence against

41

the storm of fire, and their mounts were stampeding in tight circles as fiery droplets hit their hides. Paul's horse now began to buck, and a splash of silver burned the hand which held the rein, causing him to jerk it back in pain. His horse reared and he was catapulted from the saddle.

He stumbled to his feet as the firestorm reached its full fury, searing his head and face. Kate's igloo was beginning to melt under the onslaught, and he knew that none of them except Teresa would last long unless he did something. . .

He snatched the talisman from his belt and looped the golden chain over his neck. His face was burning from the hot rain, and he could scarcely see in front of him. But he did not need to see: he needed to concentrate all his mental energies on conjuring up a protective shield of mental energy around them.

Paul thought of a transparent blister which would envelop them all. He thought of it, then began to conjure up as vivid an image of it as possible. For a moment nothing happened, but then he felt the talisman begin to pulse on his chest like a rapid heartbeat. His concentration almost broke but he recovered in time, resisting the temptation to open his eyes and holding the image of the force-shield in his mind as clearly as he was able.

He did not know how much time had passed before it dawned on him that his body was no longer assailed by the hot rain. The talisman was still pulsing rapidly on his chest. He opened his eyes.

The fiery rain was still falling, but it did not reach them; an invisible protective umbrella prevented it from hitting the ground in a wide circle around them. The bright drops exploded in the darkness directly above their heads, snuffed out by the power of his mind.

The milky stone of the talisman flashed grey, then white as it throbbed on his chest, and he continued to hold the image of the force-shield in his mind, knowing that if he did not it would immediately dissolve. Justin and Willie had succeeded in recovering all the horses, and Kate had emerged from her half-melted ice-dome and was standing alone, staring up at Teresa.

Teresa was swooping and darting at the boundary of the force-shield like a trapped insect. It was clear that although in her ethereal form she could pass through solid objects, a psychic barrier would evidently hold her in check. Presently Teresa flitted downwards, and as she touched the earth her body shimmered and became flesh once more. It was not necessary for her to strike the bracelets together to reverse her transformation; the moment she stopped concentrating on flight, her body became solid once more.

Paul continued to hold the force-shield while the storm raged above. It lasted only a few minutes more, then ceased as abruptly as it had come. The bloody clouds seemed to dissolve rather than drift away, leaving an ordinary cloud-flecked sky lit by the red-veined moon. Only then did Paul let his concentration lapse.

The talisman had stopped pulsing on his chest and the invisible shield was gone, dissolved into nothingness the instant he had stopped imagining it.

Justin was gathering the horses together.

'There are hills in the distance,' Teresa said, pointing in the direction in which they had been riding. 'I saw them when I was flying.'

'Go,' Justin managed to say. 'Now.'

Willie nodded. 'I think the sooner we get off this plain, the better.'

They immediately began to mount. Paul was too exhausted to say anything, but he was amazed that they were accepting what had happened so matter-of-factly. They had just been inundated with a hail of rainbow fire, and yet they seemed to take it for granted and were eager to press on. It was as if they had simply negotiated the first danger in one of Justin's fantasy worlds. But the fire might have actually killed them.

Paul felt not a little aggrieved that none of them had thanked him for saving them. Was this another thing that they were already taking for granted, that their unusual powers would get them out of any scrape? If so, it was the kind of bravado which courted disaster.

Still, everyone looked remarkably unscathed after the storm. It dawned on Paul that while the bright drops had burned them, they had left no lasting marks or pain; even the horses looked unscarred. It was as if the rain had been an irritation, a test, rather than a real threat to their lives.

The effort of sustaining the force-shield had drained him considerably, and as they rode off Paul began to hope that he might find a comfortable bed to rest his head that night. How far away was Madrimar? He had a feeling that it was not a place they would reach in a day of riding, let alone a single evening.

Presently Kate drew alongside him on her horse, and he felt the chill which emanated from her cloak. Her silver hair shone under the pinkish moonlight.

'You did well,' she told him.

It was a statement of fact rather than a compliment.

He saw that there was a faint smile on her face – a detached, ironic smile. Her eyes went to the talisman which he was still wearing on his chest.

'So,' she said, 'you've become one of us at last.'

# 3

# A Movable Feast

They reached the hills after a further hour of riding. These were rugged and bare, gaunt outcrops of reddish stone interspersed with scree. Behind them the plain receded to the horizon, looking more than ever like a vast lake of solidified blood.

Justin rode ahead, urging his horse up escarpments and narrow ravines while the others took a more gentle path along the bottom of a dry valley. He was scouting, he told himself, seeking a suitable place for them to camp for the night. But he was also hoping that perhaps a ferocious animal might leap out of the darkness so that he could engage it in combat; he was keenly aware that he had not yet blooded his hammer. It felt great to be a warrior, more powerful than his old man could ever have imagined. If only he could see him now, astride a horse in a harsh land, and fearless in the face of whatever dangers might lie ahead of them.

While Justin prowled the slopes, Willie led the rest of them along the valley floor. The moon still shone low in the sky between patches of cloud. Both Teresa and Kate had started to sag, while Paul was practically asleep in the saddle. They had all given up hope of reaching Madrimar that night; it was time they found a sheltered place to sleep.

The valley had been bare of vegetation at first, but presently they began to encounter what looked like rounded balls of fluffy barbed wire. They were evidently shrubs of some sort, looking dry and brittle in the arid earth. Ahead a flat ledge of rock jutted out in front of them. Willie thought that it looked a good spot for a camp.

The others were quick to agree that they should bed down for the night on the ledge. Justin was summoned, and he also gave the place a grunt of approval. The ledge was flat enough to sleep on with a minimum of discomfort, protected at its rear by a sheer rockface, and affording a good view out over the valley. Paul, exhausted by his mental labours on the plain, immediately bedded down, using his saddle as a pillow in time-honoured fashion. He quickly fell asleep.

The others had decided that they needed some sort of fire, and Willie was quick to show his initiative by attempting to uproot one of the fluffy shrubs which grew in clusters about the ledge. But its thorns pricked his right hand as he pulled the bush free, making him yelp with pain. Willie removed his tunic and wrapped it around the stem of the bush before carrying it back to the others.

'I think this will burn,' he said.

'Fine,' said Kate without expression, 'except that we don't have anything to light it with.'

Willie had not thought of that. He rummaged in his belt pouches, but they were all empty. Then a possible solution occurred to him, and he grinned.

'We've got Justin's hammer,' he said.

'What good can that do?' asked Kate.

But Justin already knew. Paul's uncle had told him that the hammer would grow hot when he wielded it in battle. Having not yet faced any enemy he had had no opportunity to test this. But what was to stop him from imagining an enemy?

He walked over to the rockface, hefted the hammer and smashed it against the rock. There was a tremendous crack, but the rock was evidently as hard as granite and it did not break. Justin swung again, and again and again, imagining that it was the face of some terrible monster which would devour him if he did not kill it first.

The hammer began to glow a dull red, which quickly deepened and brightened. Justin stopped pummelling the rockface and held the hammer out in front of him, feeling its heat on his face. Then he strode proudly across the ledge and plunged the glowing head into the centre of the plant.

It took fire immediately, the downy coating bursting into flame. The coiled stems took longer to catch, but they began to drip some kind of resin which was itself inflammable. Within minutes it was giving off a healthy amount of heat and light, its yellow flames making their shadows loom large on the rockface. Paul, awoken by Justin's hammering, moved his saddle closer to the fire and promptly fell asleep again.

Warmed, the others began to think of food. They were all hungry, but Willie, Kate and Teresa were reluctant to sample any of the items in the saddle-bag. Justin, however, bit into one of the green carrots.

The others watched him chew, and Willie asked, 'What does it taste like?'

Justin swallowed. 'Nuts.'

None of them were quite sure whether this was a description or an insult, but they all realized that they couldn't risk going without food. In Justin's games they always lost stamina points if they did so.

The saddle-bags were emptied and the provisions laid out for inspection. Kate suggested that they be prudent and each try a single, different item in case any one of them proved poisonous. But somehow they all preferred to be guinea-pigs together, and everyone sampled most of the contents of the saddle-bags.

As it turned out, Justin had indeed been describing the taste of the green carrots, which had a distinctly nutty flavour. The grey bread was stale but yeasty, the 'cheese' tasted like a beef stock cube, and the bell-shaped fruits had a fragrant flavour which none of them could quite describe.

Only the clusters of tarry grapes remained un-eaten; when Justin broke off a globule it exuded a kind of jelly, the colour of bile, which gave off a fetid smell that was distinctly unappetizing. They threw the objects on to the fire, and watched them swell and pop and char in the flames until finally nothing was left.

Though they were all tired, they continued to sit around the fire for some time after eating. Only Kate kept her distance; the heat had soon begun to make her feel uncomfortable, and it dawned on her that fire had become her chief enemy; it was the chill embrace of her cloak in which she felt sheltered and protected.

A heavy silence hung over them as the burning bush crackled and spat. It still seemed remarkable that they were now in another world and in different identities, and they were all aware that they should be discussing what had happened to them and trying to decide why they had been brought to this strange

49

land – and how. Yet a mood of caution and reticence prevailed. While they had not exactly become strangers to one another, they had each changed, and the cosy assumptions of their former relationships could no longer be taken for granted.

No one felt this more keenly than Justin. He was studying Kate as she sat apart from the rest of them and thinking how composed and statuesque she looked in her new identity. She had scarcely spoken to him since they had been transformed, and it seemed a calculated snub. He felt the urge to bring her to heel as quickly as possible, but he knew he was severely hampered by his inability to express himself with the barbed eloquence to which he was accustomed. Willie, meanwhile, was still fascinated by the new Teresa, whose every movement was now filled with grace and beauty. When she spoke, he listened more to the fluting sound of her voice than her actual words; it was hard to credit that only several hours ago she had been a plain, dumpy figure whom no man would have looked at twice.

Teresa herself had little thought of the others at that moment. She was recalling the profound delight she had felt when she had finally taken flight, the delirious pleasure in being a creature lighter than air. She knew that she had become a beautiful figure, and she longed for a mirror in which she could study her face. She was tempted to ask Kate if she could conjure up a reflective surface of ice, but the idea smacked of immodesty and she said nothing. Besides, there was something rather forbidding about the new Kate.

Kate herself was thinking how agreeable her new identity was. She sat with her cloak wrapped tight around her, and watched the red-veined moon as it began to set over a distant line of hills. Though this had been the strangest day of all their lives, she felt an inner tranquillity which she had not experienced in years, a sense that she had finally acquired the independence of spirit which she had always desired.

The bush began to burn out, and Justin uprooted another one, carefully avoiding its thorns. As the fire blazed anew, Teresa said, 'We should sleep.'

'Look-outs,' Justin grunted.

Willie was quick to agree. 'We'll take turns to stand guard while the rest of us sleep. I think two hours each per watch should be enough.'

Willie liked the unfamiliar sense of taking decisions and organizing things, but then Kate said, 'Who's going to do the counting?'

'What?' said Willie.

'How do we know when the two hours are up? None of us are wearing watches.'

It was an obvious omission, and suddenly Willie had a dismaying sense of being his old, witless self again. But at the same time he realized the solution.

'The first bush burned for about an hour,' he said. 'We'll make each watch two bushes long.'

Justin volunteered to take the first watch, and the rest of them settled down around the fire, using their saddles as pillows. Bare rock was not the most comfortable surface on which to sleep, but they were all exhausted after the unexpected rigours of the long evening.

Justin sat with his back to Kate, studiously ignoring her. Since his early teens Justin had always had a parade of attractive girlfriends, and they had always given him a feeling of confidence and power. Few, however, had lasted more than a month or two; Justin quickly grew bored with them. Kate was the first girl he had gone out with for any duration, and he wasn't going to let her dump him just because she had acquired special powers and a fancy costume.

Paul had once tried to suggest that Justin cultivated an image as a lady-killer because his mother had walked out on him and his father when he was six years old; according to Paul, he was trying to compensate for his maternal insecurities with sexual conquest. But as far as Justin was concerned, that was just psychological claptrap: he simply liked women a lot but had a low boredom threshold. He also liked to be sure that he got out of their clutches before they put the knife in. Women were fickle; you couldn't trust them.

Justin was gripping the handle of his hammer tighter and tighter, and he saw that the hammerhead had begun to glow. He set it aside and concentrated on keeping his eyes peeled for any potential danger. The landscape looked uninhabited, but they were strangers to this world and had no idea of what threats might lurk in its nooks and crannies. After a rain of fire, anything was possible.

If Justin had glanced over his shoulder at that moment, he might have seen a movement in the saddle-bag which Paul was using as a pillow. Paul was too exhausted to be awakened by the movement, and presently a dark mass rolled out from under the flap.

It was the object resembling a bunch of grapes, which the rest of them had taken to be an unpalatable fruit. It lay there for a moment on the rock like a pulsing lung. In the moonless sky the canopy of stars was now brilliant, and nothing moved save for the object which lay beside Paul. It throbbed and heaved and distended until it had quadrupled in size. Then it flopped on to Paul's abdomen.

Paul awoke with the sensation that his innards were being torn from his body. He saw the heavy black mass on his belly and was possessed with terror. A greenish-yellow ichor was dribbling from cracks in its bulbous surface, and a disgusting aroma reached his nostrils. He cried out.

Justin rushed across to Paul and saw the black mass on his chest. Paul was shrieking with pain, and the thing was twitching. Justin plunged his hands into the mass and tried to pull it off. But it was fixed limpet-like to Paul, and Justin couldn't get a proper purchase on its slimy surface. The others had staggered up from sleep and were staring in horror at the thing.

Justin tried to shout, 'Do something!' but all that emerged was a strangled groan of frustration. Willie had instinctively pulled a knife from his belt, but he knew that he could not plunge it into the creature without the risk of harming Paul. Teresa was simply too repulsed by the sight of it to think of doing anything.

Then Kate knelt beside Paul and placed her hand over the creature. Ice-tendrils began to flow from her fingers, spreading and combining until the creature was entirely enveloped in it. Its movements ceased and Paul lay still, the agonized expression slowly fading from his face.

'How are we going to get it off?' asked Willie. He had already rejected the idea of trying to prize it away with one of his knives.

Though weak, Paul knew that he would have to remove the creature with the power of his mind. He had been too taken by surprise and terror to think of using the talisman when the creature had attacked.

He closed his eyes and concentrated on lifting the frozen mass from his belly. For a moment nothing happened; then he felt a sudden relaxation of pressure accompanied by a sound like a rubber sucker being detached from a wet surface.

He opened his eyes and saw the thing suspended above him, the bile-coloured ichor still dripping from its underside. Disgust overtook him, and he flung the creature aside with his mind.

It landed near the fire, and Willie was quick to run across and kick it into the flames. As the ice dissolved the creature began to twitch once more – to twitch madly, like an animal in its death throes. Willie backed away, thinking that it might suddenly leap from the fire. But then it flared up and shrivelled away to nothing in the flames.

Justin was helping Paul sit up. There was a patch of slimy wetness on his scarlet shirt where the creature had attached itself, but apart from a slight inner strain he felt unhurt. Underneath his shirt his skin was unmarked.

'What was that thing?' Willie was asking, though he had already recognized it as a bloated and flattened version of the grape-like objects they had thrown on the fire.

'Just imagine if we had eaten them,' Teresa said, revulsion manifest on her face.

'What if all the other stuff we've eaten is some kind of creature?' Willie said, feeling sick at the thought. 'What if it starts to incubate inside us?'

But the rest of them were quick to agree that was unlikely. The other items had looked and tasted like ordinary food, whereas the grape-objects had been immediately off-putting. But why, then, had they been included?

'Perhaps we were supposed to use them in some way,' Teresa offered.

'Perhaps,' said Paul. 'Though perhaps they were a warning.'

'What do you mean?'

'Whoever provided the horses also provided the food but made sure that one item which would be dangerous to us was included.'

'What would be the point of that?' asked Willie.

'I'm not sure. But it could be that whoever brought us here wants to ensure that we don't have an easy time of it.'

'But why would they provide us with food and horses in the first place in that case?'

Paul shrugged. 'To get us started on our journey, perhaps.'

'But why?' Willie insisted.

'That's what we're going to have to find out.'

# 4

# *Conversations with a Hermit*

Paul was excused guard duty that night. After Justin's watch, Willie took over, and was followed by Teresa and finally Kate. The night passed uneventfully, though during her watch period Teresa flirted with the idea of taking to the air once more and exploring the hills. She had not spoken of it to the others, but she had felt a great frustration when she had been penned in by Paul's psychic shield during the firestorm: in her ethereal form she had a craving for complete freedom of movement. Now she wanted to fly high up into the night, to soar far away; but she resisted the temptation, reminding herself of her responsibility towards her sleeping friends. When Kate took over and Teresa slept, she dreamt of her pretty younger sister, Michelle, dreamt of appearing before her in flight and in all her glory. She was now more beautiful than Michelle would ever be.

During the second bush of Kate's watch, dawn broke – a blood-red dawn. Kate sat on the end of the ledge, watching a distended red sun rise into the sky through purple clouds. It was twice the size of Earth's yellow sun, but it gave off far less light, colouring the sky a watery maroon.

Crouched, unmoving, on the edge of the rock with her cloak wrapped around her, Kate resembled an outcrop of snow-streaked stone. Paul awoke to the crimson dawn and saw her sitting there, as still as a statue. His midriff still felt a little tender, but he was rested after his long sleep. He stood up, his leg muscles beginning to ache from the unaccustomed strain of riding.

The huge red sun was at least an hour past rising, and yet everything looked gloomy, twilit. The hills were filled with deep shadows, and violet clouds streaked the pale, lowering sky. The entire scene had a sombre beauty; it was compelling in its very alienness.

Willie awoke at the same time, and immediately realized that he was feeling feverish. He sat up, and his head began to swim. His right hand was burning, and he saw that it was puffed up and reddened. It was the hand that had been scratched by the thorn-bush.

Kate, on examining Willie's hand, rapidly confirmed that something in the thorns must have caused a severe allergic reaction. What she did not tell Willie was that it might actually endanger his life. They knew nothing about the plants in this world, and everything might be highly toxic to their systems. And yet they appeared to have digested the food from the saddle-bags without ill effects. Perhaps Willie had nothing worse than the local equivalent of a severe nettle-sting. But they could take no chances; they had to try to find some native person who could help him.

Justin and Teresa were roused, and they mounted and rode on. They continued along the dry valley, heading in what was presumably an easterly direction since the swollen red sun hung directly ahead of them. It was now quite high in the sky but the light remained dusky and wan. Kate drew her horse alongside Teresa's and was about to suggest to her that she take a reconnaissance flight in the hope of finding a settlement; then there was a flash of white light over a hill in the near distance.

All of them saw it, and they spurred their horses. Teresa knew that she should fly ahead and try to discover what had caused the flash, but for some reason she was reluctant to do so; none of them knew what dangers might lurk in this world, and she was fearful that it might be some sort of trap.

The hills were becoming more rounded, and they began to encounter patches of short vegetation which looked like dark candy-floss but was clearly some kind of grass. Soon the patches had blended together until they completely covered the hills. Here and there flowers like pink splashes of paint could be seen, and at length squat trees like twisted shuttlecocks began to adorn the hills, pendulous growths like walnuts hanging from their branches.

All of them were awestruck by the strangeness of the environment. The pale crimson sunlight tended to swamp the more subtle shades of colour, but the landscape had an eerie beauty nevertheless. Only Willie was unreceptive to it, for he was barely conscious in his saddle. His fever had been mounting as they rode along, and his swollen hand was extremely painful to touch.

Paul and Justin flanked Willie's horse and were ready to catch him if he started to slip from the saddle. But Willie remained grimly conscious, his eyes fixed ahead as they began to round the brow of a hill.

They were greeted by the sound of rushing water.

A stream tumbled down the mountainside over rounded white rocks. It had been hidden from them until the very last moment, but now they saw that it broadened as it plunged down the valley, becoming a river which curled away through hills to the east.

Their horses immediately cantered forward and splashed into the water. It had been a dry morning's ride, and all of their flasks were empty. Justin, not one for doing anything by half measures in his new guise, leapt off his mount and plunged into the stream. The water was clear and cold, immediately refreshing him. He let it run into his mouth, swallowed. It tasted as pure as the mineral water which had been in their flasks.

The others joined him in a more restrained manner, splashing their faces and filling up their flasks. The water revived Willie a little, but he continued to feel dizzy and feverish. He dragged himself back to the bank of the stream and sat down. The sun was warm on his head. He was about to lie back and close his eyes for a few minutes when he saw a thin line of yellowish smoke rising into the sky over the brow of the hill.

'Look!' he shouted to the others, pointing.

Justin, seeing the smoke, immediately hefted his hammer and began to advance up the hill.

'Wait a minute!' Paul called. But Justin was not to be delayed. Willie dragged himself to his feet and scrambled after him.

Paul and the others followed, catching up with them as they reached the crest of the hill. They stared down on what at first sight looked like a burial-mound built of stones and covered with the dark turf of the hills. But a chimney protruded from the centre of the turf, and the smoke was rising from it.

It was a squat cylindrical building with walls of the rounded white stones from the stream, piled higgledy-piggledy upon one another and cemented together with a copper-coloured mortar. There were no windows, but a small arched door of dark wood could be seen, and from this ran the trodden path which wound its way down to the stream.

Teresa and Kate joined the rest of them on the top of the hill. Before they could say anything, Justin began advancing down the hillside. Paul, nervous of his tendency to stalk off at the slightest provocation, called to him but was again ignored. After a moment's hesitation, he and the others hurried after him.

Justin strode up to the door and pounded hard on it with the side of his fist. There was no response. He pounded again, and heard a snorting sound from within, as though someone had abruptly been awakened from sleep.

'Eh?' came a startled voice from inside.

The others joined him outside the door. Paul was supporting Willie, who felt dead on his feet. His swollen hand was on fire.

'Who's there?'

It was the voice of an old man, and its tone contained a mixture of suspicion and irritation. All five of them had a sense that the words were not English, and yet they understood them perfectly.

'We are travellers, strangers here,' Paul said. 'We need your help.'

It occurred to him that perhaps none of them had been speaking English since their arrival in the twilight world but had been made fluent in one of the local tongues – so fluent that they spoke and thought in it as if it was their native language.

'How many are you?' came the voice with the same note of irritable caution. It was closer now, as if the speaker was standing on the other side of the door.

'Five,' said Paul. 'We mean you no harm. One of us has a swollen hand and a fever which needs attention.'

There was no immediate reply. Willie was sagging against the wall, looking awful.

'I live alone,' said the voice, 'and do not welcome strangers across my doorstep. Go away.'

'We mean you no harm,' Paul repeated. 'We are strangers to this world and yours is the first place we have come upon.'

Silence. Paul saw that Justin was looking increasingly impatient. He was flexing his hammer and seemed ready to smash the door down.

Kate stepped forward.

'Let us in,' she said in a commanding voice. 'Otherwise we'll bring the building down around your head.'

They heard a grumbled oath from within, and then there was the sound of a bolt being drawn back. The door creaked open.

A small old man dressed in threadbare green robes stood before them. His hair and beard were long and white and scraggly, his face withered and gaunt, his pale blue eyes lying deep in their sockets. He was stooped over a staff of the same dark wood from which the door had been built. He was undeniably human.

The resentful look which had been on his face when he opened the door immediately disappeared on sight of them.

'Well,' he said gruffly. 'What have we here? Five feathered friends, done up in all their finery. Warriors, by the look of it.' He jerked his head like a chicken as he spoke. 'I am just a poor old man living out his last years alone. If you are going to kill me, be done with it, but you will find no riches here.'

'We have no wish to kill you,' Paul said. 'Our friend is ill, and we need your help.'

He indicated Willie. The old man looked at him with narrowed eyes. A creature strongly resembling a tabby cat stared out from between his legs. Its eyes were the colour of egg-yolks.

'We are not of this world,' Paul said, 'but were brought to it by mysterious means. We know nothing of your customs but we would welcome whatever help you can give us.'

The old man's eyes seemed to twinkle with a renewed curiosity, and Paul wondered if it had been wise to reveal that they were not natives of the world.

The tabby cat began to sniff at them, and the old man shooed it inside.

'I suppose you'd better come in,' he said.

The interior of the house comprised a single room, gloomily lit with candles in wall brackets. There was a strong smell of something resembling formaldehyde, and a fire blazed in a central stone hearth. The room held several rough tables all cluttered with flasks, retorts and a variety of other equipment. Strange animal shapes floated in jars of clear liquid on shelves, and books and parchments littered the earthen floor.

It was like entering the den of some medieval mad scientist, and even the simplest object did not quite look as it should have done. The chairs were like bowls cut in half and mounted on splayed legs, the books resembled flattened accordions, the tables were of greyish wood with a stony appearance and the candles looked like cylinders of Stilton cheese. Everything in the room was similar to objects which they knew on Earth but subtly different; strangest of all, the fire was fuelled by the 'walnuts' from the thorn-trees; they burned like coal, giving off a healthy heat. Another cat-like creature with tortoise-shell markings sat before the fire, lazily regarding them.

The old man cleared a low couch of parchments and made Willie lie down on it. Willie was by now barely conscious. The old man examined his swollen hand and asked what had happened. Paul explained about the bush.

'A venom-thorn bush,' the old man said. 'Even a dolt would not put his bare hand into its briars.'

'We are strangers here,' Paul repeated patiently.

The old man shambled over to an array of ornate bottles mounted on a long shelf. He selected a phial of dark blue glass, unstoppered it and put it to Willie's mouth, forcing him to drink.

'That's for the fever,' he said. 'I'll need some turf for a poultice.' He was addressing Justin. 'Take care that it's not torn from my roof.'

Justin stood there for a moment, then grunted and stalked outside. By the time he had returned with a clump of grass, the old man had filled a porcelain bowl with milky liquid from another of his bottles. He doused the clod in the liquid before wrapping it around Willie's hand. Willie was unconscious by this time.

'What now?' Teresa asked.

'Now we let him sleep,' the old man said impatiently, as if it was obvious. 'He'll wake before evening, and feel recovered.'

'That quickly?' said Paul.

63

'Didn't I say so? The liquid I used is a specific antidote to the poison, and it acts quickly. But it is just as well you came upon my hut. By sunset he would have been dead.'

'Are you a physician?' Paul asked.

The old man smiled. 'Not exactly.'

'A scientist, then?'

The old man shook his head. 'Let us say that I am a student of the world – in all its natural and unnatural forms. My name is Therion.'

Hobbling on his stick, he sat himself down on the bowl-shaped chair beside the fire. Paul and the others were obliged to find stools for themselves amongst the clutter of books and parchments.

'Now,' the old man said when they were all seated around him, 'you have availed yourself of my services, so it is only fair that I request something in return from you. I am a seeker after knowledge, a man of some education, and yet I am puzzled. You tell me that you have come from another world and yet you speak my language and look no different from me. I ask myself – how can this be?'

It was not a question that could easily be answered, and Paul realized that they would have to tell Therion the whole story.

The old man's hands were cupped over the top of his stick, and he rested his chin on them and listened without speaking as Paul did his best to explain how they had abruptly been transported from Earth to Therion's world and transformed into warriors with special powers. He did his best to omit no significant detail while being as succinct as possible. The word 'Earth' sounded foreign on his tongue, confirming that they now thought and spoke in Therion's language.

The old man remained silent when Paul had finished, tapping the top of his stick and staring down at the tortoiseshell cat. The cat yawned and closed its egg-yolk eyes.

'A remarkable tale,' Therion said at last.

'Do you believe it?' asked Paul.

'Had it been any less remarkable, I might not have done.'

'You mean you do?' said Teresa; her face shone in all its elfin beauty before the fire.

'A demonstration of your powers might convince me,' Therion said.

Kate was quick to accept the challenge. Raising a cupped hand, she created a ball of snow in it. Then she tossed the ball on to the fire. The tortoiseshell cat scuttled away as the fire erupted in a hiss of steam.

Now Justin raised his hammer and thought of enemies and battles and revenge. The hammerhead began to glow a dull red. He plunged it into the earthen floor, and it smoked.

Paul was about to demonstrate the power of his talisman when Therion said: 'Enough, before you bring the roof down on our heads!'

He studied them with renewed interest.

'Where are we?' asked Paul. 'What is the name of this world?'

A cat striped like a zebra emerged from the shadows. The old man reached down and hoisted it into his lap.

'It is called Xhandarre,' he told them, 'an ancient word which simply means The Land. Once it was a world of beauty and ripeness, but now it is a twilight realm of shadows and darkness.'

He began to stroke the cat distractedly while staring into the fire.

'Shadows and darkness,' he repeated. 'So much has changed. There were always wars and struggles for power, but a balance was maintained until Avron Kromar established his dominion over Xhandarre. He is a sorcerer of singular and frightening power.'

'A sorcerer?' said Teresa.

There was wonderment in her voice, but Therion took it for scepticism.

'Do you doubt that they exist?' he asked.

Before Teresa could reply, Therion stretched out his hand and gestured. From his fingertips came bright green tendrils which coiled together into a knot before slowly dissolving into nothingness.

'A rudimentary trick, I must admit,' Therion said sourly, 'but I am an old man now and my powers are not what they were. In my prime I might have challenged Avron Kromar himself, but I was old when he was an apprentice. And when he began to destroy all his rivals I had to flee for my life. So I came here, to a land on the edge of human habitation where I could live out my years in peace with my pickled animals and my household pets.' The zebra cat had begun to purr under his stroking. 'And now Avron Kromar reigns supreme in Xhandarre. I have no doubt that it was he who was responsible for bringing you here, for only he has such power.'

'But how?' said Paul. 'And why?'

'Who can say for sure? I am not privy to his thoughts. But it is possible to make an educated guess. He has long searched for other worlds which lie in parallel to our own, and I can only assume that somehow he discovered your world and used his sorcery to create a threshold between the two. When he tricked you into stepping through the mirror you were transported here in the guise of the characters which he fashioned for you.'

'You mean we've become his creations?'

'In a bodily sense, perhaps. But no sorcerer, no matter how powerful, can control other human minds against their will. You are free agents here, and will be able to use your powers as you wish.'

'I still don't understand,' said Paul. 'Why should he want to bring us here as warriors with special powers in the first place?'

'Who knows?' Therion scratched his goatee. 'Avron Kromar is renowned for his delight in manipulating others to his own ends, and you would do well to take nothing for granted on your quest.'

'Quest?'

Therion nodded. 'If you wish to return to your own world then you must track him down and confront him. And since he is unlikely to return you voluntarily, it will doubtless be necessary to impose your will on him by force.'

There was a long silence. The fire crackled in the hearth.

'Madrimar,' said Kate. 'Is that where we will find him?'

'Indeed,' said Therion. 'It is the capital city of Xhandarre, on the eastern shore of the continent. Avron Kromar dwells in a castle on the island of Dremund in sight of the city. From what you have told me of the signs and portents which you have already received, I have little doubt that he will be anticipating your eventual arrival there.'

'Is it possible for us to defeat him?' Kate asked.

Therion studied her. 'Anything is possible, given sufficient ability and determination. You have been granted rare powers, and even if they were bestowed

67

by the dark sorcerer, that does not mean that they cannot be used against him. And Avron Kromar may well relish a real challenge to his power. He has been the absolute master of Xhandarre for twenty orbits or more, and it would be unlike him to bring you here simply to squash you like flies.' He paused. 'But then again it might be more prudent to relinquish your own world and find a quiet corner of Xhandarre in which to live out the rest of your lives.'

'No,' Justin grunted, banging his hammer on the floor.

'Avron Kromar has great powers,' Therion said. 'It is he who is responsible for the perpetual twilight in which we live. He is attended by four demon familiars, who are formidable opponents themselves. If you confront him, he is likely to know everything of your weaknesses.'

Therion told them that Avron Kromar had managed to summon the four demons from a nether region and strengthen his powers by entering into a pact with them. Then the dark sorcerer had rapidly established his power over Xhandarre, defeating the armies of King Qhoron, who had formerly ruled the land, and having him killed in the most grisly fashion. The king's son, Prince Jarmassad, had also been defeated and made a permanent captive on display in Madrimar; and all rival sorcerers had been destroyed.

Twenty orbits, or years, had passed since then, and Avron Kromar had ruled Xhandarre with an unassailable authority and ruthlessness. The population was cowed, reduced to a subsistence economy, their lives prone to disruption or danger at any time through some whim of the sorcerer or the four demons who served him.

The more Therion talked, the more Paul's apprehension grew. The old man theorized that Avron Kromar must have temporarily seized control of Paul's uncle's mind to trick them through the mirror, and Paul went cold at the thought. But Justin's hammer was glowing, and he brandished it to indicate that he was determined to fight. Kate and Teresa were quick to agree that they had no choice but to press on to Madrimar and confront the sorcerer. Presently Willie awoke, his fever gone and the swelling in his hand diminishing. When the others had explained their situation to him, he was also eager to ride on to the capital. Only Paul had misgivings about the enterprise, but he said nothing in the face of his friends' determination. But Therion was quick to sound a cautionary note:

'Since Avron Kromar established his rule,' he told them, 'Xhandarre has become a world where all evils are possible and creatures of any sort may dwell. He has moulded the world after his own image, and it is a world filled with sorcerous threats to cow the common folk and daunt even the bravest of souls. You will need to draw on every reserve of your courage.' He explained that they would have to travel through forests and farmlands until they reached the second city of Xhandarre, Sharalidor. Then they would have to continue through rugged country before they finally reached Madrimar. It was a journey of perhaps ten days on horseback, and dangers might beset them at any turn.

But there was no daunting them. Justin was eager to engage his enemies in battle, Willie was keen to prove his mettle with his whip and knives, Teresa simply relished the prospect of being able to fly and was confident that she could avoid any dangers by fleeing from them, while Kate took the practical view that if their only hope of getting back to Earth was to overcome Avron Kromar, then they would have to do just that. In the meantime she was going to master and refine her powers so that she would be as formidable an opponent as possible.

Therion, increasingly warming to their company, prepared a thick vegetable stew in a black cauldron which would have done credit to a witch. While he cooked, he explained how he survived alone in the mountains, taking berries and root plants from the fertile slopes of the river valley, and using what remained of his magical powers to lure small animals into traps so that he could add meat to his diet. None of them had yet seen any evidence of animal life, but the old sorcerer assured them that they would find life in abundance once they descended into the river valley; they had come from the Glazed Plain, now the most desolate part of Xhandarre, though a city had once stood where only the ruined tower now remained. The city and all the land around it had been obliterated by Avron Kromar during his rise to power. More fertile land lay ahead of them, though it might be even less hospitable.

Under their urging, Therion was persuaded to display a few simple spells. A silver-grey cat had joined the tortoiseshell beside the fire, and the old sorcerer spun both animals in the air with a wave of his hand and made them bark like seals. He conjured a black ribbon out of nothingness, made the cauldron stalk across the room on suddenly animated legs, and caused a piece of parchment to dissolve into dust.

'Mere tricks,' he said with a grumpy fatalism, 'I am reduced to mere tricks in my dotage. Once I lived in Sharalidor and was the most renowned sorcerer in the city. But those days are long gone and my powers are only a shadow of what they were.' He yawned expansively. 'The simplest spell tires me and I spend much of my days dozing beside the fire. Magic should not be used frivolously, for it becomes like a well dipped into too often which runs dry when it is most needed. Your powers are akin to magic, and you would also do well not to spend yourselves too wantonly.'

Nevertheless, when pressed Therion admitted that he had used magic to build his house, binding the stones together with a sorcerous cement which made the building far sturdier than it looked. He was also able to make the walnuts burn much longer than normal so that a summer crop would provide sufficient fuel to last the whole year, though a side-effect of this spell was that a walnut would occasionally flare white and shoot up the chimney into the air. The flash which they had observed earlier had been caused by this.

'Good magic is like good cooking,' Therion told them as they spooned their rich-tasting stew from smoked glass bowls. 'The recipe has to be just right.'

The old man's potion and poultice had enabled Willie to make a rapid and complete recovery from the effects of the venom-thorn, and his stew nourished all of them. Paul would have been happy to spend the rest of the day and night with Therion in order to learn as much as possible about Xhandarre and the perils they might have to face on their quest; but the others remained eager to press on.

From a cold-store dug into the earthen floor, the old sorcerer provisioned them with various vegetables and dried fruits. He also gave them each a flat loaf of the greenish bread he baked from a wild cereal resembling rye which grew amongst the grass of the mountains. Finally, as they prepared to mount up, he jabbered out details of what vegetables and fruit they could pick and eat in the wild along their way to supplement their rations.

He stood in the doorway, his various cats crawling around his heels.

'Should you succeed in defeating Avron Kromar,' he told them, 'the whole of Xhandarre will rejoice. Would that I could go with you, but I am too old for battles and my aged bones would sit badly in a saddle.' He paused to consider, then said, 'Still, there may be a way of aiding you, if you are willing.'

He was addressing Paul, who lingered, still feeling that they were being foolish to hasten on their journey.

'We are young and know very little of this world,' he said. 'We would welcome any help you can give us.'

'Hold out your talisman,' the old man said.

Paul did so. Therion took the stone in his cupped hands and closed his eyes. For a moment there was nothing; then Paul felt a brief pulse of energy pass through him.

'I have made a link between us through your stone,' Therion told Paul. 'Should you need to summon me, call out with your mind, and if I am able I will come to you and help you as best I can.'

'It will be an invaluable link,' Paul said. 'We are sure to have need of your wisdom and your knowledge of Xhandarre.'

'I would not place too much reliance on it,' Therion told him. 'I am old, and I tire easily. Don't you be surprised if you try to summon me in a moment of peril and hear nothing but snores. Now, begone with you all and travel safely!'

With this gruff farewell, the old man turned and entered his house, his four cats scurrying after him. The arched door closed behind him with a resounding thud.

# 5

# *Creatures of Water and Woodland*

The mountain streams had converged, and now a fast-flowing river ran to their left as they rode along. Strange-looking trees and shrubs sprouted amongst the dark grass, bearing berries or pendulous fruit. Everything was dim, shadowy, and the sky was beginning to darken towards night after the long twilit day. It was summer here in Xhandarre, as on Earth, and the daylight hours were roughly the same.

With the fertility of the land had also come insects – small, gnat-like creatures which buzzed around them but seemed harmless. From time to time they would spot birds like black swallows swooping low over the gleaming water of the river, and there were movements amongst the tufted grass as if unseen animals were scurrying along.

Kate rode apart from the other four, urging her mount along the very edge of the river bank. The horse seemed rather nervous of the water, but Kate held it under a tight rein. She had noticed silver fish darting through the water, and she was keen to test the speed of her reactions.

Kate was prepared for the next flash of silver in the

74

water. Jets of frost sped from her fingertips, plunging into the water and instantly freezing it into a small blob of ice. As the ice bobbed back to the surface of the water, she searched for evidence of the fish inside it. But there was none. Her aim had not been as good as her speed of reaction. Well, then, she would have to keep trying until it was.

Willie was thinking along similar lines. Both the swelling and the tenderness was gone from his hand and it felt as good as new. He unfurled the whip from his belt and switched it, searching for any movement amongst the grass. For a while there was none, but then he suddenly saw a brief flurry just to his right. He immediately flicked the whip and felt it catch around something moving.

With another flick of the wrist, he brought the whip back. Its end was coiled around the neck of a small rodent like a black hamster – coiled so tightly that it had cut into the fur and drawn a milky-grey blood. The creature was dangling lifelessly from the whip: it had died immediately.

Willie unleashed the whip again and the dead animal spun away, disappearing into a tuft of grass. Willie's only emotion was a sense of triumph at his own dexterity. As he stared at the spot where the animal had landed he saw a sinuous movement in the grass nearby – the track of a scavenger come to claim Willie's prey for its own.

Justin had watched all this, and frustration continued to mount in him. He had still had no proper opportunity to display his own prowess, and almost longed for an attack by some large predator who would be a worthy opponent for his hammer. He was also angry at his continued inability to master more than the rudiments of speech: he had to leave all the talking to the others and stand there like a dumb brute. Well, when the time for real fighting came, he would show them all his mettle.

Unlike the others, Teresa was irritated by the small insects which buzzed around them. They seemed to have a liking for her delicate skin, and their bites had begun to itch. The urge to transform herself into flight continued to grow as they rode along but she tried to deny it, knowing that she should keep her power in reserve for real threats to herself. But the saddle was rough between her legs, the bites continued to itch, and the contrast between the discomforts of flesh and the delights of weightless flight grew stronger and stronger.

Paul, meanwhile, felt more composed than he had done since they had entered Xhandarre. The thought that he could summon Therion for help and guidance through his talisman was a comforting one, despite all the sorcerer's qualifications. He had never had much confidence in his own abilities, but with Therion's help he might be able to live up to the others' expectations of him. Not that he wasn't still daunted by the thought of having to battle for their lives with a sorcerer who ruled a world; but he hoped that Therion would provide some extra backbone when he needed it most.

Paul rode between the other three and Kate. Formerly convivial and gregarious, Kate now seemed to prefer to be alone in her new guise, but Paul took every opportunity to watch her from afar. As an ice maiden her girl-next-door attractiveness had been transformed into a regal beauty which still drew him, forbidding though it was. More than ever he wanted to tell her how attractive he found her, but the fear of meeting with a contemptuous rejection remained his dominant emotion, and he kept his distance.

Kate was intent on the water, seeking the flash of silver which would mark the presence of another fish. Her horse continued to twitch its green head under her reins and tried to draw away from the river. She pulled it back, watching the ripples and eddies for the merest hint of silver. . .

Suddenly a fish leapt straight up out of the water. Kate reacted instantly, sending a spurt of ice from her fingertips which transformed the fish into a jagged ball of ice before it hit the water again. But Kate had no time to register her triumph, for suddenly the water foamed and out of it reared a monstrous serpent's head.

It was like a huge copper snake with slitted orange eyes. Kate's horse bucked and flung her from the saddle. The serpent arched its long neck and flicked out a barbed red tongue through a jagged array of teeth. It gave a hideous hiss and loomed over Kate's sprawled form. The fetid smell of rotting fish reached her nostrils. She was too dazed by the fall to summon up her ice powers and thought she was done for. The serpent reared once more, preparatory to striking. Then its head exploded.

This was Paul's doing. On seeing the threat to Kate's life, he had immediately summoned up as much mental energy as possible and destroyed the creature with a devastating burst of his power. He spurred his horse over to Kate, dismounted and helped her sit up.

'Are you all right?' Paul asked. Her body felt cold to the touch.

She nodded slowly, staring at the headless corpse of the serpent, which was draped on the bank. The bulk of its body was still underwater, and a sudden surge of the current carried it away, submerging it in the river so that it was quickly gone.

Kate got to her feet.

'I'm grateful,' she told Paul. 'I owe you a debt.'

'Debts have nothing to do with it. We're all in this together.'

She made no reply to this, and her face remained impassive. Paul was still holding her by the shoulders, but his hands had begun to feel frozen against the chill material of her cloak. He removed them.

Justin and Willie joined them, Justin standing poised on the river bank with his hammer raised as though willing another serpent to appear so that he could dispatch it himself. Damn Paul, he thought, he's not giving me a chance.

A single orange eye remained intact amongst the bile-coloured mess that had once been the serpent's head. Willie prodded it with his foot and found that it was like hard rubber. He picked it up and took it over to Paul and Kate.

'Look,' he said, grinning. 'A battle trophy.'

Both Paul and Kate regarded the eye with distaste. With an urge to shock them, Willie took a dagger from his belt and stabbed it into the eye. A thick, yellow-green fluid began to seep from the punctured sac. Willie let it drip into the palm of his hand.

'Mmm,' he said, licking his lips and making as if to taste it. 'Lime-flavoured custard.'

Kate and Paul looked revolted. Willie laughed, then casually flung the eye into the river before splashing his hand clean.

'Where's Teresa?' said Paul.

The roan horse was cropping the turf near a dense

copse of feathery trees; but there was no sign of its rider.

They waited for ten minutes or so before deciding that they would have to search for her. Paul took charge of her horse, reining it to his, and they rode into the copse. Darkness was falling rapidly now, and it quickly became apparent that the copse was just the outpost of a more extensive woodland, filled with an undergrowth of bracken and squat shrubs. As with everything else in Xhandarre, the vegetation was fundamentally similar to that on Earth but different in its details: the trees were black and gnarled, many with moss-like foliage in place of leaves, while the bracken resembled ragged seaweed. Strange woodland noises reached their ears, and insects whirled by, unseen in the darkness.

As the light faded completely, they began to glimpse tiny flickering white lights amongst the trees. They drew tightly together in a diamond formation with Justin at the apex and Paul at the rear. The walnut trees grew everywhere, their branches snapping under the cloven hoofs of the horses. The flickering lights revealed themselves as shining moth-like creatures, and when one of them settled on Justin's hand, he snatched it away abruptly.

'Hot,' he said.

At that moment Paul was urging his horse through a tangle of foliage when something heavy landed on his back and pulled him from his horse. He felt a thorn-like stabbing at the back of his neck, and immediately a numbness began to spread through his body, preventing him from calling out. He tried to raise himself up, to throw off his squat assailant, but he was too weak to move. His eyelids drooped, and he blacked out.

Scant seconds later two more dark shapes dropped from the tree branches on to Willie and Kate, hurling them from their mounts. Something hard and spiky prickled their skins like tiny anaesthetic darts which rapidly drugged them. Willie glimpsed a grimy, crumpled face with yellowish eyes and matted hair, and Kate saw her assailant grin mischievously, jabbing a short stick on which was mounted a spiky object like a horse-chestnut casing. Then they were both unconscious.

Justin succumbed immediately afterwards, a further attacker dropping on to his back. The barbs of its weapon scraped Justin's cheek. With a shrug of his powerful shoulders he flung the creature from his back. But the numbness quickly began to overcome him. He slid from his saddle to the springy turf. Fighting the effects of the barb, he managed to rise. Then another dark creature dropped from the trees, and a further barb pierced his neck. This time he could do nothing to resist the deadening tide which swept over him. The dark forest floor rushed up to meet him. . .

Willie opened his eyes to find himself trussed to a stake in some kind of forest clearing. He felt hungover, weakened. His whip and belt of knives were gone.

As his thoughts began to clear, he saw that Kate, Paul and Justin were strapped to stakes, as he was himself. Kate's cloak, Paul's talisman and Justin's hammer were also gone.

Overhead the bloodshot moon was full, highlighting the clearing to which they had been brought. At its opposite end a huge shining web was hung between two trees; and at the centre of it Teresa was spread-eagled like a giant butterfly.

Even in captivity her face was radiant, and her eyes were focused on the group of creatures who were squatting in front of her. They were the same creatures who had attacked Willie and the others in the forest – squat proto-humans with straggly hair and crude animal skins covering their dirt-grimed bodies. As Willie's fogged head cleared a little more he began to register the high-pitched ululations they made as they pressed their faces to the earth and covered their heads with their hands in an attitude of supplication. To all appearances they were worshipping Teresa.

Only one of their number was standing – an old woman with matted grey hair, the only female amongst them. Kate's cloak and Paul's talisman hung around her neck, Willie's belt had been strapped about her waist and she held Justin's hammer and Willie's whip aloft in each hand as she added her cries to those of the others. The sound they made was like a chorus of squealing birds.

The clearing was not large, but a pile of dry grass and firewood had been gathered at its centre – a fact which Willie noted with considerable apprehension. In the trees fringing the clearing he saw oval structures which resembled huge roofed nests, and even as he stared one of the squat people emerged from a nest, scrambled across a branch with the dexterity of a squirrel and vanished into the star-shaped foliage of the trees.

Beyond the clearing the forest was dark, but Willie glimpsed the flickering white lights of the moths which they had encountered earlier. Then, in another tree, he saw what was evidently the female of the species of tree-dwellers, holding four small babies to her breast as she stared out into the clearing from her leaf-shrouded perch.

Willie tested his bonds, but found them securely tied. Primitive though the tree-dwellers appeared, they clearly knew how to tie a knot. Kate, Paul and Justin were still unconscious, so he couldn't expect any help from them. But he wasn't going to stand there like a trussed animal and wait until they woke up. . .

At the other end of the clearing Teresa tried vainly to escape the glutinous web. She had been hanging there for what seemed like hours, and she still felt very weak. She knew that she had been foolish to fly off into the forest on her own, but when the serpent had suddenly reared up out of the water, something in her had snapped; she could no longer bear the thought of remaining in her insect-bitten fleshly form for one more second, and so she had struck her wrists together and taken flight into the forest.

At first its tranquil shadows had been comforting, and she had flitted through the undergrowth like a woodland creature in its natural environment. But then she had begun to sense vague movements at the periphery of her vision – rustlings and scurryings which immediately ceased as soon as she turned her head. Soon afterwards a faint fluting sound had reached her ears – delicate, lilting sounds which had immediately made her want to pursue them to their source, banishing her fears.

So she had darted through the forest, the fluting sounds growing louder until she had abruptly emerged into a clearing where a grey-haired woman stood. The sounds were issuing from her. Spellbound, Teresa had sped forward, whereupon the fluting suddenly changed into a piercing shriek which shattered her concentration and her power to remain in flight. She had felt her body becoming flesh once more as she plummeted to earth.

When she had regained consciousness she found herself pinioned by the arms and legs to a sticky web of shining gold. A host of little people were prostrate in front of her. They were inhabitants of the wood, and she immediately understood that the crone who had lured her to the clearing and caused her to black out was their leader and their sage.

She understood this because her mind was suddenly opened to the fleeting thoughts and emotions of the forest-dwellers. With her friends she could sense only vague impressions of their moods, and these only intermittently; but the minds of these primitive creatures were far more open to her.

They were a reclusive people who dwelt in the trees and feasted off fruits and small animals; their trilling, songlike sounds were their equivalent of speech, though much cruder in vocabulary and nuance. They built large egg-shaped nests of grass and twigs high in the trees, and the females produced up to five offspring in one brood, hatching them from eggs the size of grapefruit. All this Teresa discovered simply by opening her mind to the random thoughts and feelings of those around her. But the clearest and sharpest thoughts of all belonged to their leader.

It was apparent to Teresa that her thought patterns were of an altogether higher order than those of the rest of her people. She was the only one of the forest-people to have given herself a name – it sounded like 'Shree-vla' – and this was the most obvious indication of her more advanced mental development. Whereas her people were scarcely capable of holding a coherent line of thought in their minds for more than a few seconds, she was able to think in a manner which might be basic but which was at least consistent and logical on its own terms; whereas the average forest-dweller reacted chiefly out of raw instinct to the immediate aspects of his environment, Shree-vla was capable of detached contemplation and understood the concept of action and consequence. She was also capable of envisaging the future.

From Shree-vla's mind Teresa discovered why she had been captured, and what lay in store for her. The forest-dwellers were perfectly at home in their chosen domain, but their only enemies were the luminous moths whose bodies gave off heat as well as light. Their burns were very painful to the forest-people, and a mythology had grown up amongst them that the glow-moths originated from a single great Moth-Mother who was hidden somewhere in the forest. The Moth-Mother was at once revered and hated by the forest-people; they worshipped her as a goddess, yet believed that if they could destroy her, all the glow-moths in the forest would die, never to plague them again.

When Teresa had flown into the forest her presence had quickly been detected and Shree-vla informed. The crone was immediately convinced that she was the Moth-Mother and determined to lure her into the clearing and stun her into unconsciousness with the raw power of her voice. That she had succeeded did not surprise Teresa now that she knew that the forest-people habitually used their shrieking notes to immobilize the small animals they hunted for food.

Afterwards she had been pinioned to one of the webs which the females of the species spun from the sap of a tree, and which were used as a larder for prey. Now she would be worshipped before being cast into a ceremonial fire and destroyed forever.

On learning all this, Teresa's natural instinct had been to try to escape immediately. But she was still weak after her fall, and could not conjure up any terrifying images with which to frighten off her captors. And just as she was beginning to hope that somehow the others would find her, she saw them being dragged into the clearing by a host of the forest-people who were skipping and trilling with triumph.

For a horrifying few moments she thought all four of them were dead; but as she saw them being tied to stakes she realized that they were simply unconscious.

Shrec-vla was quick to claim the spoils of victory, adorning herself with Willie's belt, Kate's cloak and Paul's talisman. She took the whip and hammer, too, flourishing them above her head as she trilled out orders to her followers. Teresa sensed a subtle and sinister presence in her mind, which was making sure that the crone disarmed her friends. A cold feeling of apprehension filled her; unknown to herself, Shree-vla was being manipulated by another presence, and Teresa had little doubt that it was Avron Kromar himself.

The web still held her tightly, and she could not move her arms. Shree-vla had now gone over to the pile of wood and grass. There was a flickering light in one of the trees, and a female leapt to earth, holding a lighted bunch of kindling. Shree-vla took it from her and plunged it into the middle of the wood-pile.

The dry grass took fire quickly, dense grey smoke billowing up and obscuring Teresa's view of the others. Now the fluting sounds of her captors grew louder and louder. She was trapped, doomed. A terrible fear came over her at that moment, and she would have sacrificed anything to be able to fly away.

Willie, meanwhile, had not ceased in his efforts to free himself from his bonds. The ropes had been spun from tough vine and could not be broken; but the prime physical characteristic of his new body was its suppleness, and he was determined to squirm free. He began to flex and relax his hands.

To his left, Justin awoke. He looked groggy, but he quickly took stock of the situation and gave a bellow of rage. Suddenly Willie's right hand was free from its bonds. At the same instant Justin gave a great grunt and wrenched his whole stake from the ground.

Willie quickly freed his other hand as Justin crouched and then charged the startled forest-dwellers like a one-man battering ram. The little people squealed and scattered in all directions, Justin pursuing the largest knot of them across the clearing. Willie saw that the old hag, in trying to flee, had promptly tripped over Kate's long cloak and now lay sprawled, in all her regalia, face-down on the grass.

Willie dashed across the purple grass and hurled himself on top of her. The old woman began to struggle. She was surprisingly strong, grappling with him like a wild animal. Willie's whip had fallen out of arm's reach, but he managed to pinion her by the shoulders. The old woman's face was squashed and grimy, and an odour of soil and dead leaves issued from her – a sweet and sickening smell. Willie was repulsed by it, and as the woman hung on his neck he suddenly felt that she was a crazed invalid, desperately clinging to him. A wave of disgust overtook him, and he lunged for the belt, pulling one of the daggers free and plunging it into her belly.

The old woman's yellowish eyes rolled in their sockets, and her hands fell away. They were like claws, black-nailed and hideous. Her mouth opened in a gasp, and her breath smelt like rotting meat. Willie twisted the dagger in her belly, and she slumped dead beneath him.

Only then did Willie register what he had done. For a moment he was paralysed by the enormity of it, thinking that he could have easily subdued the old hag without killing her. But there was no time for remorse – Justin needed help. He was at the other end of the clearing and had dispatched several of the forest-people by knocking them over with the stake. Willie pulled a fresh knife from his belt and darted forward, snatching up his whip.

He used the knife to cut the ropes which bound the stake to Justin's back. Freed, Justin immediately rushed to recover his hammer. The forest-people had regrouped and were now advancing around the whole circumference of the clearing. Justin and Willie moved to its centre with the blazing fire at their backs. They both awaited the onslaught almost with eagerness, Willie keen to cut down his opponents with his whip, Justin wanting to crush a few skulls with his hammer. Justin could feel a renewed physical power flooding through him, and the hammerhead began to glow a dull red in anticipation of battle.

But then one of the forest-dwellers gave a keening cry and pointed to the body of the old hag. His cry was quickly taken up by all the others, and suddenly they scattered and darted up the flanks of trees like squirrels in flight. The battle was over; without their leader they had no more relish for the fight.

Willie immediately hurried over to Teresa and began to cut her free from the web. In consistency it was like hard, sticky plastic through which even the sharp blades of the knife could cut only slowly. Willie was working on the bonds at her ankles when Teresa said, 'Free my arms.'

Close to, she looked more radiant than ever, and the melodious sound of her voice captivated him. He did her bidding as speedily as possible. Once her arms were free she struck her bracelets together. Willie stepped back in wonder as she shimmered and took to the air as an insubstantial creature whom no web could hold.

Meanwhile Justin was furious that he had once more been denied the chance to wield his hammer in battle by the abrupt flight of their attackers. As he watched them scurry amongst the trees overhead, he still craved revenge. Snatching flaming logs from the fire, he began to hurl them into the trees.

The foliage took fire immediately, and within a matter of minutes most of the trees around the clearing were ablaze. Justin yelled with triumph as he watched the flames consume the forest-people's nests; the forest-people themselves scurried in panic along boughs, seeking escape routes wherever they could find them.

Paul had awoken just after Justin, and he had seen everything. He watched the mothers with children clutched to their breasts desperately trying to flee the flames, and he felt the hapless sense of being an involuntary participant in some atrocity. True, the forest-people had attacked them in the first place, but they were a primitive people and did not deserve such retribution. It was all very well to destroy goblins and ghouls in their weekly games, but this was real and it was not noble at all. And yet he was conscious that he had not even called out to Justin to stop.

Suddenly Willie was at his side, untying his bonds. On his face was the satisfied grin of someone who has successfully blooded himself in battle, but Paul could not share an iota of his triumph. Teresa had materialized beside Kate and was now untying her. As soon as she was free, Kate hurried over to the body of the crone and unceremoniously pulled her cloak from her neck. Without the cloak she had felt naked, exposed, but as soon as she draped it over her shoulders its chill enveloped her and she could feel her poise and confidence returning.

Paul stood over the old woman, staring at the dagger handle which protruded from her belly. Willie pulled the dagger free and wiped the dark blood from its blade on the grass.

'It was self-defence,' he told Paul. 'She tried to stab me, and in the struggle the dagger went into her.'

Paul had seen everything, and he knew Willie was lying. But he said nothing.

Justin was still running around, tossing firebrands into the branches of the trees, and the whole clearing was ablaze; the harsh, flickering light gave the scene a nightmarish quality. Paul could not bring himself to take the talisman from the old woman's neck. He wanted to ride away without it and forget the ridiculous idea that he could be a warrior.

He saw that their horses were tethered to a burning tree just beyond the clearing. He hurried to them and freed their reins, dragging them into the clearing. Leaping up onto the cream horse, he shouted to the others: 'Let's get out of here!'

'You've forgotten something,' said Teresa, coming forward.

She held out the talisman, innocent of his reluctance to reclaim it.

Paul hesitated, then took it from her.

# 6

# A Plague of Scavengers

'*Voilà*,' said Willie, as the dry grass in the fire they had built erupted into flame. Therion had supplied each of them with a small bundle of matches resembling sparklers, which gave off a bright white flame when struck against a rock. During their ride out of the forest, Willie and Justin had gathered several walnuts from the trees and these now took fire, quickly giving off a comforting heat.

It was a chilly night, the stars like gleaming diamond-points in the sky, the red-streaked moon lying low on the horizon. They had camped on a hillside within sight of the river but some distance from it. The river snaked across a gently undulating plain as far as the eye could see, and in the near distance a rough chequerboard pattern could be discerned: cultivated fields, though they had not as yet come upon any farms, and had decided to sleep in the open that night. They were all exhausted from their travails in the forest.

Paul had led all the way, urging his horse along even when it grew nervous as the glow-moths began to flit out of the undergrowth to investigate them. Kate had kept the creatures away by chilling the immediate air around them.

Any fears that the forest-people would regroup and pursue them had proved groundless, but Paul had been relieved when they had finally emerged from the forest; he wanted to put behind him the disturbing memory of the blazing trees and the families fleeing in terror. Teresa had told them of her intimation that the crone had been manipulated by some superior mentality, and it was a revelation which comforted none of them. Would Avron Kromar's sinister presence be following them every step of the way?

Justin was the only one of them who rejoiced in their victory over the forest-dwellers. The rest of them were subdued, even Willie feeling uneasy about stabbing the crone to death now that the heat of the battle was over. In the final moments of their struggle a mad desperation to escape from her clawing hands had overcome him, and his revulsion had given way to something like relish as he plunged the dagger home. To recall it now made him feel an obscure guilt which went beyond the bare fact of the old woman's killing.

They were all too tired to talk. Paul volunteered to take the first watch. He slipped away to relieve himself, and when he returned the others were all asleep. He sat down beside the fire, the talisman nestling against his chest as if it had always belonged there. In the end he had had no option but to put it on again; he had a responsibility to the others as well as himself, and they might have need of his powers.

It was a clear night, and Paul gazed up at the canopy of stars. Suddenly he saw what was unmistakably the outline of The Plough.

He had only a limited knowledge of astronomy,

but he could recognize the most prominent constellations. Scanning the sky, he quickly spotted the W of Cassiopeia. He searched for the bold upright bow-tie that would be Orion, but failed to find it. Then he remembered that Orion was more visible in winter. What he had already identified was confirmation enough that Xhandarre's night skies were the same as Earth's. Therion had mentioned Avron Kromar's search for 'other worlds which lie in parallel to our own', and he realized that this statement was literally true: Xhandarre was an alter-ego of Earth, perhaps occupying another dimension or timestream, but having similar physical characteristics. That was why they could breathe its air and eat its food; that was why it was inhabited by human beings. They were in the northern hemisphere of Xhandarre in summer, and day and night were the same duration as on Earth. It *was* another Earth – an Earth where science remained rudimentary and sorcery was the dominant force.

The night passed uneventfully, and they set off late the following morning. It was another dim, twilit day, and the river was like watery blood under the distended sun. The others greeted Paul's news that they were on another Earth rather than a different world entirely with none of the surprise which Paul had anticipated; they had taken Therion's words more literally than he, and in any case were not so concerned about the niceties of their situation. It didn't matter much where they were, they told him, so long as they succeeded in their quest and were able to return to Earth.

To Paul, however, it did matter. Xhandarre was a

sister planet to Earth, yet it had a bloated red sun instead of a yellow one, and its moon was like a bloodshot eye. Therion had told them that Avron Kromar was responsible for the perpetual twilight by day, and Paul began to wonder if this meant that he could use his sorcery to alter the appearance of heavenly bodies. If so, it would mean that he was an even more formidable opponent than they had supposed.

Leery of serpents, they continued to keep their distance from the river. They were therefore surprised when, on rounding a bend, they came upon three fishermen standing waist-deep in the middle of the river.

That they were men like any on Earth was immediately clear. Their skins were swarthy, their hair dark, and they wore rough shapeless tunics. Each held a corner of a fishing-net, but on catching sight of the riders they began to scramble towards the opposite bank.

Justin, in the lead, shouted, 'Wait!' But his booming voice made it sound like a threat rather than a request, as he had intended.

Kate spurred her horse past him and gestured at the river. Bolts of ice sped from her hands, and the river immediately froze about the three fishermen, trapping them.

'There was no need for that,' Paul said.

Kate stared at him. 'We do not know who our enemies might be.'

'Our enemies will be everyone if we treat them as such.'

He spurred his own horse to the river bank. The fishermen looked at him without expression, as though expecting to be cut down at any moment.

Paul reached out with his mind and cracked the ice around them. The talisman began to pulse on his chest as he did so, the fishermen stared at it with a mixture of fascination and fear. Finally they clambered up on to the bank.

Paul crossed the river to them.

'We mean you no harm,' he said as the others followed him.

'Are you sorcerers?' asked the youngest of the three, a boy in his teens.

Paul shook his head. 'We are travellers, on our way to Madrimar.'

'You are Avron Kromar's agents,' another of the fishermen said defiantly. He was black-haired, and blind in one eye, a sunburst of white scars surrounding it.

'Far from it,' said Paul, thinking that their accent was quite unlike Therion's but still perfectly understandable. 'We are warriors who are travelling to Madrimar to do battle with the sorcerer.'

The half-blind man exchanged a glance with his older companion, a stout fellow with a hint of grey in his hair.

'Warriors,' said the boy, as though savouring the word. 'No one has dared challenge the sorcerer since before I was born.' He began to stare at Paul and the others as though in the presence of gods.

'It's a trick,' the half-blind man said.

'It's no trick,' Paul assured him.

'If we meant you harm,' Kate interjected, 'rest assured that you would be dead by now. You have seen something of our abilities.'

The two older men seemed to consult silently with one another. Then the stout man spoke: 'What do you want with us?'

'Our horses need rest and food,' Paul said, 'but we want nothing that you do not wish to give us. If you ask us to, we will ride on.'

Paul sensed that the others were not happy with such a diplomatic approach. But it was he who had begun their dialogue, and he felt that it would be better to gain the fishermen's help by persuasion rather than force.

'Madrimar is many days' ride from here,' the stout man said.

'Do you truly mean to do battle with Avron Kromar?' asked the boy.

Paul decided to take a gamble. 'He brought us here from another world. If we are to return home, we must overcome him.'

'Another world?' the boy looked astounded. 'You have come from another world?'

'Enough, Maric,' the stout man said, as though he still doubted that they were friendly and did not want the boy to be too familiar with them. He stared at Paul, and it was as if he was trying to peer into Paul's mind, to see whether he and the others could indeed be trusted. Then he indicated the half-blind man.

'This is my brother, Eren,' he said, 'and I am called Leshtu. Maric is my son. We are farmers and fishermen, no more, no less. It is the custom in these parts to invite innocent travellers to share the hospitality of the dinner table. Our farm is but a short walk from here.'

There was a slight emphasis on the word 'innocent', as if Leshtu was still suspicious of them. But the hospitality, if grudging, would be welcome; they were not used to travelling by horseback and sleeping out in the open. Paul felt as if every bone in his body was aching.

The net was drawn in from the river, but it contained only one small fish, insufficient to feed a single person.

'Even the waters are cursed,' Eren said bitterly.

'Don't you fear that you might snare a water-serpent?' Paul asked, thinking that they had shown considerable courage in braving the river in the first place.

'A water-serpent?' Leshtu regarded him quizzically. 'There are no serpents in this river.'

Paul was tempted to tell him of their encounter with the creature further upstream, but some instinct made him hold back. Perhaps the river was shallower here, or perhaps the serpents avoided its inhabited stretches.

Leshtu led the way through crop-bearing fields, with Eren and Maric at his heels. In deference to their hosts, Paul and the others dismounted to ensure that their horses did not damage any of the crops. It was clear that Maric was profoundly intrigued by them and was only restrained from enquiring about their powers by his father's caution. Eren, meanwhile, remained remote and taciturn, as if he still mistrusted them.

The fields were all small, divided from one another by simple mounds of earth. In many of the fields the crops were damaged, their foliage ragged or whole plants torn from the ground as if by vandalizing hands. Where they survived they looked weak and sickly, with pale, wilting leaves. Little wonder, Paul thought, for they could hardly be obtaining adequate sunlight; overhead the sky was a washed purple colour, and the dim, swollen sun produced no more light than that of a heavily overcast day on Earth.

97

Presently they came in sight of a series of squat buildings: farmhouses and barns, with duck-like creatures scurrying about in an enclosure. There were crouched figures in the fields nearby, and Leshtu began calling out to them that they had visitors and that hospitality must be proffered. They immediately stopped what they were doing and began hastening from the fields.

In all there were fifteen of them sitting around a long table of speckled grey wood. Leshtu sat at the head of the table, with Eren and Maric on either side of him. At the opposite end of the table sat Leshtu's wife, Peris, flanked by her two daughters, both of whom looked to be in their late teens. Eren's three young daughters and a son not yet in his teens made up the numbers. It was conspicuous that there was no mention of Eren's wife.

They had eaten some kind of roast fowl with vegetables and a savoury jelly, accompanied by grey bread and a yeasty ale the colour of brass. The meat resembled a spicy chicken and came in small portions, the vegetables constituting the bulk of what was on their plates. It was clear to Paul that Leshtu and his family barely managed to survive off the land and had been forced to spread their meagre rations even further so that their visitors could receive the traditional hospitality of the farmlanders.

There was a subdued atmosphere at the table during the meal. Leshtu and his family were polite but unforthcoming, and they showed no curiosity about their visitors, despite their claim to have come from another world and the evidence of their unusual powers. In their gaudy uniforms they made the farmlanders look drab, and the older daughters cast admiring glances at both Teresa and Kate as they ate; it was as if they were royalty being entertained by peasants.

Paul began to wish that they had simply ridden on instead of accepting Leshtu's invitation to eat with them; as it was, they were depriving the family of food which they badly needed themselves. But it was too late now, although when Justin made to give himself a second helping of vegetables from the pot, Paul mustered the courage to say to him: 'I think we should not place too great a strain on the family's provisions for the sake of our stomachs.'

He sweetened the comment with a smile. Justin paused and stared at him, his hand already on the bowl. Then he gave an affirmative grunt before pushing the bowl aside.

When pressed, Leshtu admitted that their crops had flourished in the distant past but the land had long ceased to yield its former bounties. They did not mention Avron Kromar directly, but it was clear that they blamed the sorcerer for all their present difficulties, while remaining chary of actually saying as much. They lived, Paul realized, in continued fear.

'I noticed,' Paul said conversationally to Peris, 'that in several of your fields the crops are damaged. Do you have problems with insects or worms?'

Peris glanced at Leshtu before saying, 'Birds. Sometimes flocks of birds descend on a field.'

'Birds?' said Kate. 'They must be large to cause such damage.'

'They are no ordinary birds,' Peris said slowly, then stopped at a look from her husband.

Kate looked around the table. It was clear that no

one was going to say anything further. As strangers they were still mistrusted.

'They killed my mother,' the little girl sitting opposite Kate said matter-of-factly.

Everyone seemed to freeze around the table. The little girl was one of Eren's daughters, and Eren himself had gone rigid. No one spoke for several moments, and then Leshtu said, 'It is a painful subject, and you will forgive us if we choose not to discuss it with strangers.'

No more was said on the matter, but the brief frankness of the exchange seemed to permit a greater conversational relaxedness, which Maric immediately exploited. He was sitting between Willie and Justin, with a whip and hammer on the floor at either side of him.

'Will you kill the sorcerer when you've defeated him?' he asked Willie.

'Would you want us to?' Willie replied.

'Yes. Everyone would. He is evil and hated everywhere.' The boy paused, peering at him. 'Are you afraid that you might die?'

There was an unnerving quality about the boy's questions. Willie shrugged and essayed a light-heartedness he did not feel. 'We will all die sooner or later.'

'All of us are very aware of the dangers,' Paul said from across the table. 'It would be foolish not to be afraid.' It was he who had introduced them as warriors in the hope of dispelling the farmlanders' fears that they were sorcerers, but he felt it important that the boy should not romanticize them.

Maric turned to Justin. 'Can I try your hammer?'

Justin gave a short nod and the boy, with difficulty, managed to raise it from the floor. He stared at the stony metal of the hammerhead, and in his eyes Paul could see dreams of battles and of opponents slain. Both Leshtu and Peris were looking at him with a hint of anxiety, but neither said anything.

Then, out of the silence, they heard distant screeching sounds, raucous and flock-like. The family's reaction was instantaneous. Without a word they surged from the table and made haste for the door.

'What's happening?' said Teresa, but all the family were suddenly too busy to take heed of her. Peris was ushering the smaller children into a voluminous cupboard beside the hearth, while the rest of the family were snatching up brooms and rakes and mattocks.

Paul and the others followed them outside. Leshtu, Eren, Maric and Eren's son, Jalel, were each armed with a mattock. Jalel could have only been ten or eleven years old, but he hurried after the others across the farmyard and out into the fields. He was closely followed by Peris and her two daughters, armed with rakes and knives attached to broom handles.

The screeching sounds were louder now, and a flock of large, dark creatures were flying out of the sun towards the farm. Framed by its bloated red hemisphere, they looked like a cross between bats and true birds. And they were the size of eagles.

'Come on!' said Paul, racing after the farmlanders.

The birdbats had reached the fields before Leshtu and his family. They were black and leathery, with reddish claws and serrated beaks. They immediately began to tear the crops from the fields with both beak and claw, working not instinctively but methodically, as if their prime purpose was not to scavenge for food but to destroy as much of the crop as possible.

When Leshtu and the others reached the field, they

immediately began flailing with their mattocks. The birds took to the air before soaring back and attacking them.

They were not invulnerable: as Paul raced across the field he saw Leshtu plunge his mattock into the breast of one of the creatures and watched it flap lifelessly to earth; but they were clearly very dangerous opponents, attempting to stab at the eyes with their beaks and rake the flesh with their claws. But the family were fearless, the women batting the birds from the air with brooms and rakes, and even young Jalel swinging his mattock at any bird that dared come near him. But none was more enthusiastic and fearless in the fight than Maric, who swung and jabbed and parried with his weapon as though he relished every moment of danger.

The family were, however, greatly outnumbered by the birdbats and could fight a holding action only. But at last Paul was in range. He picked out half a dozen of the birds who were presenting an immediate danger to the family and willed them to explode. They promptly did so.

Moments later bolts of ice crackled through the air and several more birds fell in frozen death as Kate added her powers to the battle. Willie and Justin ran on into the thick of the fray, Willie cracking his black whip, Justin's hammer already beginning to glow.

The birdbats were clearly disturbed by this unexpected resistance to their attack, but they continued to harry their human opponents. Willie lashed and slashed with his whip, a delicious sense of vengeance filling him each time he brought a birdbat to earth. Justin bellowed and swung his hammer at the head of one of the creatures. There was a grisly crunch, and the birdbat fell lifelessly at his feet, lime-coloured blood spreading from it.

Only Teresa hung back. She felt repulsed by the hideous sight of the creatures, just as she had done with the water-serpent, and she experienced the same instinct to transform herself into her airy form and fly away from the horrors. In her new guise she was sensitive to all forms of ugliness and brutality; she longed to live in a world of grace and beauty. It would be so easy to flee, to escape forever. She only needed to strike her wrists together.

The others, in the thick of the fray, were unaware of Teresa's absence; they knew nothing except that they were swamped by the birdbats. They struck out as best they could, bringing creature after creature to earth. But always there were more, screeching and hissing and flapping their leathery wings, snapping with their dark beaks and grasping with their red claws. Then suddenly all the birds' cries seemed to coalesce into a single shriek before the whole flock took off as one and sped as fast as they could fly into the sunrise.

'I filled their minds with the image of a terrifying predator,' Teresa told them all as they sat around the table in the aftermath of the fight. Leshtu had fetched a barrel of ale from his cellar to celebrate their victory, and they were drinking from mugs of the smoky glass which seemed common in Xhandarre. All five of them were now completely accepted by the family as friends.

Teresa felt somewhat abashed that she had only joined the fight belatedly, and she was glad that none of the others had noticed. What had stopped her from flying away was the realization that she could dispatch the birdbats without having to go near them. Summoning up her powers of illusion, she had filled their minds with an image of an enormous flying dragon, swathed in glittering red and gold plumage and intent on devouring them. They had instantly fled.

'Those creatures have harried us ever since Avron Kromar conquered Xhandarre,' Leshtu told them. 'They will doubtless return, but it is enough for the moment that we dispatched them more vigorously than ever. You have our thanks.'

'Where do they come from?' asked Paul.

'They nest in caves in the mountains to the east,' Leshtu told him. 'They harry all the farmlands roundabouts, destroying crops and making our lives more of a misery than ever. Avron Kromar does not want his subjects to rest easily under his yoke.'

'He controls them?'

Leshtu shrugged. 'They are products of his sorcery, creatures conjured by him to keep us cowed. Once, these lands were fertile and without dangers. We were able to raise healthy crops and sell our surplus in Sharalidor. But it is in the sorcerer's interests to keep us poor and weak. At first he sent men to collect heavy taxes, but there were rebellions and several were slain. So he installed the creatures as a more effective means of policing us.'

'I was one of those who rebelled,' Eren said abruptly. 'He sent a flock of the creatures to my farm. My wife was slain protecting my children, and a claw took the sight from my eye.'

The radial scars around his dead eye were a graphic emblem of what had happened. Paul could imagine the claws raking the eye socket before plucking the sight from the eye itself.

'Eren and his children have lived with us ever since,' Peris said. 'His land lies derelict and the creatures come regularly to destroy the best of our harvest.'

'You say the birds nest in caves to the east,' Paul said. 'Would we pass them en route to Sharalidor?'

'Have no fear,' Leshtu said. 'If you travel through the valley by day it is unlikely that you will disturb them. They are nocturnal creatures, who are most active at dusk or by night.'

'It was not our safety I was thinking of,' said Paul. 'I was thinking that perhaps we might rid you of these creatures once and for all.'

# 7

# *Death by Drowning*

'I say we should press on to Sharalidor,' Willie told
Paul. 'We can come back later, when we've killed
Avron Kromar, and get rid of the birds.'

'No,' Paul replied.

'We haven't got time for mercy missions.'

'I promised,' Paul said firmly, then spurred his
horse ahead of Willie.

He disliked arguing and was even more uneasy
that he was imposing his will on the others. But, apart
from Willie, the others appeared to be quite happy to
go along with him in his intention to destroy the
birdbats in their nests. Justin was always game for
adventure in his new guise, while Kate and Teresa
had expressed neither reservations nor enthusiasm for
the task. So he was determined to go through with it.

It was an overcast morning and a thin, ordinary
rain was falling. Draped in oilskin cloaks which Peris
had provided, they had already entered the rocky
valley where the birdbats were said to have their
roosts. They had spent the night at Leshtu's farm,
telling Maric and the other children stories of Earth,
and finding it surprisingly difficult to communicate a
sense of what their world was like.

Afterwards Peris had shown them to their sleeping quarters, a large room with blankets draped over bales of brown straw. Before they had bedded down, Paul persuaded the others to swap their various weapons and articles of power. It soon transpired that they would not work for anyone else. Kate's frost-cloak remained at room temperature on all the others, Justin's hammer failed to glow when wielded by anyone but himself, Willie's whip was as inflexible as wire, and Teresa's bracelets – too small to fit on any wrist but her own – produced nothing but a metallic ring when struck together. Finally Paul's talisman was no more than an ornament on the shoulders of his friends. Their powers were not transferable.

They had set off again shortly after sunrise. Peris had insisted on feeding them a breakfast of brown, nutty grain moistened with a fragrant milk from a creature which was presumably the Xhandarrean equivalent of a cow. Maric had pleaded with his parents to be allowed to accompany them as a guide, but Paul was quick to assure the disappointed boy that this would not be necessary. With full bellies, they had ridden off into the rain.

To Willie the breakfast had merely been an added part of the emotional blackmail which the family was putting on them to destroy the birds. In theory he wasn't against helping them, but you had to be practical; they needed to secure their own futures before they started dashing off like knights in shining armour to help all and sundry. What if there was a time-limit to their quest? What if the sorcerer had ensured that they would remain permanently in Xhandarre unless they killed him in a matter of days? Several of Justin's role-playing games had entailed them achieving their goals within a specified time, otherwise they lost. The real thing might be no different.

They rode on, Willie disgruntled with Paul's stubbornness, but not wanting to make an issue of it in the face of the others' tacit support for Paul. Presently they came in sight of the pitted rockface where the birdbats' caves were clustered.

Though the creatures were asleep inside, Teresa began to sense their presence. It began as a vague feeling of unease which gradually built up until she could almost see the creatures hanging in the dark recesses of their caves. A horde of rapacious consciousnesses, created by sorcery to plunder and despoil, they had no thoughts as such but were merely filled with a ravening urge to destroy. Their unconscious instincts writhed like worms inside her head, and Teresa closed her mind to them.

Paul was in the lead, and she drew her horse alongside him. The honeycombed rockface rose up to a great height, a crag festooned with overhanging vegetation.

'They're in there,' she said in a whisper.

Paul nodded, staring at the rockface. Despite his insistence that they should destroy the creatures, he was suddenly afraid. It was the same kind of fear which had possessed him when his cousin had drowned . . . a paralysing, helpless sense that all that mattered was to preserve his own safety no matter what happened to anyone else.

The previous night he had dreamt again of Brian, as he did on many nights. In most of his dreams he merely saw his cousin as he had been when still alive; they had always been close when young. But last night he had returned to the afternoon of Brian's

108

death and had awoken from the nightmare consumed with guilt at his drowning.

They had been on holiday with his aunt and uncle in Cornwall, staying at an isolated beach-house on a rocky stretch of coast. His aunt and uncle had gone into the local town one afternoon to buy provisions, and Brian had insisted on launching the small dinghy which they had brought with them. Unlike Paul, Brian had never learned to swim, and the currents offshore were treacherous.

Paul had made his first mistake by not insisting firmly enough that Brian shouldn't take the dinghy out. His second mistake had been to refuse to accompany his hot-headed cousin. Instead he had remained on the beach, watching Brian paddle out to sea. Then Brian had stood up to wave at him; at the same instant the dinghy had overturned, plunging him into the water.

Paul had raced along the coastline to get as close to his cousin as possible. Brian had fallen into the water amongst rocks where the tides were fierce. As Brian flailed about, crying out for help, Paul found himself rooted to the spot. He knew that he should try to swim out and rescue his cousin, but he knew also that there was a real danger that he too would drown.

That fear had held him back until Brian had finally gone under and had not reappeared. Clawing his shoes from his feet, Paul had immediately flung himself into the water and swum out to where he had last seen him. The tides were strong and the jagged rocks presented a constant danger, but Paul had submerged himself again and again, searching the turbulent waters for his cousin, but without success. In the end, exhausted, he had no choice but to scramble on to a high rock and cough water from his lungs as the sea continued to rage around him. He had still been there when his aunt and uncle found him.

No blame was ever attached to him for Brian's death; both his aunt and uncle knew Brian as a headstrong boy who had always got his way with Paul. In fact they praised Paul's efforts to save him. But Paul was not mollified. He knew that it was his fear and indecision which had been the cause of Brian's death; if he had dived into the water immediately, he could have saved his cousin. He was a coward, plain and simple.

His aunt was devastated by her son's death, and she had died of grief six months later. This only added to Paul's guilt, for she had taken him in and raised him after his own parents had died when he was a small boy. His uncle had continued to treat him generously in the years that followed, but that only made him feel more unworthy and despicable. And as his uncle grew increasingly frail and eccentric, Paul became determined to shoulder the burden of the toyshop as much as possible; he was going to stand by his uncle until the bitter end.

Paul had awoken from the nightmare filled with shame and self-loathing. But then he had sensed a stirring in his mind, and a sleepy and irritable voice had said, 'What is it?'

The voice was Therion's, and Paul realized that somehow he had transmitted the powerful emotions associated with the dream to the old sorcerer, rousing him from his sleep.

'It's only me,' Paul said with his mind. 'I was having a nightmare. I didn't mean to wake you.'

'What sort of nightmare?' Therion asked.

'It was about someone I used to know.' Paul didn't want to talk about it.

Therion seemed to sense this. He grunted, then asked to be told what had happened to them so far on their journey.

Paul wondered if the old sorcerer had actually relived the nightmare with him. But he was eager to be distracted from it, and he told Therion about their encounters with the water-serpent, the forest-people and finally the birdbats.

'The serpent was an unnatural creature, doubtless conjured by Avron Kromar,' Therion told him.

This confirmed Paul's own suspicions and emphasized how innocent all five of them were of this world.

'Do you think I was right to promise the farmlanders that we would destroy the birdbats?' he asked Therion.

'You are a grown man,' came the reply, 'and you must take your own decisions on these matters. Make your choice, then stick to it. If you have told the farmlanders that you will eradicate the creatures, then it is now your obligation to do so.' He paused. 'Or to take an equally firm decision to change your mind. Just don't dither.'

There was a teasing note to the old man's voice, but Paul knew he was right; it was his indecision that had caused Brian's death.

'Now,' said Therion, 'do you think you will permit me to sleep in peace? I am going to need my rest if you decide to call on me for help tomorrow.'

Then the old man was gone.

As he faced the honeycombed rockface, Paul recalled Therion's words and realized that the old sorcerer expected a summons. Paul concentrated and began calling out to him even as he spurred his horse forward.

111

A few moments later he sensed Therion's presence, sensed him peering out through his eyes. The rain had now ceased, and a mist hung over the top of the crag. Paul waited while the sorcerer took in all the details of their environment.

'Fire,' Therion said at last. 'Fire will consume them. Throw blazing bushes into the caves and they will burn like dry straw.'

Paul had vaguely formulated a different plan, but he bowed to the sorcerer's superior knowledge of Xhandarre.

'Is Therion here?' Teresa asked, coming up beside Paul; she had sensed his presence.

Paul nodded. 'He says we should throw burning bushes into the birdbats' caves.'

The valley floor was dotted with the venom-thorn bushes. The others were consulted and they agreed to the plan. Assuming that the bushes would burn when damp, Paul could then use the power of the talisman to hurl them into the caves. A lighted match was applied to a test bush, and it quickly erupted into flame.

There remained the problem of trying to ensure that all the cave entrances were sealed with fire more or less simultaneously, so that the birdbats from one cave could not be alerted by the fire in another and escape. Paul knew that he lacked sufficient control of his power to achieve this unaided; the caves lay at different levels, and there were over a dozen in all. Various suggestions were made – Kate could construct gantries of ice from which to hurl the flaming bushes, or Teresa could try to keep the birdbats hemmed in their caves with some terrifying image of a predator. Justin also wanted to be involved in some way, indicating that he was more than prepared to

112

charge directly into the caves with burning bushes.

'What is all this foolishness?' Therion said abruptly to Paul. 'The simplest plan is always the best. Use the talisman to hurl the burning bushes into the cave-mouths. I will help in securing speed and accuracy.'

Paul conveyed this to the others. Justin looked disgruntled, but there was no time to be lost.

Protecting their hands with the oilskins, the five of them uprooted more than twenty bushes. They were speedily lit, while Paul stood back and allowed Therion to add the power of his mind to Paul's own.

'Now!' said Therion.

Paul had accepted the old man's counsel that he should concentrate on accuracy, while Therion himself provided the speed. He lifted all the bushes into the air, slowly but steadily; they glowed bright orange against the muddy red-grey sky, rising up and up *en masse* until suddenly he felt Therion propelling them forward.

Most of the caves were small enough for one bush to fill their entrance; to the larger cave-mouths Paul added a second bush. He was surprised and pleased at the skill which he displayed in manoeuvring the two dozen or so bushes; even with Therion's help, it was something of a feat. Every cave-mouth was filled with a ball of fire.

Then the screeching began.

From every cave came the harsh cries of the birdbats. They quickly rose to a terrifying and inhuman crescendo – the creatures were trapped and panicking, screaming in fear and pain.

Then they began to burst through the cave-mouths.

Paul and the others stood rooted as the flocks emerged. Each birdbat caught fire as it issued through the wall of flame, but none fell. In blazing swarms they descended on their attackers.

Kate created a barrier of ice in the air, but this was quickly breached by the burning horde. Willie flashed with his whip and Justin with his hammer, but they could do no more than pick off a few of the birdbats at a time, whereas there were thousands of them in all, more dangerous than ever before as they harried and lunged with their fiery beaks and claws. Teresa tried to conjure up another vision of the predator which had scared them away in the fields, but they were too crazed with pain to take notice of it. Terror overtook her, and in an instant she had struck her wrists together and was flying away as fast as her weightless body could carry her.

Paul stood frozen at the centre of the swarm, unable to understand what had gone wrong. He saw that the birdbats were being consumed by the fire, but not quickly enough; he and the others would be dead before all the birds fell. Then he noticed that the fires in the cave-mouths were already flickering out. And dark, flapping shapes were still emerging, now unscathed by flame. They would not even have the satisfaction of having eradicated the creatures.

Paul's original plan had been to bring down the crag overhanging the caves, to seal them in forever under an avalanche of rocks and earth. He was now profoundly wishing that he had done so at the outset. And the plan was still a good one.

Concentrating over the screeching and the flapping of wings, he managed to create a protective bubble around himself and the others. The few birdbats who were trapped inside it were quickly dispatched, and then Paul turned to the others.

'I'm going to pull down the crag,' he told them. 'I

want you to get a safe distance away from here.'

'Where's Teresa?' Willie asked, not having noticed her departure.

'She flew away,' Kate said.

'It must be done as quickly as possible,' Paul said. 'You have to get away now.'

'Can't you do it from a distance?' Kate asked.

Paul shook his head. 'At long-range I don't think I'd have the power. Even this close it's going to be difficult. But it's the only chance we have.'

The others stared at him.

'Don't worry,' he told them. 'I'll look after myself. Go! Now!'

Willie was the first to move. Kate and Justin hesitated, until Paul pushed them after him. Reluctantly, they went.

He protected them with a psychic shield for a few hundred yards as they hurried down the valley, the burning birdbats flapping around the invisible bubble about their heads. Finally he dismissed the shield, spinning around and peering upwards towards the overhanging crag. He gave the mental equivalent of a huge scream, pouring all the powers of his mind into imagining that the crag was splitting, cracking, tumbling down upon him and the birds.

There was a pause, and then everything seemed to happen in a furious slow-motion. A huge chunk of outcropping rock topped with trees and bushes began to separate itself from the main mass, the bloody sky appearing like a vein in the crack. It started to descend as other massive chunks came away, and fell towards him.

The fiery birdbats flapped about his head. He had intended to protect himself from the onslaught with another force-shield, but suddenly he felt exhausted of will-power and knew that he could not possibly hope to escape the avalanche. He made a half-hearted attempt to summon a shield, but nothing happened; he could only stare helplessly as the fruits of his mental labours came hurtling down upon him.

# 8

## *Sharalidor*

As soon as Paul released the others from the protection of the force-shield, the birdbats descended on them.

Willie, Kate and Justin were prepared, and they reacted instantly by flailing, freezing or bludgeoning the creatures from the air. Within a matter of seconds, none remained. At that instant they heard a tremendous cracking and splitting of rock. They turned and saw the crag fracture as if hit by an earthquake.

Rocks, soil, grass, shrubs and trees all came tumbling down in an irresistible tide which engulfed the burning swarms below. Willie, Kate and Justin hurriedly scrambled on to a tall outcrop of rock as the torrent of earth and stone flooded past them, surging down towards the bottom of the valley. Huge clouds of dust rose up, obscuring the sun, obscuring everything.

Presently the dust began to settle. A tide of debris stretched all the way down to the river. The roots of trees protruded incongruously from the earth, flowers and grass lay beneath rocks and boulders, and everywhere lay the black corpses of the birdbats.

Willie, Kate and Justin did not move for some time, nor was there any movement in the path of the avalanche. Then a few straggler birdbats who had escaped the avalanche began to emerge and flap around aimlessly. Very deliberately, Kate picked each one off with a fierce burst of ice from both her hands.

Then there was a rushing of air, and Teresa flew out of the sky, landing on the outcrop beside them. She shimmered, became flesh and blood once more.

'I saw it,' she said. 'I was right overhead. He was trapped in the middle of it. Do you think he managed to protect himself?'

The others said nothing; all of them knew only too well that Paul could not possibly have survived.

Another birdbat flapped out of the dimness. Willie slashed viciously at it with his whip, bringing it to earth. It lay close by, injured but not dead, screeching at them with a feeble fierceness. A knife flashed in Willie's hand, and the creature skittered across the rocks as the blade plunged through its breast.

Retrieving the knife, Willie twisted it in the birdbat's breast as he pulled it free. Lime-yellow blood stained the blade, and Willie wiped it clean on his thigh with two swift movements. He felt irritated that Paul had been so stupid as to get himself killed quite needlessly; if only they had ridden straight through the valley as he had wanted to, instead of playing Good Samaritans to a bunch of farmers. . .

Justin felt a similar sense of helpless irritation towards his dead friend. It was as if Paul had been determined to play the hero and the martyr while denying anyone else the chance to exhibit bravery. Justin knew that in Xhandarre his only way of

118

displaying his mettle was through his hammer, and yet he continued to be thwarted at every turn. Damn Paul; there was no need for him to have died. There was no need for him to have been a hero.

Kate had felt numb immediately after the avalanche. But with Teresa's return an icy anger filled her.

'You ran out on us,' she said. 'You fled.'

Teresa started, as though physically wounded by her words.

'I didn't,' she said. 'I tried to create an illusion, but it didn't work. There was nothing else I could do to help. I was only trying to protect myself with my powers, just as you all were.'

'All you thought about was your own safety.'

'That isn't fair.'

Teresa looked at Willie and Justin, but both were silent, offering her no support. She was keenly aware that she had got the rest of them into trouble after her earlier flight into the forest; and now she seemed to have let them down again.

But what else could she have done? In her new guise she was continually tempted with the urge to fly, and under stress this urge often became irresistible. Was that cowardice or just a natural characteristic of her new self? She didn't know. But she disliked the thought that a butterfly nervousness and timidity might have ousted the doughtiness which she had always prized in her old personality.

At that moment she began to cry. The urge was as sudden as it was uncontrollable. Willie took her in his arms, made her sit down, and held her as she sobbed over Paul, over everything. Kate watched, part of her despising Teresa for her weakness, part of her wishing that she could let out her grief as well. Meanwhile

Justin's shock over Paul's death was translated into a burning anger which made him stalk away.

The horses had been tethered a safe distance along the valley. They had been in no danger from the avalanche and had escaped the ravages of the birdbats. Kate and the others approached them with the keen awareness that there were still five mounts, whereas only four riders remained. Up to now, and despite everything that had happened to them, it had been possible to imagine that they were engaged in some kind of ultra-realistic role-playing game. But Paul's death had finally banished that comfortable illusion.

The horses snorted, as though impatient to resume the journey. They were immune to human tragedy, creatures of basic instincts and appetites. At times their white eyes would seem to glint with intelligence, but then the nictitating membranes would blur them as if to deny the fact. Kate thought again of Paul, lying crushed and broken beneath tons of earth and rocks. If they survived the journey and succeeded in conquering Avron Kromar, she hoped that it would fall to her to kill the sorcerer.

In the meantime there was nothing for it but to ride on.


The rain began to fall again, and as they continued east in their oilskins, they looked as drab and miserable as they felt. Emerging from the ravine, they found themselves in a broader river valley, thickly forested with dark conifers resembling cedars of Lebanon. They avoided the forests, in which the glow-moths fluttered, and climbed to higher ground, where only grasses and shrubs prevailed.

Night fell, and the rain finally ceased. They continued riding, bleakly and silently, until hunger finally made them stop on the crest of a hill fringed by tall trees with dry, spade-like leaves, which they discovered were an excellent substitute for paper tissues.

They lit a fire in a hollow on the hilltop and attended to their rations. Afterwards Kate excused herself, and Justin went off to check the horses. Willie studied Teresa, whose face flickered like a ghost in the firelight. A beautiful ghost. Despite the tragedy of Paul's death, he felt a strong stirring of desire. Discreetly he moved closer to her.

She was nibbling on a succulent fruit which resembled a large blue raspberry. A trickle of juice ran from one corner of her mouth. Willie tore a leaf off a branch and offered it to her. She smiled, took it, and dabbed the juice away.

'Do you know something?' Willie said.

'What?'

'You're beautiful.'

Willie felt a kind of thrill at saying the words, knowing that in his old guise he had been gauche with the opposite sex and would never have mustered the courage to be so frank.

'I mean it,' he said, moving closer and taking hold of both her arms. She did not resist. He lowered his head and kissed her on the lips.

Teresa was taken by surprise more than anything else. She was still numb over Paul's death, and while Willie's compliment delighted her, she felt that it was inappropriate under the circumstances.

Willie pressed her back on to the grass and continued kissing her. As his lips crushed hers, she began to feel oppressed by the sheer physicality of him, pinning her down, flattening her, his heavy male smells suffocating. . .

She struggled free and sat up.

'What is it?' he asked.

She shook her head. 'It's too soon. After Paul.'

'I didn't mean any disrespect for him,' Willie assured her. 'I just wanted to show you how I felt.'

Before Teresa could say anything, Justin came blundering through the dense strand of trees.

'Come,' he said to them.

They followed him back through the trees, and suddenly emerged on the far slope of the hill, which looked down on a broad plain. Kate was standing there, staring down at what was clearly a city nestling in a bend in the broad river which coiled across the plain.

'Sharalidor,' said Teresa.

All four of them were weary from their dismal travels that day, and Teresa suggested that they bed down for the night in the hollow and ride into the city in the morning. Willie, however, was keen to reach the city that night.

In the end it was Willie who prevailed, simply because he was the more adamant. He told them that they owed it to Paul to press on with as much determination as they could muster; he stressed that it might rain again and that they would be more comfortable in a warm bed than on a soggy hillside. And they would be that much closer to Madrimar.

With Paul's horse in tow, they descended the hillside towards the plain. Sharalidor had looked as if it was no more than a few miles distant, but appearances were deceptive; they rode for perhaps three hours before they came in sight of it again, by which time all of them were exhausted.

The city was surrounded by a wall of dark stone on which pale, vine-like plants clung. They approached it from the south, riding towards a broad gate flanked by towers. There were several soldiers on duty there, garbed in purple tunics and cloaks. They carried spears and swords fashioned from a bronze-coloured metal. Willie and the others were still draped in their oilskins, and they hid their weapons from sight as they rode up to the gate.

A soldier with greying hair at his temples greeted them.

'State your business,' he said in an accent similar to Therion's.

'We are travellers,' Willie told him. 'Bound for Madrimar.'

The soldier studied them. His face was grimy and unshaven.

'Indeed?' he said. 'What business do you have there?'

Willie sensed that he should not have told them that much. But before he could say anything further, Kate spoke:

'We are seeking a relative to give him news of a death in the family.'

Still he looked suspicious; he seemed interested in the colour of her hair.

'Where do you come from?'

'The farmlands west of here,' she told him.

'You do not look like farmlanders to me.'

'We are not all yokels,' Kate said tartly.

A smile slowly formed on his craggy face. 'That I can see.'

He stared at the others, then turned back to her.

'You have five horses, and yet there are only four of you.'

'Our relative in Madrimar will be returning with us to the farm,' Kate said. 'Would you expect him to walk all the way?'

The smile returned, and then the soldier motioned to another guard, who came forward with something resembling a ledger and a wedge-shaped pen sitting in a square pot of green ink.

'I will give you passes for one night,' he said, and began to scribble in the ledger before tearing out the page and handing it to Kate. 'Be sure that you depart the city by sunrise on the morrow. Travellers without the proper passes are arrested on sight, and the dungeons of our city are not hospitable.'

Kate took the pass without comment and waited while three others were written for her friends.

'One more thing,' said the soldier, looking at Willie and Justin. 'Should you feel the urge to use those weapons you have hidden under your oilskins, do your utmost to resist it. Brawling as much as vagrancy is punished by summary arrest.'

The wooden gate was opened, and on this chastening note they rode into the city.

'Do you think he suspects us?' Willie asked Kate.

Kate shrugged. 'Of what? He probably doesn't give a damn who we are as long as we behave ourselves.'

The name Sharalidor had conjured up romantic visions of graceful buildings and stately parks, with inhabitants dressed in rich clothes, but the reality proved utterly different: Sharalidor was mean, cramped and dirty. The main road into the city was little more than a dirt-track fringed on either side by the refuse of its people. The buildings were shabby and dilapidated, clustered together with narrow alleyways twisting between them. All their windows were shuttered for the night, and the few inhabitants who were abroad hurried along as if eager to get off the streets.

The impression of poverty and decay was profound, and would have been apparent to a blind man, for stagnant smells assailed the nostrils immediately on entering the city. The smells of human waste and neglect were only partially masked by the woodsmoke drifting from chimneys or from open fires in sidestreets around which a few bedraggled people clustered. Sharalidor was bordered on the south by the conifer forest, and evidently the trees were the most easily available source of fuel and warmth.

Willie and the others halted just inside the gate, peering around them with dismay. Purple-uniformed soldiers patrolled in small groups, their swords prominently displayed; the ordinary people kept their distance from them wherever possible.

Suddenly a man dressed in a long ruby-coloured robe stepped out in front of them. He had been lingering by the gate, and was holding a crumpled dark blue handkerchief under his nose as he stumbled forward, taking care not to trip in the mud, while hoisting his cloak with his free hand so that its edge would not be soiled.

'Terrible, terrible,' he murmured as he came forward, obviously referring to the squalid conditions around him. 'To think that I would have to descend to this – begging for custom at one of the gates of the city. But I must fill my rooms or be cast out into the street myself. Such a poor season – I cannot remember such a poor season. You are four travellers, I see, and must be seeking warm beds for the night. I beg you to accept the hospitality of my own establishment.'

This monologue was conducted by way of an introduction, the man peering anxiously into each of their faces in turn. He was a plump, middle-aged figure, with the pointed beard of a cavalier and auburn hair bound by a copper band into a topknot.

'I cannot pretend that it is an establishment of the highest class,' he went on, 'but I do promise you that it lies in somewhat more salubrious surroundings than we find ourselves in at present. I listen at the gate, you know, and I overheard you tell the guard that you are bound for Madrimar. A splendid city in many respects. I have often thought that my fortunes would improve if my business interests could be transferred there, but alas. . .' He shrugged, as if it was common knowledge why a move to Madrimar could not be accomplished, and dabbed the handkerchief to his nose. It was strongly scented with an aromatic oil, to mask the smells of the city.

'We have passes for one night only,' said Willie.

'A silver piece would suffice for one night's lodging each,' the man replied.

'Far too costly,' Willie said on an instinct. 'We will have to seek accommodation elsewhere.'

The man spread his hands in a gesture which was at once imploring and resigned. 'I am a reasonable man and you seem like honest travellers. You may have the pick of my rooms for three silver pieces.'

'We require only one room,' Willie said. 'We sleep together, for safety.'

The man nodded, as if prepared to agree that this was indeed wise. 'By chance, my largest guest-room is available. At two silver pieces you will find no more economical accommodation in the whole of Sharalidor.'

'Alas, we are poor farmlanders,' Willie said. 'We carry no more than a silver piece between all four of us.'

The man gave a long sigh and shook his head fatalistically. 'You have the advantage of me, for I have already confessed that I am in sore need of lodgers. So be it – one silver piece.'

Willie was pleased with himself; he had been determined to make up for his near-gaffe with the guard at the gate, and felt that he had haggled perfectly with the hostel-keeper. He saw that Kate was looking at him with a questioning expression. They carried no money, and she was clearly concerned that they would be unable to pay even a single silver piece for their beds. But Willie had other ideas, and he indicated that she should not worry.

They dismounted, and the plump man led them off down narrow streets. As they went he continued to jabber, introducing himself to them as Aremktesh and extolling the virtues of his humble but well-kept hostel. Whenever they approached a group of soldiers, he would fall silent and press himself against a crumbling wall until they had gone past; Willie and the others followed his lead, wanting to do nothing to make themselves conspicuous. Afterwards Aremktesh would fall to grumbling about the soldiers, whom he claimed were everywhere, disrupting honest citizens in their ordinary lives. Gradually the impression emerged that the soldiers were policing-agents for Avron Kromar himself and that they kept the population cowed with indiscriminate arrests and executions. Aremktesh did not refer to the sorcerer by name but merely called him 'our ruler' or 'the master of our destinies' ; at the same time he would dab his scented handkerchief to his mouth as if to muffle the words.

There's something phoney about our fat hostel-keeper, thought Willie as they went along; he's too eager to ingratiate himself with us. But they needed a room for the night, and Willie was determined to procure the rent from Aremktesh himself. When they had been bargaining he had noticed a small purse strapped to the hostel-keeper's belt, and he was confident that he would be able to pick the purse without the fat man noticing. He need only wait until an opportune moment presented itself.

As they progressed further into the city, the general surroundings began to improve somewhat. Streets became broader, houses sturdier and the general air of neglect less apparent. Buildings had been painted in pastel colours in an attempt to offset the general urban gloom, flat stones had been laid over the mud-tracks as walkways, and there was no refuse in the gutters. They began to enter streets which were lit with lamps comprising globes in which glow-moths fluttered. The insects were evidently collected from the forest and put inside the globes until their light and lives gave out.

Though the interior of Sharalidor was less seedy than its perimeter, there still remained an underlying sense of neglect and decay. Broken towers which once must have been graceful still jutted above the humbler dwellings around them, though they were succumbing to climbing plants and the ravages of the weather; houses with splendid façades displayed cracks and patches of damp; small parks between streets, where the inhabitants might once have relaxed, were now neglected and thick with weeds. The abiding impression was of a city where all pleasure and dalliance had been banished, a city reduced to the exigencies of survival by the harsh and unrelenting rule of the sorcerer who had conquered it, and the purple-robed soldiers who served him.

The soldiers were everywhere, patrolling the streets like the forces of an occupying army, though Aremktesh told them that Avron Kromar had chosen his men from the ordinary citizens of the city, and that they now served him with unquestioning devotion, suppressing their former fellows with as much ruthlessness as any foreign invader. No doubt the sorcerer had provided them with favoured living conditions, something which was to be prized in such a mausoleum of a city.

'Not far now,' Aremktesh kept telling them, 'not far.' But they had already walked at least a mile from the city gate, and Justin began to find it hard to curb his impatience. Like Willie, he mistrusted the hostel-keeper and kept a hand on the hilt of his hammer. Teresa meanwhile was close to complete exhaustion. The sights and smells of the city repulsed her, and she was profoundly wishing that they had spent the night on the hillside.

Then they reached a square and Aremktesh said, 'It is just around the corner.' As he spoke a body of soldiers marched across the square and came hurrying past them. They pressed themselves against the wall, and Willie finally saw his opportunity. While Aremktesh was distracted by the troops, he pretended to stumble against him. In one deft movement he had slipped his hand under the fat man's cloak, unclipped the purse and slid his hand inside.

His fingers encountered no more than half a dozen coins. One felt noticeably bigger and heavier than the others. He slipped it between his middle fingers, withdrew his hand, and reclipped the purse with his thumb and forefinger before letting his arm fall away.

Aremktesh noticed nothing untoward. Willie glanced at the coin under the streetlamp and saw that it was indeed a large, gleaming silver piece.

When the soldiers were gone, Aremktesh began leading them across the square. Willie hung back, studying the coin. It showed not the sorcerer, as he had anticipated, but the profile of a woman with flowing hair. He looked up to see that Kate was staring at him. He winked at her before slipping the coin into one of his belt pouches.

The hostel was a squat, square building with a concave roof of dark tiles which gave it a faintly oriental appearance. There were horizontal lozenge-shaped windows set at intervals around its walls, and the main entranceway was an arch shrouded with pendulous ivy. This led into a small vestibule with a dusty wooden floor and faded drapes hanging around the walls. It was lit by candles, and an adolescent boy was asleep behind a counter of whorled green wood. Aremktesh promptly strode forward and clipped him around the ear.

'Uzo, you wretch!' he shouted at the startled boy. 'Any rogue or vagabond could have walked in here and stolen what few valuables we have left while you snored your life away.'

The boy was still recovering from his abrupt return to consciousness. He blinked and regarded the hostel-keeper without speaking.

'Well?' said Aremktesh. 'What do you have to say for yourself?'

The boy struggled, but he could not prevent a yawn from escaping him.

'Have we had any customers tonight?' Aremktesh asked in an exasperated tone.

'None,' said the boy.

'How would you know?' demanded Aremktesh. 'How would you know if an entire army had marched in here asking for rooms, only to march off again when they failed to rouse you from your profound slumber?'

The hostel-keeper sighed, then indicated Willie and the others. 'It falls to me to find guests. I am forced to prowl the city at the risk of my life and to the detriment of my clothing so that we might keep a roof above our heads.'

The boy's face had now relaxed into a careful neutrality; he was clearly used to such tirades.

'Our guests' horses require stabling,' Aremktesh told him. 'See to it immediately!'

The boy slipped off his stool and hurried outside.

'My only son, Uzosiat,' Aremktesh told them, not without a trace of pride. 'Alas, his mother died soon after he was born, and the burden of raising him did not rest lightly on my shoulders with all the responsibilities I have here. I often feel that I spoiled him as a child and encouraged his laziness.'

More likely nagged him into inertia, thought Willie. Aremktesh continued to prattle on, finally asking them if they required food or a hot drink before they retired.

'Beds are all we need,' Willie told him. 'Just take us to our room.'

Aremktesh nodded, and led them up a narrow stairway which gave out on a carpeted corridor with elaborate lamps resembling Chinese lanterns hanging from the ceiling. The whole place had an air of having seen better times: the carpet was threadbare, the walls in need of a fresh coat of paint or whatever passed for paint in this world.

Their room was at the end of the corridor. It

proved to be spacious, with a window overlooking the square. There were two beds at its centre, with cushions and blankets piled on them, and flanking the window on each side were long couches like *chaises longues*.

Aremktesh put the lantern, which he had fetched from the corridor, down on a pedestal beside the door.

'Alas, I am no longer able to provide the luxuries for which my hostel was once renowned,' he said. 'But I think you will find the quarters comfortable enough for one night. Payment is naturally in advance. Will you require breakfast?'

'All we require at the moment is sleep,' Willie told him, pressing the silver piece into his hand and bundling him towards the door. 'We will summon you when we are awake.'

He pushed the hostel-keeper out into the corridor, then closed the door behind him.

The others were taking off their oilskins, which had proved useful in preserving their anonymity. Willie felt thoroughly pleased with the way he had handled the whole transaction with the hostel-keeper. He removed his own oilskin and let it fall to the floor. Teresa had already fallen asleep on one of the beds.

'You take the other one,' he told Kate.

'Since when are you giving us orders?' she said.

'I got you in here, didn't I?'

'I can't say I liked the way you did it. You cheated him.'

'He's a rogue. What else can he expect?'

'How do you know he's a rogue?'

'Come on, Kate. Would you buy a used car from him?'

'Perhaps he was just nervous of us. We're strangers, after all.'

'Look, Kate, I'm too tired to argue. Do you want the bed or not?'

'You take it.'

So Willie did just that. Kate lay down on one of the couches, and her qualms about Willie's behaviour were swiftly overcome with sleep.

Only Justin remained awake. Soft snores were issuing from Willie, but otherwise everything was still. And yet Justin was suspicious. He didn't like the convenient way that the hostel-keeper had been on hand as they entered the city, and he felt that the others had taken it far too much for granted. Everything that had happened to them so far indicated that the sorcerer was following them every step of the way, leading them into traps and presenting them with continual dangers. Was it so unlikely that the hostel-keeper might be one of his agents, or even Avron Kromar himself in disguise? It wasn't, and Justin was angry that he had not been able to communicate this possibility to the others. He was angry that he could only speak in grunts and monosyllables, angry that the others were developing the habit of talking around him, as if he didn't exist.

And yet he recognized that it was partly his own fault, his fear of sounding like a Neanderthal making him reluctant to speak up. It was ironic that he, who had always had a whiplash tongue, was reduced to this, while the bumbling Willie had become the schemer and conniver. But he was sure that Willie wasn't really clever enough to bring it off successfully; he was more likely to get them all into trouble while he, Justin, stood by helplessly, wanting to tell them what to do but unable to get his words out. The continual frustration made his blood boil.

He glanced at Kate as she slept, and his resentment

of her was stronger than anything. She was continuing to give him the cold-shoulder, acting as if he meant nothing to her. But he was biding his time. He wasn't going to make a big issue of it in front of the others, but there would be a reckoning, sooner or later.

His hammer lay at his side. Around him everything was silent, as if the whole city had finally fallen asleep. His eyelids drooped, but he forced them open. He sat up on the couch, drawing a blanket around his shoulders more for comfort than warmth since the night was mild. They'd left their saddle-bags with the horses, he realized, and he told himself that he would check them first thing in the morning to make sure that nothing had been pilfered. There was an unhealthy atmosphere in this city, and they were behaving like rank amateurs. He was determined to stay awake until dawn at least, just in case; he had more stamina than the others and was confident that he could see out the night. . .


There were shadowy figures clustering around him, pulling at his arms and legs. He flailed out at them even as he became conscious, realizing that he had fallen asleep and that it was a dream. Only it was no dream. He came fully awake and knew that the dark shapes were really there, forcing him down, pinioning his arms and legs. He tried to struggle and succeeded in throwing off one of his assailants. But there were too many of them. He heard Willie cry out, then felt two simultaneous blows on either side of his head which sent him plummeting back into unconsciousness.

# 9
## *Captivity*

Justin awoke with an aching head to find himself in a stone chamber with a small barred window set high in the wall. Manacles were attached to his hands and feet. Pale red sunlight filtered through the window, dimly illuminating the cell. The floor was covered with a thin layer of dirty straw, and Willie, Kate and Teresa were slumped in a corner, staring disconsolately at him. They, too, were manacled. Willie had lost his whip and belt of knives, Kate was without her cloak, and Teresa's bracelets were gone. Justin did not need to check to know that his hammer would also be missing.

There were lumps on either side of his head from the blows which had knocked him out. He had the strength of three men, but at least twice that many had come upon him during the night, overwhelming him by sheer force of numbers. The others looked unscathed but utterly defeated. He asked the obvious question: 'How?'

They knew little more than he. A body of purple-robed soldiers had burst in on them during the night, pinioning them to their beds and quickly disarming them before they had a chance to use their weapons or their powers. Justin had been dumped on a barrow, and they had been forced to wheel him through the streets to a gaunt building which was plainly a prison. Then they had been pushed down a long flight of stairs to the cell they were now in.

The soldiers had been brutal and uncompromising, refusing to offer any explanations for their arrest. They had departed, bolting the door of the cell behind them. Several hours had passed since then, and the day was already well advanced.

Justin rose painfully and went to the door. He tried to rattle it, but there was no handle on the inside and he could not get a purchase. He felt weak, drained. The others continued to sit slumped against the wall, as if they had already investigated the cell and decided that there was no possibility of escape.

Captivity is in some senses the most mundane of all human conditions, and for the rest of the dim daylight hours they did nothing but exchange morose, desultory conversation. Everyone was convinced that Avron Kromar was in some way responsible for their imprisonment, the guards having been quick to disarm them not only of obvious weapons, such as Justin's hammer and Willie's knives, but also Teresa's bracelets and Kate's frost-cloak. One of two outcomes seemed likely: they would be either executed or left to rot in their cell. Either way, it would be an ignominious end to their colourful quest.

A large, battered bucket stood in one corner, and this was the only toilet facility. It was humiliating for each of them to have to relieve themselves in the corner while the others discreetly turned their backs, but there was nothing for it. The drab, mindless hours wore on, and still no one came to their cell. Finally the light began to fade. They made themselves as comfortable as they could on the straw and surrendered to a fitful, haunted sleep.

Early the following morning there was the thud of bolts being drawn back, and a scruffy jailer entered carrying four bowls of gruel on a rough wooden tray. He was accompanied by two guards, armed with swords, who flanked the doorway while the jailer dumped the tray on the floor and departed without a word. The guards slammed the door shut behind them and the bolts thunked into place.

Justin and the others studied the gruel, which looked like grey mud. But they were all ravenous after a day without food and grabbed a bowl each, relieved that at least they were not going to be starved to death. There were no spoons, and they were forced to hold the bowls to their lips and tip the contents into their mouths.

The gruel was cold, but it did at least have a distinctive if watery flavour. Even Teresa, who had at first been horrified by the conditions of the cell, emptied her bowl and licked it clean. Then they sat in silence and waited to see what would happen next. Without their weapons they felt naked, at the mercy of everything. Like innocents suddenly confronted with the harsh facts of life in a savage land.

The day wore on, and finally they heard footsteps on the stairs. The bolts on the door were drawn back, and half a dozen guards marched into the cell, armed with both spears and swords. The four of them were pushed and prodded up the stairway and marched down a long stone corridor. As they went, Justin flirted with the idea of bursting free and making a run for it. But the guards were vigilant and he had no doubt that they would use their spears and swords at the slightest provocation. Besides, he still felt weak.

They were marched into a room hung with purple drapes. At a small table resembling a lectern sat a man of middle years with a shaven head and a profuse black beard. He wore robes which matched the drapes, and as they were lined up in front of him he regarded them with open contempt.

'Bring the witness,' he said.

One of the soldiers went to a side door and returned with Aremktesh, dressed in a faded brown and gold robe and doing his best to look dignified.

The bearded man indicated Justin and the others. 'Are these the ones you have accused of theft and fraud?'

Aremktesh nodded without looking at them.

'State your case,' said the bearded man.

Somewhat unnerved by the man's peremptory tone, Aremktesh began a hesitant and expansive account of how he had met them at the south gate of the city and offered them board for the night. They had agreed a fee of one silver piece before proceeding to his hostel. He dwelt at unnecessary length on the journey, still not daring to look at Justin and the others but keeping his eye on the bearded man, whom he referred to as 'Judge Kevaldol'. Kate thought that he gave every impression of being a man as much on trial as they were.

'I took them to their room,' Aremktesh said at length, 'and there the payment was made. I was given this – '

He approached the table and held out the silver piece to Kevaldol. The judge took it from him and examined it cursorily before his eyes returned to the hostel-keeper's face.

'It is a medallion of my wife which I had minted

138

after her death some years ago,' Aremktesh told him. 'I keep it with me constantly in memory of her. It was in my purse that night, and when it was presented to me I knew it had been stolen from my person. So I summoned a detachment of night-guards, who arrested them.'

'You have a witness for all this?' asked Kevaldol.

Aremktesh nodded. 'My son, Uzosiat.'

Still holding the medallion, the judge turned to look at the four captives, a humourless smile forming on his face. With his free hand he reached into the folds of his robe while saying, 'You are most evidently strangers to our city. Should you wish to cheat its inhabitants you would do well to find out more about its customs and commerce.'

He produced a coin from the folds of his robe and held it up for their inspection. It was smaller than the medallion and made of some alloy which resembled zinc more than silver.

'A silver piece,' Kevaldol said, his smile broadening and becoming even more sinister. 'As you can see, it is not made of silver. Our coinage has been debased these many years, and what we call silver pieces are minted from base metal.'

Kevaldol returned the coin to the folds of his robe, but he did not give the medallion back to Aremktesh, who looked eager to reclaim it.

'The facts of this case are clear,' he said, 'and there are no mitigating circumstances. You came here and attempted to steal money from the person who had offered you shelter for the night. You have abused the laws of the city and must pay the price. . .'

'Are we not to be given the chance to speak for ourselves?' Kate said.

It had required some courage to speak up, and

Kate had felt her newly acquired self-confidence beginning to desert her since their capture. Kevaldol looked a fearsome, uncompromising man, and she had little hope that he would show them any mercy.

'What do you have to say for yourself?' he asked.

But it was Willie who spoke. 'It was my doing. I stole the medallion and tried to cheat the hostel-keeper. The others knew nothing about it. Punish me, but let them go free.'

Willie had spoken out of a sudden urge to redeem himself for having got the others into trouble with his thievery. He was responsible for their plight, and he was the one who should pay.

'Your belongings were searched,' Kevaldol said, 'and no money was found in any of them. How were you and your friends to find board for the night without fraud or thievery?'

Before any of them could muster a reply to this, Kevaldol waved his hand dismissively. 'Enough. There are other cases waiting to be tried and I cannot waste any more time with you. Tomorrow you will be taken to the labour market and sold into bonded service for a period of not less than five years.'

There was a ledger on the table in front of him, and as he noted down the details of their sentence with a long stylus, the soldiers clustered around the four of them as if to forestall any protest. But none of them said anything; it was all so alien, so foreign to their expectations of justice that they were too numbed to react.

Then the judge turned to Aremktesh, fingering the medallion as if it was a thing of great value.

'This was printed from a coin?' he asked conversationally.

140

'Indeed,' Aremktesh said with pride. 'I have long cherished it.'

'Do you know the penalty for defacing the city's currency?'

The hostel-keeper's jaw sagged.

'This man will also be taken to the market on the morrow,' he told the guards. 'The sentence is one year's bonded service.'


With a further gesture of careless cruelty, Aremktesh was placed in the same cell as the rest of them. As soon as the door closed he began to blubber and plead with them not to harm him; he had only being doing his duty and he had no idea that the sentences would be so harsh.

He huddled in the corner with his robe wrapped around him as if for protection. Justin and the others felt too defeated to think of revenge, and they ignored him. They were all surprised that Kevaldol had made no mention of their special powers and seemed unaware of their mission to destroy Avron Kromar. In fact, he seemed to consider them ordinary criminals, worthy of only routine punishment. Was it simply luck that the night-guard had managed to disarm them? And what had happened to their weapons?

At sunset the jailer returned with further bowls of gruel, which even Aremktesh did not demur at eating. The hostel-keeper had begun to weep periodically, while wondering aloud what would happen to his son now that he was to become a slave for a year. It was impossible not to feel sympathy for him under these circumstances, and Kate regretted that they had tried to cheat him. He was no rogue, but a simple businessman who had been over-eager to attract trade and had unwittingly encouraged Willie's worst instincts. And yet the stony anger which she had initially felt towards Willie had given way to a similar sympathy; Willie looked disconsolate, and clearly regretted his rashness.

Aremktesh, sensing a lessening of their hostility towards him, gradually became more voluble, bemoaning the harshness of the city authorities and the injustice of the bonded-labour system. The system had been introduced on Avron Kromar's orders, he told them, and all the purple-robed judges served him. The sorcerer had not visited the city for some years, but through his minions he continued to rule them with as much severity as ever.

Aremktesh's fastidious nature was appalled by the crudity of the toilet bucket, and for hours he refused to relieve himself. Finally, however, nature could not be denied; but a modicum of dignity was preserved by using his cloak as a makeshift screen.

Though by now the cell was rank with human odours, in their gloom they hardly noticed it. Justin was particularly despondent, so consumed with frustration at their hopeless situation that he could not talk to anyone. Only Teresa tried to sound a positive note. At first she had been mortified by their surroundings, but now she found herself trying to raise the others' spirits by enumerating its advantages: at least it was dry, tolerably warm and not infested by vermin. At least they had not been beaten up or tortured. At least they were still alive.

'Let's not forget Paul,' she told them. 'Compared to what happened to him, we should consider ourselves lucky.'

None of them had forgotten Paul; but his death now only made their sense of failure more abject. They would have no chance to avenge him, to honour his memory by killing Avron Kromar. And they would never be able to return to Earth.

Eventually they lapsed into an uneasy sleep. Willie dreamt of his mother lying in bed at home, calling out for him. He awoke and realized that she was alone, without him to minister to her. It seemed incredible that he could have forgotten her until now, and he was filled with a profound sense of his own stupidity and selfishness.

Late the following morning the jailer returned with a detachment of guards. A strong rope was slung through their manacles, harnessing them together, and they were led from the prison like a team of horses, down streets filled with ordinary citizens of Sharalidor who paused to gawp at the specimens bound for the human meat market.

The market was held in a large square, a wooden stage being set up at one end; the prisoners congregated behind the stage under guard. The seller was a large, severe-looking woman of middle years, her brown hair dragged back into a tight bun behind her head. She was seated at a table on the stage and shouted out details of each prisoner or group of prisoners as they were marched up and displayed before the crowd. The crowd itself comprised the usual raggle-taggle of ordinary citizens drawn by sheer curiosity, and a smaller number of more wealthy folk who were presumably prospective buyers of the human merchandise on offer.

Kate stared up at the stage. The seller's muscular arms were decorated with tattoos of centaurs and snakes. She looked stern and uncompromising, a harridan who would get the best prices for her customers.

The first prisoner, a young woman, was led up on to the stage, bound in manacles like all the rest of them. She was thin and pale. The seller studied the ledger in front of her and said to the audience: 'Nineteen years old, convicted of thievery. Two years' indentured service. Recommended as a cook or washerwoman.'

'Three silver pieces,' a merchant in green at the front of the crowd said immediately.

'Four,' called another voice from further back.

'Six,' said another.

There were no further bids. The seller looked displeased.

'Six silvers for two years' service?' she said. 'The woman is healthy, free from disease or pregnancy. She is worth twice that.'

There was a silence from the crowd.

'Take her back,' the seller told the guard. 'We'll try again tomorrow.'

'Ten,' shouted the merchant in green.

The seller studied him for long moments before saying, 'Done.'

The merchant approached the stage and gave his name to the seller, who entered it into the ledger.

'She is to be set free two years exactly from this day,' the seller said. 'Is that clear?'

'Of course,' said the merchant.

Then the young woman was unchained and led away by the merchant and two of his retainers.

Kate had watched the entire transaction with a horrified fascination. It appeared that all sorts of crimes in Sharalidor were punishable by varying degrees of servitude, after which the citizen was free to return to ordinary society. But that was no comfort whatsoever. They were already unwilling captives of this world, and now the last shreds of their liberty were to be taken from them for five long years. She could not imagine how they could possibly survive the sentence; they would be driven mad with despair.

The morning wore on, and other prisoners were displayed and sold. The bidders spoke of silver pieces and coppers, but only rarely was a gold piece mentioned, for a male slave who looked especially strong or a female slave who was especially attractive. There appeared to be twenty coppers to a silver piece, and twenty silver pieces to one gold. Kate kept herself from sliding into abject despair with such calculations; the whole proceedings were an offence to human dignity.

Then, suddenly, she and the others were being marched up on to the stage.

'Four outlanders,' said the seller, after pausing to look at them. 'Robbery and attempted fraud. Five years' indentured labour. All are strong and healthy and would be useful for manual labour or breeding.'

*Breeding*, thought Kate, aghast. Did slaves lose all their sexual liberties? Were she and Teresa to become mares or whores for some fat richman? The idea repulsed her.

'Ten silvers for the big man,' said a merchant, with reference to Justin.

'Fifteen for the two women,' cried another.

'Eighteen for the two,' cried a third.

'Three gold pieces for all four,' said a muffled voice from the back.

Numerous heads turned to regard the last speaker. He stood right at the back of the crowd, wearing a grey hooded cloak which covered his head and shadowed his face.

'Three gold and ten silver for the four,' said a bejewelled merchant with rings on his fingers.

'Five gold,' said the man in grey. The cloak enveloped him completely, and there was no means of telling whether he was a rich man himself or was merely acting for one.

'Six gold,' said the merchant with the rings.

'Ten,' said the cloaked man.

The whole crowd had gone silent, and attention was focused on the two bidders. They were clearly offering large sums.

The merchant fingered his rings before saying: 'Twelve.'

'Fifteen,' the cloaked man said instantly.

A kind of muted gasp escaped from the crowd, as if this sort of price had never been offered before. The merchant twisted his rings more furiously, then suddenly stalked off through the crowd and departed the square. All eyes were now on the cloaked man.

'Done,' said the seller with a heavy note of irony.

The cloaked man approached the stage. The hood covered his eyes, and even close up his face could not be made out.

'Your name?' asked the seller.

'Yelsrennik,' the man murmured.

'Occupation?'

'Bursar to the city-guard. In Madrimar.'

The seller stiffened momentarily and made haste to scribble in her ledger. The hooded man glanced up at the stage, looking not at Kate and the others, but at Aremktesh, who was awaiting his turn to be led out.

'Who is that man?' he asked the seller.

She studied her ledger. 'A hostel-keeper,' she told

him. 'A man of some education and business-sense.'

'What is his crime?'

'Defacing the coinage.'

'And his sentence?'

'One year.'

'I'll give you an extra gold piece for him.'

A greedy gleam appeared in the seller's eyes. 'He is worth twice that.'

'He is not worth half it. You have obtained an excellent price from me for the other four, and I have no intention of being fleeced further. I am sure your superiors would be interested in an account of your conduct if you fail to give me satisfaction.'

The woman looked sullen. 'One gold piece it is, then.'

Kate, watching and listening to this, was sure that she recognized the hooded man's voice, disguised though it was. But it simply wasn't possible.

'Will you take them now?' the seller was asking.

The hooded man nodded. 'Remove their manacles and tie them together with ropes.'

'Do you have a guard?'

'They are waiting beyond the square.'

The hooded man's instructions were quickly carried out. Their manacles were removed and replaced with ropes, and then all five of them were led down from the stage. Without further ceremony, the hooded man took the end of the rope which bound them together and led them off through the crowd. The crowd itself was all curiosity as they moved back to provide a pathway. Then the seller called the next prisoner out, and their attention gradually returned to the platform.

On leaving the square, the hooded man led them across a broad street, then down a narrower one, and finally into an alleyway which was shadowy and deserted. Justin had already begun to think that the man was showing a foolish bravado in leading them off alone and not having his guard close at hand. What was to stop them now from falling on him and escaping? The alleyway was a cul-de-sac, which made it even better.

Then he saw a movement in the dark entranceway to a stable at the end of the alley. Uzosiat was standing there with their horses. The cloaked man threw back his hood.

It was Paul.

# 10
# *Narrow Escapes*

As the crag began to tumble down on him, Paul had thought of trying to teleport himself out of the path of the avalanche. But it was a thought with no real will-power behind it, and he had stood frozen like a small animal entranced by a predator and awaiting the death-blow without resistance. Then he had sensed a surge of energy from something that was within him yet not part of him, a surge of energy which had enveloped his consciousness, causing him to black out.

He awoke to find himself on a hillside, exhausted but undeniably alive. Therion was present in his mind, and he knew that the old sorcerer had come to his aid at the last moment, adding his powers to Paul's own and enabling him to teleport himself away from the rock-face at the last instant.

The intense effort had exhausted both of them, and Therion had slept for several hours while Paul was unconscious. Paul saw that he had been transported less than a mile from the avalanche, landing in a secluded gulley where the others would not have been able to see him. They were long gone. And they had taken his horse.

Paul still felt weak from the tremendous mental effort of displacing himself in space. He sat down on a rock, not knowing what to do. Therion, still present in his mind, then told him that if he was prepared to surrender his body to him temporarily, the sorcerer would try to work some magic through him in the hope of speeding his passage to Sharalidor.

Paul had distinct qualms about the idea of surrendering his body to anyone, but he knew that he had little choice. In his present weakened state it would be hours before he had recovered sufficiently to set off in pursuit of his friends, and without a horse he was sure to tire again quickly. Not without misgivings, he had laid back and allowed Therion to flood into his mind.

When he next became conscious, Paul found himself sitting in a shallow wooden boat which was travelling along the river. He had a dim recollection of Therion fashioning the boat by sorcery from a tree, uprooting it, then reforming it into a kind of canoe. The memory was a startling one, and yet it seemed like a dream, something that had not really happened to him.

It was a clear, calm night. The river was placid, without rocks or rapids, and Paul made steady progress along it with only the occasional use of the oar which Therion had fashioned from one of the tree branches. Was the sorcerer helping to keep the boat on a steady course with his magic? If so, it was sorcery on automatic: the old man, evidently still exhausted by his magical labours, was asleep again.

As he drifted on through valleys thick with trees and flickering glow-moths, Paul reflected on what had happened. He was grateful for Therion's help, but his mistake had been to assume that the old man knew best regarding how to dispose of the birdbats. Therion had been wrong in believing that fire would immediately destroy them, whereas Paul's original plan had ultimately proved effective. But he could not blame Therion; it was his own fault for not having the confidence even to suggest his idea in the first place.

The experience had been chastening in more ways than one. Apart from demonstrating that Therion was not infallible, it had also crystallized a vague feeling of unease which he had felt from the outset of their adventure. They knew that they were being manipulated by the sinister presence of Avron Kromar, but what they did not know was how far his influence extended over them. Now Paul began to wonder if they were being manipulated far more than they had imagined. They had been lucky enough to come upon Therion's house in the wilderness of mountains, but what if it hadn't been luck? What if they had been led there by Avron Kromar himself? What if they were meant to enlist the old sorcerer's help? What if Therion was just another dupe who would unwittingly lead them into danger?

Paul decided to say nothing to Therion about these misgivings. Judiciously used, the old man's wisdom and sorcery could still be of great advantage to them; but he was going to have to be careful to take nothing for granted.

Late into the night, Paul brought the boat ashore; he had given up hope of catching up with his friends before they reached Sharalidor. Not wanting to risk being attacked by some wild animal during the night, he turned the boat over and crawled underneath it. Sleep came surprisingly easily. Sometime during the night he was awakened by the scratching sound of a small animal on the roof of the boat. With his mind he caused the boat to shudder, and he heard the animal scampering away. He was not disturbed again.

The following morning he took to the river once more. The waters remained shallow and slow-moving, the land gradually flattening around him. Towards midday he emerged from the forest and saw the grey-walled city looming ahead.

He summoned Therion. As a former resident of Sharalidor, the old man would be able to advise him on what to expect there. It transpired that Therion had made a few surreptitious visits to the city since Avron Kromar had established his rule there, and as they drifted the last few miles towards the wharves and jetties of its harbour, the old man told him a great deal of Sharalidor and informed him of how best to conduct himself. His pressing need would be to obtain coinage, for money was a powerful social lubricant in the city. He would also need to move with great caution.

To Paul's surprise there was little traffic on the river around the harbour: a few small fishing vessels, and the occasional barge carrying grain or wicker baskets filled with glow-moths which, Therion explained, were used to light the city's streets. Sharalidor had apparently once been a busy inland port in the days of King Qhoron; but commerce in Xhandarre had suffered greatly since Avron Kromar's accession to power.

Ignored by other sailors and the various groups of peasants clustered around the rotting wharves, Paul brought his boat up against a deserted landing-stage and clambered up a ladder. He watched the canoe float away, then suddenly saw it shimmer and become a tree once more, a tree carried away by the tide. He heard Therion give a dry chuckle in his mind.

'Sorcery can twist the fabric of nature,' he told Paul, 'but things always return to their natural shape in the end.'

The sorcerer stayed with him, alert and watchful through his eyes. The wharves were centered around the west gate of the city, through which Paul would have to pass. Therion told him that the guards on duty there were less rigorous in their inspection of strangers and quite willing to sign passes permitting entry into Sharalidor, providing their palms had been lined with a suitable amount of silver pieces.

Not far from where Paul had landed, a group of merchants were watching the offloading of sacks of grain from a barge. A tall, barrel-bellied man with long russet hair and a disdainful expression on his hawk-like face was overseeing the operation. He supported himself with a stick, and as Paul watched he hobbled forward and used the stick to swipe one of his servants across the head when he stumbled with a sack of grain. A pouch obviously containing money hung at his belt.

'Do you want me to spirit the pouch into your hand?' Therion asked him.

'No,' Paul answered. 'I'll do it.'

With his mind he focused on the pouch, testing its weight and the strength of the leather thong which bound it to the merchant's belt. He concentrated on the knot in the thong, delicately beginning to untie it, little by little. As it came free he supported the pouch so that it would not fall to the floor. He let it descend slowly, until it was inches from the greenish wooden boards of the quay. Then he began to draw it towards him.

Neither the merchant nor any of his retinue noticed a thing. The merchant had taken his stick to yet another hapless servant, and Paul felt a perverse sense of pleasure at this further display of the man's vile temper. It made him easier to steal from.

The pouch floated slowly towards him, then dropped neatly into his hand. Paul slipped it inside his oilskin and slowly walked away from the wharves.

'You are learning,' Therion told him.

Paul paused before he approached the gate to inspect the contents of the pouch. Therion identified the coins as forty-six gold pieces, twenty-two silver pieces and a handful of copper coinage.

'You found a very wealthy man,' Therion told him. 'It is a small fortune – enough to keep an ordinary man of the city alive for years.'

He advised Paul not to offer the guards any gold pieces, for that would be too ostentatious and suspicious a display of wealth. Three silver pieces would suffice.

'When were you last here?' Paul asked him.

'Not for some time,' Therion admitted.

'Then perhaps I should offer five silver pieces. In case of inflation.'

The old sorcerer made no reply.

The main guard proved to be a bored, slovenly man who did not rise from the rough wooden stool on which he was sitting when Paul approached the gate. Paul was grateful that the oilskin hid his uniform and his talisman.

'What do you want?' the guard asked without looking up.

'A visitor's pass for one night,' Paul said.

He was hoping that it would take him no longer than a day to find his friends. Therion had explained

154

that strangers to the city could only obtain passes for more than a day by applying to a magistrate; and this might mean awkward questions.

The guard opened his palm, still without looking up. Paul dropped five pieces of silver into it. The guard did not move. Paul added a further piece. The guard snatched the money away and reached for a ledger.

Once inside the gates Paul was immediately assailed by the sights and sounds and smells of the city. An atmosphere of squalor and overcrowding prevailed; the cramped streets were filled with people who looked poor, dirty and cowed. And everywhere there were groups of purple-robed soldiers.

Therion had warned him in advance of what conditions were like in the city, but suddenly Paul felt daunted by the prospect of tracking down his friends in this great rat-hole of humanity.

'Find a room,' Therion told him. 'Then perhaps I will be able to locate your friends for you. There's a hostel opposite.'

Paul followed the old man's gaze and saw a grubby building which looked more like a barn than anything else. But on entering it, an old woman took him to a squalid room on payment of five copper pieces. All curiosity had been leached from her by her dismal existence, and she asked nothing of him beyond payment for the room. Paul closed the rickety door behind him and studied the lumpy bed, which was draped with grey blankets and grimy sheets; the pillows were filled with straw.

'Lie down,' Therion told him. 'Then I will be able to send my mind out in search of your friends.'

Paul wondered if such a feat was possible, even with the aid of sorcery.

'It is,' Therion assured him tartly. 'I am not necessarily saying I will be successful. But if we don't try, we will never know either way.'

Once again, Paul was reluctant to surrender himself to Therion's power.

'The alternative is that you search the city on foot,' he was told.

There was nothing for it. Paul spread himself somewhat squeamishly on the blankets and did his best to relax. Gradually he felt Therion's presence growing stronger in his mind, enveloping his own thoughts. Then it began to expand outwards into the room and beyond it, spreading through the streets of the city that it knew so well, touching every mind it encountered, searching for Kate and Justin and Teresa and Willie. Then Paul was no longer thinking at all.

He regained consciousness with the sense that Therion had only just returned to his mind. The old sorcerer was weary, and Paul knew that some hours had elapsed while he had scoured the city. But he had found them.

'They are in prison,' Therion told him.

The sorcerer had been fortunate enough to find Kate and the others just as they were being brought before Judge Kevaldol. By listening to their interrogation, he had rapidly gleaned what had happened. He gave Paul a full account of it before finally saying:

'In some respects they were fortunate.'

'Fortunate?' said Paul. 'They were captured while they slept, and disarmed before any of them could use their powers. I don't call that fortunate.'

'But the guards who stripped them of their weapons were not aware of the powers they possessed. Nor is Kevaldol. That part was sheer bad luck. Their belongings have been impounded as a matter of course, but Kevaldol did not inspect them and he does not consider their case worthy of special note. No one knows who they really are.'

'But they are to be sold into slavery.'

'Tomorrow morning, according to Kevaldol's ledger.'

'Did you manage to let them know you'd found them?'

'They would not be able to sense my presence.'

'Not even Teresa?'

'Without her bracelets she can sense nothing.'

Paul considered. 'I have to rescue them. Tonight. I could blast a hole in the wall of their cell and free them.'

'And alert every soldier in the city. Why do you insist on using the power of the talisman as a bludgeon when it might be employed more subtly and effectively? Remember how you procured the purse of coins. It was not necessary to blast the merchant into submission – you lifted the purse without his knowledge. We can secure your friends' freedom in a similar manner.'

'What do you propose?'

'First of all I would suggest that you pay a visit to the prison repository.'

Less than an hour later, Paul was standing outside the walls of the repository, a sturdy-looking building which stood opposite the forbidding bulk of the prison itself. Therion had succumbed to a profound sleep after his mental endeavours on Paul's behalf, but his words still lingered in Paul's mind. The old sorcerer had suggested that the talisman might be

157

used to influence minds as well as physical objects, and Paul was now intent on testing this supposition in the hope of recovering his friends' belongings. But his heart was beating rapidly as he strode up to the guard who was on duty at the entrance to the building.

'I am Judge Kevaldol and I wish to inspect the repository,' he told the guard, concentrating on making the man believe what he was saying. Paul was still wearing his oilskin for camouflage, but he could feel the talisman throbbing like a heartbeat against his chest.

It worked. The guard gave a curt bow, which was evidently the equivalent of a salute, and said, 'Follow me, sir.'

He unlocked the door and led Paul inside. It was a place of bare stone walls, with a long corridor which led to a descending flight of stairs. At the bottom of the stairs the guard unlocked another door to a large room filled with all manner of objects: clothing, furniture, jewellery, books, paintings, and even a stuffed animal resembling a bear.

'Wait outside,' Paul told the guard, while subtly commanding him to do so.

The guard went out, closing the door behind him.

The whole room was a great clutter of confiscated goods, the flotsam and jetsam of a police state. Paul prowled its haphazard corridors and finally spotted Kate's frost-cloak draped across a chair; Teresa's bracelets lay underneath it. After a few more minutes of searching he had also found Justin's hammer and Willie's whip and belt of knives. Not a knife was missing from the belt, and Paul was surprised to find everything untouched. He had been concerned that Kate's cloak and Teresa's bracelets might have been taken by some official as a present for a wife or mistress. Did the strict authoritarianism of the city authorities discourage such pilfering? Or was there some other reason for his good fortune?

Paul had bundled everything into Kate's cloak and tied it into a knot when the door opened and the guard entered with another man, who had a dense black beard and a shaven head.

'What are you doing here?' the bearded man asked.

'I am Judge Kevaldol,' Paul told him. 'I require these items for a prosecution I am to undertake tomorrow.'

'Indeed?' said the man. 'How curious that I, too, am called Kevaldol.'

The guard suddenly looked confused.

'Arrest him!' the bearded man said.

The guard moved forward, but Paul reacted instantly, pole-axing them both with a blast of mental energy.

He snatched the keys from the unconscious guard and locked both men inside the room before hurrying up the stairs. Then he locked the outer door, walked casually down the street and dropped the keys into a thick patch of weeds. Night was already falling, and with luck both men would sleep until well past dawn. By which time Paul hoped to be gone from the city with his friends.

Therion had also discovered the address of Aremktesh's hostel from the judge's ledger, and after disposing of the keys, Paul made straight for the hostel, following the directions which the old sorcerer had given him. He was keen to recover their horses, which the night-guard had neglected to impound and which were presumably still in the hostel stable.

But he was also hoping to introduce himself to Aremktesh's son. He had agreed with Therion that the simplest plan would be to buy his friends' freedom at the slave-market in the morning with the money he had lifted from the merchant at the harbour; then they could simply depart the city with a minimum of fuss. But he also wanted to secure Aremktesh's freedom. True, the hostel-keeper had got his friends into trouble in the first place, but only because Willie had behaved dishonestly. Paul felt a moral obligation to set things right.

It was approaching midnight when he arrived at the hostel, and the place was locked and shuttered. He circled the building cautiously, checking for guards, before going to the front door and knocking hard on it. After several attempts, he finally roused Uzosiat, who was red-eyed and disconsolate.

Paul had already decided that he was going to reveal his powers to the boy, if not tell him that he was from another world. Taking care not to do anything dramatic, he demonstrated the power of the talisman – lifting chairs and rolling up carpets with his mind. He was quick to assure the boy that he was not a sorcerer, but an ordinary man with special powers who wished to secure the freedom of his friends and the boy's father.

Uzosiat, facing confiscation of all his father's property now that Aremktesh was in prison, needed little persuasion to assist Paul. He took him immediately to the stables, where their horses were untouched. There were also two mule-like creatures, which belonged to Aremktesh. As part of their bargain, Paul agreed that the boy and his father would be allowed to accompany them to Madrimar; this was a cherished ambition of both Uzosiat and

160

Aremktesh, and there was no longer any future for either of them in Sharalidor.

Paul slept in the stables that night, and in the morning went early to the market square with his purse of gold, leaving Uzosiat in charge of the horses and mules and a sack containing all their belongings.


Paul recounted a potted version of this story after the others had finished hugging him and slapping his back with surprise and delight. Kate was particularly demonstrative, crushing him in her arms and planting a big kiss on his cheek.

'Paul, Paul,' she kept saying. 'I can't believe it! You're alive!'

'And kicking,' he told her, grinning. 'To think I got the lot of you for sixteen gold pieces. Do you reckon you're worth it?'

'You were terrific. You had that woman in the palm of your hand at the end. Fancy telling her that you were a bursar from Madrimar. Is his name really Yelsrick or whatever it was?'

'Yelsrennik,' Paul told her. 'It's Kinnersley backwards.'

The others were equally delighted with his nerve – all except Justin, who was staring somewhat stonily at Kate.

'Have you got our weapons?' he asked Paul.

Paul indicated one of the mules. 'They're in that sack.'

As Justin went to retrieve his hammer, Paul realized that he had spoken normally. And the others were more themselves, too – more their old selves. Kate's eyes were moist with the emotion of their reunion, Teresa had a wry grin on her face which he remembered well, and Willie looked rather dazed and confused by the rapid turn of events.

Paul was quick to conclude that their separation from their articles of power had made them begin to revert to their old characters. But now they were all eager to reclaim them.

Justin had been too morose to do more than grunt during their time in prison, but it also dawned on him that he had spoken without difficulty, and he came to a similar conclusion. He hoped the effect would be a permanent one, but nothing was going to stop him from reclaiming his hammer. He delved into the sack, found it and pulled it free. The power of the weapon immediately began to flood through him, invigorating him, making him whole once more.

Willie did not delay in following Justin's lead. He had felt awkward and guilty ever since their imprisonment, but he knew that as soon as he recovered the whip those feelings would pass away. He was eager to feel sharp and devil-may-care again. He thrust his hand into the sack, and found his belt of knives first. Quickly he put it on, and felt more confident at once. But he needed his whip. He thrust his hand into the sack again, groped, and finally encountered the tautly coiled weapon. It seemed to relax the moment he touched it, like a living thing. He pulled it out, cracked it, and it was as if something vital had been restored to him.

Teresa, meanwhile, went over to her roan and stroked its muzzle. She, too, was aware that while in prison she had begun to revert to type by displaying the sort of determined optimism which had been one of the prime characteristics of her former self. She did not want to lose this, to sacrifice it for the uncertain courage of her Xhandarrean character. But the bracelets promised so much – the indescribable beauty of flight above all. Before she knew it she had reached into the sack, found them, and slipped them on her wrists. Straight away she was possessed with the urge to abandon her dirty, exhausted body and fly. But a residue of self-discipline remained and she suppressed her desire.

Kate was the last to go to the sack, and only after some hesitation. She also knew what had been happening to them in prison, and her ice-maiden identity seemed fearsomely aloof even to her when she thought about it now. But she knew that in the cell she had begun to feel nervous of Justin, nervous that he might recover all his powers of speech and launch a scathing attack on her. Without the cloak her self-confidence was fragile; without it she could not defend herself.

Kate wavered, a confusion of emotions filling her. But the others had all recovered their articles of power, and she would be foolish to think that she could survive without her frost-cloak.

The cloak was at ambient temperature when she removed it from the sack, but even as she was unfurling it she felt it beginning to cool. She draped it over her shoulders, and suddenly the exhilarating chill enveloped her, calming and clarifying her thoughts in an instant, making her wonder why she had hesitated before reclaiming it.

Paul watched the others as one by one they became the warriors of the figurines once more. In each a transformation was immediately noticeable, but in none was it more stark than in Kate. Suddenly her face was no longer animated; all the emotion drained out of it, and the brightness of her eyes seemed to become diamond-hard. Paul felt an obscure disappointment, as if an opportunity had been snatched from him before he could grasp at it.

He allowed the others a few moments to come to terms with the recovery of their powers, then explained his plan to get out of Sharalidor as quietly as possible. He had brought the oilskins with him, and the others were persuaded to don them and keep their weapons hidden. Paul returned the hooded cloak to Aremktesh; he had borrowed it from the hostel-keeper's wardrobe to disguise himself.

Aremktesh, overcome with joy at being reunited with his son, leapt at the chance to accompany them to Madrimar. Uzosiat, for all his father's complaints about his laziness, had shown foresight in filling a second sack with as many valuables from the hostel as the second mule could carry, to ensure that they would have some collateral to establish themselves in the capital. Aremktesh himself seemed not at all daunted by the prospect of living so close to the sorcerer's citadel.

'Madrimar is a fine city,' he told them, 'and I would rather sit on Avron Kromar's doorstep than crawl in the gutters here.'

He led them off through the city streets. Therion had earlier advised Paul that it would be best to leave the city via the north gate, which would allow them a speedy departure through a savannah of tall grasses which would not hinder their mounts but would quickly shield them from any pursuers. It was Paul's plan that they would lead the horses to the gate on foot, pretending to be ordinary travellers, and he would engineer their departure with some mental sleight of hand. Though there was no evidence that the city authorities knew who they really were, it was important to get away as quickly as possible before Kevaldol and the guard were freed from the repository and a general alert raised. There was also the ever-present possibility that Avron Kromar might intervene to make things difficult for them in some way which they could not anticipate, added reason for making as prudent an exit from Sharalidor as possible.

All this was true, but Paul was also aware that he was keen to demonstrate to the others just how effective the subtle use of his powers could be. For the first time since his arrival in Xhandarre, he had begun to appreciate what he could accomplish through the talisman. Potentially he had more power than any of them, and his abilities were not so very different from those of a real sorcerer.

Keeping to sidestreets and alleyways, they approached the gate after less than an hour of walking. Two guards were on duty, one dark and gaunt, the other ginger-haired and florid.

'Your passes,' the gaunt guard said.

Paul produced his own pass, but immediately concentrated on the guard, willing him to believe that he saw seven passes, all issued only the previous morning. The talisman pulsed against his chest.

Once more its suggestive influence worked. The guard nodded, and made to hand the pass back to Paul. His companion, watching from close by, frowned and stepped forward.

Paul was about to fill his mind with the same conviction that he was seeing seven passes. But Justin acted first. As they made their way through the streets to the gate, Justin had realized that his powers of fluent speech had deserted him once more. A silent fury of frustration had mounted in him, compounded by his reluctance to take a back seat to Paul in engineering their escape. He had decided that since it was Paul's moment of glory, his friend could have things his way this once. But although he was genuinely glad to see Paul alive again, he had no intention of letting him take charge on a permanent basis, talisman or no talisman. And he hadn't liked the way Kate had fawned all over Paul. Now all these simmering resentments rose to boiling-point, and as he saw the second guard look quizzical, his immediate urge was to strike out and prevent the man from raising the alarm.

His hammer was tucked into his belt under his oilskin, and he had kept a hand on it throughout their journey to the gate. He pulled it free and brought it down on the second guard's head. The man's skull splintered with a horrible crack and he crumpled beneath the blow. The gaunt guard immediately bolted, screaming for help.

Justin ran after him, hefting his hammer. He caught the guard before he had gone a dozen paces, felling him with a blow that broke his back. But by then it was too late, for purple-robed soldiers were streaming out of every building and alleyway, their swords and spears at the ready.

'You fool!' Paul shouted, but it was too late for recriminations. Willie was the first to move, pulling free his whip. Two soldiers were advancing to his right. He swung the whip, slashing both of them down into the mud. He whooped with triumph and darted forward, eager to engage the enemy.

Kate was also quick to react. She gestured at a group of soldiers who were hurrying down a broad street towards them, freezing the mud around their feet so that they were halted in their tracks. Some

166

tripped over, while others tried to fling their spears; but without leverage they fell hopelessly short.

Paul, meanwhile, was grouping the horses around the terrified Aremktesh and his son. Teresa, feeling physically wretched after her imprisonment, had been yearning to fly ever since she had donned her bracelets, and now she could resist the urge no longer. As they backed towards the gate, with the city-guard advancing on them, she brought the bracelets together. Immediately she felt herself dissolving, becoming lighter than air. She spread her arms and soared upwards.

The city fell away from her, dwindling as she rose, its buildings blurring into one another, streets shrinking to ragged lines, the city boundaries becoming visible, and finally the whole city spreading out below her as an irregular circle nestling in a wide hook of the twisting river, with dark forests to its west and the paler expanse of scrubland stretching to another river in the east. A steady wind had sprung up, and she could feel it racing through her body.

It was only then she realized how high she had flown, only then that she remembered her duty to her friends. With a sweep of her arms, she began to descend.

But by the time she had touched down and materialized beside the gate the soldiers had been routed. Though greatly outnumbering Paul and the others, they had been no match for them. Justin's hammer had crushed the skulls of many, Willie's whip had accounted for many more, while Kate had formed barriers of ice which blocked doorways and street corners, preventing reinforcements from getting through.

The others were already mounting, and the gate

167

had been opened. Paul was helping Aremktesh get Uzosiat into the saddle of one of the mules, and she saw that the boy had been wounded in the side, presumably by a stray spear. His thigh was soaked with blood, and his eyes were closed.

'It would be better for you to stay here,' Paul was saying. 'Get him to a doctor.'

Aremktesh shook his head frantically. 'They would kill us both immediately. We must come with you.'

No one had time to say anything to Teresa. She took the reins of her roan and leapt into the saddle. All the horses appeared to have escaped injury in the fighting. Paul and Aremktesh flanked Uzosiat on their mounts, and Justin was already urging his horse forward. As they rode through the gates they saw a trio of guards, who had evidently been on duty outside, huddling behind a bush. It was clear that they had witnessed the battle and were going to do nothing to stand in the way of their enemy's escape.

# 11

# *The Revenant*

The scrubland comprised waist-high feathery grass and bushes with tough jagged foliage which they were careful to avoid. Only Paul was truly fit for riding any distance, even Justin feeling drained from their two nights in prison. Paul rode close to Uzosiat, doing his best to cushion the boy's ride while continuing to press on with all possible speed. They were riding into a stiff wind, and it had dried the tears on Aremktesh's cheeks.

Presently they came upon the tributary of the larger river on whose banks Sharalidor stood. It was swift-flowing but looked shallow. Paul turned in his saddle and stared back the way they had come. There was no obvious sign of pursuit.

'I don't think we're being followed,' he said.

Willie delved into one of his belt-pouches and produced a match, which he struck against a knife blade before dropping it into the grass. The grass took fire immediately, rapidly fanning out. The bushes also caught fire, burning like torches in the gloom. Driven by the wind, the wall of fire began to race in the direction of Sharalidor.

'Just in case,' Willie said with a grin.

They crossed the river without difficulty and rode

on for a short while before finally dismounting. Uzosiat was slumped across his mule, and blood from his wound stained the flank of the animal. Even before they had pulled him from the saddle, Paul knew that he was dead.

Aremktesh insisted on riding on and taking the boy with them; he told them that it was considered ill-luck in Xhandarre to bury someone by day and he was determined to wait until nightfall.

With the river behind them and Willie's fire consuming the scrubland, they felt confident that any pursuit would be difficult. Uzosiat was strapped to his saddle, and Aremktesh tied a dark cloth about his son's head in accordance with his religious practices. Paul could not help but feel that the boy's death was a direct result of Justin's impulsiveness.

They headed north-east, deciding to take a more indirect route towards Madrimar in the hope of ensuring that they would lose any pursuers. Though weary, they bowed to Aremktesh's insistence that they should not stop until sunset, when his son could be buried. All of them were very conscious of the dead youth strapped to the mule and aware that he would still be alive if he had not met them.

The land gradually began to rise, the grasses growing shorter and the shrubs less common until eventually they were travelling over low, rolling hills. In the distance to the south they could see Sharalidor's river like a long silvery rope under the lowering, plum-coloured sky. The river spread eastwards, as though tempting them to take the quicker route to Madrimar. But they remained in the hills, where nothing living moved, apart from birds like white hawks which soared high on gusts of wind, heedless of the grim procession below.

They were drawing on every reserve of their energies in continuing to ride on, and both Teresa and Kate dozed fitfully in the saddle. Uzosiat had filled their saddle-bags with food, and they ate as they rode, scarcely registering the exotic flavours of the fruits and vegetables and the biscuit-like bread which the dead boy had provided for them.

Finally the swollen sun slipped below the horizon, and gloom became true night. They stopped on a hilltop, and Aremktesh immediately lifted his dead son off his mule and carried him a short distance away from the rest of them. From his sack of belongings he produced an ornate dagger with a curved blade. It was evidently a ceremonial dagger, for it was laid on the boy's chest. Paul and the others watched as Aremktesh then tore rough grass from the hillside and piled it over Uzosiat's body until it was covered. Then the hostel-keeper lay down beside his son with an arm stretched over his chest in an attitude of sleep.

To Paul and the others it seemed an odd sort of funeral ceremony, but they knew practically nothing about Xhandarrean customs and religious rites. They left Aremktesh alone with his son on the mountainside, settling down in a hollow where there was some protection from the wind. Teresa fell asleep almost immediately, and Paul, fresher than the others, offered to take the first watch.

Kate was the last to bed down, and Paul lingered nearby. He had begun to wonder if the enthusiasm which she had shown for his return was evidence of a more fundamental change in her attitude towards him; he wanted to try to find some way of broaching the subject with her. But Kate, who had spoken little since their escape from Sharalidor, rolled over with

171

her back to him, drawing her frost-white cloak around her.

Apart from the rustling of the grass in the breeze and the occasional snorting of the horses, all was silent. Paul had taken up a vantage-point on the top of the hill with a good view back over the path they had travelled. He told himself that he would stay on watch for as long as possible to allow the others the maximum of rest.

The red-streaked moon appeared between a break in the clouds. It was gibbous, waning, but looked as unnatural as ever. Could they hope to defeat Avron Kromar? Could they allow themselves *not* to hope?

On the hillside below, the wind had blown the grass from Uzosiat's face and he looked placid, released from all sorrow, while his grieving father slept on.

Paul was awoken by the whinnying of the horses. He rolled over to see Uzosiat looming over him, his eyes rolled in his sockets, the ceremonial dagger in his hands. He immediately lunged at Paul with the blood-covered blade, and Paul only just managed to roll aside in time and scramble to his feet.

The boy was dead – still dead, even though he stood and moved. Bits of grass clung to his body and his face was utterly devoid of expression. He looked like a demonic sleep-walker, his rolled eyes giving him a terrifying appearance. Like a puppet or a ventriloquist's dummy he had been animated by some external force. Paul had no doubt that it was Avron Kromar's evil power.

The boy lunged again, and Paul dodged aside. Still befuddled with sleep, he was too stunned and repulsed by the sight of him immediately to use the power of the talisman.

The others were woken by the scuffle. Far more weary than he, they merely stared with a mixture of confusion and disbelief as the boy moved like a jerky puppet, a horrific parody of life itself. As they stumbled to their feet the boy halted, then began to flash and jab with the knife as if to keep them at bay. His movements were like nothing human.

Finally something snapped in Paul. Concentrating, he hurled the boy far up into the air and away from them, flung him out over the hills like a rag doll. The boy made no sound, which somehow made it worse. With a surge of mental energy, Paul used the power of the talisman to burst his body apart, scattering it widely over the mountains so that there was no hope he could ever be reassembled.

On the hillside Aremktesh was lying with his face to the stars. His throat had been slashed.


Because they could not take the risk that the hostel-keeper might be revivified like his son, Paul was forced to dispose of Aremktesh's body in a similar manner. Paul, temporarily numb with horror, did the job clinically and efficiently. He also disposed of the hostel-keeper's belongings by flinging them far away, much to Willie's displeasure. He had advised that the sack might contain items valuable for barter which should be retained; but Paul and the others wanted no trinkets which might remind them of a grisly episode. They kept only the mules.

Late into the night they all fell into an uneasy sleep, huddled together for comfort and with no one on guard. Each of them was haunted by the memory of

Uzosiat's resurrection. Though the boy had been much less of a threat to them than other dangers which they had faced, his revival had been a frightening symbol of the evil power which they would ultimately have to face if they survived the journey to Madrimar. They had been confronted with a disgusting demonstration of the disregard for ordinary human life of their foe, who continued to haunt them in a most literal sense. Even alone in the mountains you are not safe from me, the incident seemed to tell them; I can threaten your lives or your sanity at any time.

Paul continued to doze and wake throughout what remained of the night. He began to feel that he had been as much responsible for Uzosiat's death as Justin. After his success in recovering the others' belongings and then freeing them, he had become overconfident, seduced by the power of the talisman. He had wanted to show off his powers to the others, to command and control them. But the boy's death had chastened him, given him pause for thought. It seemed to him now that the powers they had gained might be their damnation rather than their salvation, if they allowed themselves to forget who they really were and became too wrapped up in the roles of heroic adventurers. They had to remember that their journey, their quest, was a means to an end rather than an end in itself.

Late the following morning they mounted up and rode on, taking the mules with them. Their success in escaping Sharalidor had been cancelled out by the deaths of Aremktesh and Uzosiat, so that a cheerless, reticent mood prevailed amongst them.

They headed in a south-easterly direction. The hills remained low and treeless, and a steady wind

174

blew. After a few hours they came in sight of the river again, and saw a barge in the distance, drifting eastwards in the direction of Madrimar. They followed a route parallel to the river but some miles north of it. At length the hills began to flatten, and presently the land became arable and dotted with small farms.

They avoided the farms, taking what food they needed from the fields and from fruit trees, deciding that it would be better if they shunned human contact and travelled as secretly as possible. It was a long, monotonous day of unhurried riding, without incident. They stopped to bathe in a broad stream, washing away the sweat and the grime of their imprisonment with a richly perfumed soap which Teresa had been prudent enough to take from Aremktesh's sack before they disposed of it. They bathed naked, without modesty or concern for one another, too worn down by the rigours of the past three days to think of anyone but themselves.

They slept in a derelict orchard that night, and in the morning helped themselves to fruit and tubers growing in a nearby field before riding on. Conversation continued to languish as they followed the looping path of the river from a distance, two more barges passing them during the day. They plucked warty fruits from gnarled trees, pear-shaped white berries from cultivated briars, grains and vegetables of many strange varieties from fields. They took only what they needed, knowing that under the bloated red sun crops did not thrive and farmers remained poor.

Each meal was something of an adventure for the taste-buds, and Kate froze fish from the streams which interlaced the region to add to their diet: they

175

joked about it coming from the freezer, but it was a rare moment of levity. Riding on, they scarcely spoke.

They spent the second night in a field of stubble. Towards dawn it rained, so they mounted up and continued on. The cloudy sky was like reddish slate. The rain was not heavy but it proved relentless, trickling down inside their oilskins. In her saddle, Teresa began to weep with the misery of her condition. It would have been a simple matter to transform herself into a flying form, but she knew only too well that she would eventually have to return to physicality and would feel even worse. Paul thought of using the power of the talisman to form a rain-proof shield around them, but he resisted the temptation, knowing that it was unwise to use their powers frivolously or simply for personal comfort when they might at any moment be needed for more urgent matters of survival.

The rain persisted a long time, then abruptly stopped. Suddenly, less than a mile ahead, they saw a town of squat buildings which was steaming after the rain.

They rode down the long main thoroughfare, intending to continue straight on; there were few people abroad, and those who passed hurried by without giving them more than a glance. But the town was deceptively large, and their resolve to avoid human contact until they reached Madrimar began to weaken. Teresa in particular yearned for some warmth and comfort. Suddenly she found herself irresistibly drawn to a large building, which was clearly an inn of some sort.

Soft yellow light spilled out of its narrow windows. An ornate hitching post ran down the side of the building, and several horses were already tethered there. The place radiated a sense of cosiness, and the others needed little persuading. They dismounted and tied their horses to the post before entering the inn, their weapons and uniforms hidden beneath their oilskins.

Inside there was a large room with a concave ceiling of grey wood, which gave it a cavernous appearance; it was hot, crowded and smoky, lit by candles in brackets and filled with the hubbub of conversation. At its far end a walnut fire blazed in a wide stone hearth, and there was an unoccupied table in an alcove beside it. Paul led the others to the table.

The place was a cross between a tavern and a canteen. At a long curving bar of the stony wood a kind of mulled ale was being served in large glass cups, along with bowls of thick stew. Card games were being played at some tables, dice at others, but mostly the patrons simply sat and talked as they drank, holding the cups of ale in both hands as they brought them to their lips. They were predominantly men – large, dark men, some as strongly built as Justin, with rugged faces and bloated eyes.

Paul and the others seated themselves around the table with as little fuss as possible. It was quickly agreed that a bowl of hot stew and a cup of mulled ale would help banish the chill and dampness of their journey. Paul still had the pouch of money which he had stolen from the merchant in Sharalidor, so he rose and went up to the bar, squeezing himself into a corner beside a large man who was hunched over a stool.

The man turned slowly to regard him for several seconds before looking away. In one corner of the room Paul saw a dwarf dressed in yellow juggling brass balls while doing a jig. He was evidently a regular, for most of the patrons looked uninterested; the felt cap which was spread out on the table in front of him was sprinkled with a few coppers, but that was all.

Paul waited until a thin, haggard woman finally appeared in front of him across the bar. She stared at him impatiently, one hand on the hip of her rough brown dress.

'Five glasses of ale and five bowls of stew,' Paul said in a quiet voice.

Again the man sitting beside him turned to stare at him. He had a thick brown beard and was puffing on a thin-stemmed pipe; harsh yellowish smoke wafted into Paul's nostrils. Paul did not look directly at him.

The woman departed, and he felt the pressure of the man's eyes on him all the time he waited. She returned with his order on a large wooden tray.

Paul waited for her to tell him the price, but she simply stared at him.

'How much?' he asked.

'Five coppers each.'

Paul rummaged in his purse. He had few coppers, so he produced a silver piece. The woman took the coin as if unwillingly accepting a bribe.

'You'll be wanting change?' she asked sullenly.

Paul debated, then said, 'Yes.'

She departed to fetch it.

'Strangers are not welcome here,' the bearded man said to Paul.

'We are simply passing through,' Paul replied, not looking at him. 'Allow us to eat and drink what we have purchased, and then we will be gone.'

He made to pick up the tray, but the bearded man

178

reached out a beefy hand and grabbed him by the wrist.

'Strangers are not welcome here,' he said again.

The woman returned and scattered Paul's change on the tray. Her face was carefully expressionless. The bearded man still held Paul's wrist.

Paul turned to look at him. He was of middle years, with a swollen face and dark eyes which gleamed with a mindless hostility.

'We don't want any trouble,' Paul said. 'But if you force us to fight, we will.'

The man gave a grimace of contempt, and began to squeeze Paul's wrist even harder.

Paul stared down at his hand and began to concentrate on it. The talisman started to pulse under his oilskin as he prised the man's fingers open, then lifted his hand. A shocked look appeared on the man's face as he tried to resist the unseen pressure that was being exerted. But Paul forced the man's hand down hard on the bar-top, before picking up his tray and walking quickly away.

The others had not noticed the incident, but he said, 'Be on your guard. This is not a friendly place.' He told them what had happened, but when he looked again, the bearded man was gone from his stool. Both Willie and Justin slipped a hand under their oilskins as they attended to their food and drink.

The mulled ale was at once fragrant and spicy, the stew heavily seasoned with herbs. They huddled around the table, steam rising from the damp uniforms beneath their oilskins. The walnuts crackled on the fire, giving off ample heat.

Then Paul felt a sensation as if someone had crept up behind him. He turned, but there was no one. A man had walked in through the main entrance, bringing a draught of colder air with him. But then Paul saw that Teresa was frowning.

'I thought I sensed something,' she said. 'A presence.'

The others stopped eating and stared at her. She seemed to listen, then shook her head. 'I can't feel it now.'

At this point the dwarf in yellow did a series of cartwheels down the centre of the room, expertly avoiding all the tables. He had a thin, somewhat impish-looking face, with large ears and a thatch of unruly ginger hair on his head. His mouth opened in a crooked grin as he offered his cap around to the patrons. Several gave him coins, and when he came to Paul's table, Paul dropped a silver piece into his hat.

'Quisp thanks you,' the dwarf said, and executed an elaborate bow before disappearing into the crowd.

Then Paul saw the bearded man push through a knot of people towards them. He was closely followed by at least a dozen other men of similar stature. They carried no weapons, but they were obviously ready for a fight.

Paul turned to Kate and Teresa. 'We'll hold them off while you two slip out of here.'

'We can defend ourselves as well as you,' Kate said with icy indignation.

'I know that,' Paul replied. 'But I think we ought to try to get out of this without using our powers. We don't want every step of our way to Madrimar to be marked by public displays of our abilities. We might have to face even more threats if our reputations go ahead of us.'

The others could see the wisdom of this, even though Willie and Justin still looked keen to use their weapons. But there was no time to debate the matter, for the bearded man and his followers had now formed a loose semi-circle around their table.

Without warning, Justin hurled himself at him.

A mêlée immediately ensued, with Paul being dragged from his seat by two strapping men and Willie leaping on to the shoulders of another fellow. Willie immediately ignored Paul's advice by unfurling his whip and wrapping it tightly about the man's neck.

Kate and Teresa reluctantly retreated into the shadows, watching Justin as he threw one man from his shoulders and punched another in the belly. The first man went careering over the bar and plunged into a pile of bottles, which shattered; the second man crumpled at Justin's feet. He dispatched two more with single blows, but others continued to come forward.

Meanwhile Willie was continuing to cling grimly to his victim's shoulders, squeezing the breath from him with his whip while the man flailed at him. Then another man hit him from his perch, sending him plummeting to the floor. Willie scrambled to his feet, trying to lash with his whip. But in the confined space, it was useless; a hand grabbed the end of the whip, and he was jerked to the floor.

Paul was submerged by three or four men nearby. He tried to use the power of the talisman subtly to increase his strength, but he was being crushed and pounded so much that he couldn't muster the necessary concentration.

Kate saw that Paul and the others would be quickly overwhelmed unless she helped them. Gesturing with her hand, she created a sheen of ice across the floor.

Immediately everyone began to slip and slide and fall over. But now a pile of bodies blocked their exit, and Paul and the others were as much in the thick of the mêlée as ever. Teresa, following Kate's lead, decided to intervene as well. She had felt uneasy ever since they had entered the inn, its muggy, hostile atmosphere profoundly oppressive to her. And now that the fight had broken out – a crude bar-room brawl – she wanted only to escape as quickly as possible. In the minds of everyone in the room she began to conjure a vision that the inn was ablaze.

The fighting immediately halted, and everyone began bolting for the door, scrambling over one another in their haste to escape. Even Kate was fooled, clutching at Teresa's hand and trying to pull her towards the door.

'It's an illusion,' Teresa whispered, though she could almost see the flames reflected in Kate's urgent eyes.

She dispelled the vision as quickly as she had created it. By now almost everyone had fled. Only Justin, Paul and Willie remained on the floor, looking bruised and battered but not seriously injured. They clambered to their feet, immediately realizing from Teresa's smile what had happened.

Outside the main entrance, the crowd's cries of alarm turned into confusion and then anger as it dawned on them that they had been the victims of trickery.

'This way,' came a voice from a far corner of the room.

It was the yellow-clad dwarf, pointing to a narrow side door. He gave them a lop-sided grin, then disappeared through the door.

They hesitated, then followed him.

Their horses were directly outside, still reined to the tethering post. They mounted, and the dwarf leapt onto one of the mules.

'Quisp is clever, is he not?' the dwarf said, and gave a cracked giggle. 'You will find no hospitality in this town. But for a small fee I will lead you to warm food and warm beds for the night.'

'A fee?' said Paul, nursing a tender jaw.

'Shall we say one gold piece?' Again there was that twisted, almost teasing grin.

There was no time to argue. They had to get out of the town as quickly as possible.

'Done,' Paul said, reaching into his purse. He found a gold piece and tossed it to Quisp.

The dwarf caught it expertly and pocketed it in one swift movement.

'Follow me,' he said, spurring the mule down the alley.

As Paul unhitched his horse he saw a knot of people surge into the alley from the front of the inn. The bearded man was at their head, and he began hurling imprecations at them as they rode off in the opposite direction. Among the more colourful of them was the malediction: 'May the night-fiends suck your skulls dry!'

# 12
# The Monastery

On leaving the town they rode for about an hour until they came to foothills which led up to a rocky crag. Along the way Quisp jabbered ceaselessly, giving them a potted story of his life. He was the son of a blacksmith, a man as large as he himself was small, and he had been thrown out of his home at an early age when it became clear that he was no use in the foundry, being unable to lift the heavy tools of his father's trade and being generally terrified of burning himself with hot metal. Forced to live by his wits, he had survived various adventures – recounted at some length – before settling in Pholvenx, the town they had just left. He lodged with a widow and her four children, paying for his keep with the coins he garnered from entertaining patrons of inns throughout the town; he juggled, danced, did acrobatics and so on, having perfected his craft during a period spent as a kind of court jester to a rich merchant in a city to the south.

The dwarf was quick to distance himself from the townsfolk. He told them that although he had lived in Pholvenx for many years, he still remained something of an outsider. His various travels had given him broader perspectives than most, and he disliked the townsfolk's narrow-mindedness and hostility to strangers. This was why he was happy to lead them to a place where they would be more warmly welcomed.

Quisp spoke rapidly and incessantly, telling them many anecdotes about himself. He seemed to accept their status as strangers without question, asking them nothing about themselves and commanding their attention with his exaggerated talk so that there was scarcely any need for the rest of them to speak. He punctuated each tale with giggles and crooked smiles, and most of his stories were so outrageous that Paul suspected he drew little distinction between facts and fabrications; like most raconteurs, he prized entertainment value above literal truth.

It was late afternoon when they came to the crag. Like a huge grey anvil it rose up to perhaps two hundred feet, stark against the iron-red sky. At the top of the crag was a squat, rectangular building built of grey stone. A sinuous path led up the foothills towards it.

'It's a monastery,' Quisp told them. 'They are a religious order who came from another continent to escape persecution and settled here. The townsfolk shun them, but they will offer a night's rest and food to any weary traveller who asks it of them.'

They began to ascend the pathway, while Quisp told them more about their prospective hosts. They came from a large island far to the south called Ilmoroq and led a joyous rather than meditative existence, worshipping not any god but life itself in all its abundance and diversity.

Paul was intrigued by such a credo, but he was even more intrigued by the mention of an island with a strange-sounding name. For some reason the idea of other continents on Xhandarre had not occurred to him, but by judicious questioning he established that there were at least four. The largest, and the one in which they found themselves, was named after the world itself, but there was also a bleak, icy continent called Meeruk, a steamy equatorial landmass with the scarcely pronounceable name of Beshphalesph and the little-known island of Ilmoroq in the far south. For a humble entertainer, Quisp was very well versed in geography. Paul wondered if the continents corresponded to those on Earth.

Closer to, the monastery resembled a large stone bunker, with inward sloping walls and slitted windows. The main entranceway proved to be a tall, thin door through which a person could barely pass without brushing both walls.

'We'll have to leave our horses here,' Quisp said, indicating a rough stone corral which had been built on the approach to the main entrance.

They dismounted and led their horses into the corral. Straw had been provided for the animals, and there was a stone trough of rainwater.

The land on which the monastery had been built was bare rock covered with a fine whitish dust, which the wind stirred into tiny eddies as it blew. The crag was an isolated outcrop, affording a good view over the lower hills all around it. A good place on which to build a haven in hostile country.

The dwarf strode up to the door and knocked hard on its black wood.

'It's me,' he called. 'Quisp.'

Scant seconds later the door was opened by a tall woman dressed in a long peach-coloured robe; her face was a coppery colour, a far darker complexion than any they had seen in Xhandarre so far.

'I bring five travellers who crave your hospitality for a night,' the dwarf announced.

The woman turned slowly to regard them. She had a handsome face, and her chestnut-coloured hair fell straight to her shoulders. Her teeth gleamed white when she smiled.

'You are most welcome,' she said in an accent similar to but not quite the same as Quisp's. Then she withdrew into the building.

Quisp went after her, gesturing to them to follow. One by one they passed through the narrow doorway and found themselves in a large stone chamber which reeked of fragrant incense. Men and women dressed in robes of gold and lavender and turquoise and apple-green were seated around a long table. Some were mending clothing, others were weaving mats, others still were painting elaborate designs on pieces of pottery. They all ceased in their tasks as Paul and the others entered.

He counted eighteen of them, and everyone had the coppery skin of the woman who had greeted them. Their hair varied from dark auburn to ash blonde, but there was none of the black hair which they had found so common elsewhere in Xhandarre; these were truly people from another land. They rose and bowed a greeting, all smiling.

Apart from Teresa, the others felt a little uneasy, not sure of what they had walked into. But Teresa was quickly to calm them; immediately on entering the monastery the weariness and irritation of their vexing day's travel had quickly given way to a sense of calm – a sense of calm which radiated from the dark-skinned inhabitants of the monastery.

'It's all right,' she whispered to the others, aware of their unease. 'We're safe here.'

187

Formalities were kept to a minimum. A smile and a bow appeared to be sufficient introduction for most of the monks and nuns – though in their bright pastel robes it was hard to think of them as such; then they all hurried away down various corridors which led out of the chamber. The woman, evidently the head of the order, sat them down in front of a large wood fire, which burned in the hearth at the far end of the hall.

'I am called Lutlenl,' she told them. 'Your coming brings us great pleasure. We rejoice in all living things, from the plants which grow in our garden to the birds which fly overhead. But other people are our greatest source of delight, and we welcome you.'

There was a sing-song quality to her voice, which somehow succeeded in defusing the rather precious sentiments she was expressing. As though it was part of the formalities of introduction, she began to tell them about the order's creed and practices. In its essence it was nothing more remarkable than nature worship exalting life as a cosmic force which transcended individual plants and animals but was to be cherished in each singular expression of its bounty.

While Lutlenl talked, the other members of the order were busy elsewhere. Presently a man in rose-coloured robes returned and said, 'Your baths are ready.'

'Baths?' said Willie.

'It is our custom to provide hot baths for our guests before they eat,' Lutlenl told them, 'if they so wish. But there is no obligation.'

They needed little persuading, however, all of them feeling intolerably unclean after their days of riding and sleeping in the open. The man led them down a cloister and opened a door to a room which was filled with steam. There were two rows of rectangular baths set into the floor and separated by a screen. Three baths had been filled with hot water on one side, and two on the other. Bars of glaucous soap and rough linen towels had also been provided.

The monk withdrew without another word, closing the door behind him. Paul and the others hesitated for only a moment, then began to undress.

The water was hot, and the sweat and grime of their journey seemed to dissolve from their bodies as soon as they immersed themselves in it. Kate and Teresa took the two baths on the opposite side of the screen from the others, and soon everyone was sighing and groaning with pleasure as they sat neck-deep in water. The soap was scented with herbs and they washed themselves thoroughly, feeling their aching muscles relax and scarcely believing that they had finally come upon a civilized place.

Only when the water began to cool did they emerge, drying themselves and dressing. They returned to the hall and found that the table had been laid with a variety of food. Evidently the order's cherishing of life did not prevent them from eating well: in addition to plates of vegetables, fruit and loaves of yellow bread, trays of small roasted fowl had been brought to the table.

'We have eaten earlier,' Lutlenl told them. 'We will leave you in peace to attend to your meal.'

'It's too much,' Paul said. 'We can't accept all this.'

Lutlenl gestured towards a hemispherical window which gave out into a large central garden enclosed by the monastery. 'We grow more food than we can eat, and we maintain animals for milk and cheese. Much of our produce is bartered for firewood and

189

cloth whenever possible. Fill your bellies and have no fear that you will be depriving us. Travellers rarely seek our hospitality, and when they do we try to provide it in profusion.'

She departed with the other monks and nuns. The meal looked sumptuous, and Quisp had already stuffed himself while they had been bathing. Paul saw that he had also filled his pockets with various fruits, vegetables and pieces of meat.

'Quisp must go,' he told them, clambering down from his chair. 'The widow will be expecting me.' He hesitated. 'Can I take the mule?'

They had left the other mule behind in Pholvenx.

'You have already been well paid,' said Willie.

'On foot it would take me hours to get home. I promise to return it in the morning and show you the best route east.'

'How do you know we are headed east?' asked Willie.

Quisp shrugged. 'Where else is there to go?'

Willie stared at him. 'Won't the townsfolk be after your blood for helping us escape?'

'For a while, perhaps. But their memories are as short as their tempers, and Pholvenx is a large town.' He grinned. 'I am used to avoiding those who wish to do me harm.'

'Of course you can take the mule,' Paul said.

'You are a kind young man. I hope that I will have the chance to repay your kindness.'

'You already have. By bringing us here.'

'My life has been a difficult one,' the dwarf went on, 'and sometimes I have been forced to do things I would not wish to do. Remember two common-places: things are not always as they seem, and the presssure of circumstances can make villains of us all.

190

I will be waiting for you at the foot of the crag tomorrow morning.'

On this rather solemn and mysterious note, he strode out of the hall.

'I don't trust that dwarf,' Willie said. 'We should have made him stay here with us. He won't be back in the morning.'

'Perhaps,' said Paul. 'But does it matter? We know which way we have to travel, and we've got food and shelter for the night.'

'I still don't think you should have given him the mule.'

Paul did not press the argument. Without further ado, they set to eating. In addition to the staples, there was also a savoury porridge, a bowl of creamy honey, finger-shaped biscuits which dissolved in the mouth like candy-floss, and a fragrant bottle-green wine.

They ate grandly and at their leisure, sampling every delicacy. The fire blazed warm at their backs, and they sat on cushioned chairs, relishing their comfort. Candles flickered on the walls, and the air was still heavy with incense; but their minds were concentrated entirely on the food, on all its strange and delightful flavours.

Lutlenl returned when they had finished eating.

'We have prepared rooms for you,' she told them. 'You must be weary after travelling.'

'We would prefer to sleep together,' Paul said gently; even in this hospitable place he felt it better to stick to their policy of not being separated.

'The rooms lie in series,' Lutlenl said, 'and there are connecting doors between all of them. Their comforts are spare, but I think you will find them adequate.'

The warm fire and the heavy meal had conspired to make them feel very drowsy. They followed Lutlenl down a long cloister, past windows which gave out on vegetable gardens, vines and orchard shrubs; a few monks and nuns still laboured in the dying light of day, using hoes and rakes to turn over the earth. Most of the crops looked surprisingly healthy, and Lutlenl told them that all the soil had been brought up the mountainside from the valley below in barrows pulled by the monks and nuns.

Their rooms proved to be small windowless cells, arranged like a partitioned corridor so that access to the inner cells was possible only through the doorway to the first cell, which gave out on the cloister. In each cell was a simple bed, covered with rough blankets and coarse linen sheets. Candles burned in brackets on the walls, and under each bed was a chamber-pot. Arched doors with wooden latches connected the cells.

'I will leave you to make your own sleeping arrangements,' Lutlenl said, and with a wide smile she departed.

Though it was barely sunset, they all wanted to sleep. Exhausted from their travels and battered after the fracas in Pholvenx, they selected their cells with a minimum of debate, Justin opting for the one nearest the cloister, Paul taking the second cell, Kate the third, Teresa the fourth, and Willie the innermost.

Relishing the modicum of privacy, they closed the doors between them, leaving the candles burning as they crawled under the rough sheets and quickly surrendered to sleep. Only Justin remained awake for a while. Despite Teresa's assurances that their hosts radiated only friendliness, Justin felt that there was something slightly creepy about the place, that the

192

hospitality they had received was too readily offered and profuse. It was a residue of his old suspicious habit of mind, he knew, the cynical attitude that do-gooders always had an angle. He dragged his bed up against the cloister door – just in case – before finally removing his boots and settling down with his hammer lying beside him on the pillow.

Teresa was dreaming again of Michelle. Her younger sister had long been the beauty of the family, tall and willowy, with blonde hair which Teresa had always admired. In fact she had admired practically every-thing about Michelle, who had never been short of boyfriends and was always able to wear the most outrageously fashionable clothing and still look stunning. Teresa, by contrast, was the ugly duckling of the family, and while she had always strived to be cheerful and matter-of-fact, her admiration for her sister was frequently tinged with profound envy. Michelle had had all the breaks and the attention, whereas Teresa was usually taken for granted by her family.

Now, in her dream, Teresa was alone with Michelle in her bedroom as her old dumpy self. Michelle was admiring herself in a long mirror, but Teresa was wearing her golden bracelets, which she promptly struck together to become her dragonfly self. Startled by the transformation, Michelle stared at her in wonderment before telling her that she was the most beautiful creature she had ever seen. Then Teresa's mother and father and older brother were also there, admiring her, profuse in their compli-ments.

Teresa stared at herself in Michelle's mirror, and

luxuriated in her family's admiration. But abruptly their manner changed, becoming at first cold and then positively hostile. They began to leer and snarl at her. She backed away, and woke suddenly to her candle-lit cell.

The sense of threat did not pass on awakening. Instead it grew. Then she heard a great crash of something heavy overturning.

The crash came from Justin's room, where Justin himself had been catapulted from bed by a surge of force. He scrambled dazedly to his feet, snatching up his hammer. The door to his cloister had been burst half-open, and in the flickering candle-light he saw what had caused it.

Clustered in the crack of the doorway were a host of feral faces, like ravening wolves with long snouts and blood-red eyes. They snarled and spat at him, clawing the air with hands like furred talons. Saliva drooled from an array of fangs as they leapt forward as a body once more, pushing the bed further back to gain entry into the room.

Justin was seized with terror at the sight. As a young boy he had been terrified of a neighbour's Alsatian, and one day his father had held him over the garden fence, his face mere inches from the barking dog, to try to cure him of his fear. Justin had wet his pants and had suffered nightmares for days afterwards. And now the sight of similar but far more fearsome creatures sparked off a Pavlovian reaction of abject horror. He fled, hurling open the door to Paul's cell.

Paul, awoken by the noise, was feeling groggy and had only just stumbled from bed when Justin charged into his cell. Through the doorway he saw the wolf-creatures overturn Justin's bed and burst into the room with their terrible snarling. There were at least a dozen, and wolf-like though they were, they wore the pastel robes of the monks and nuns.

Paul slammed his door. Justin was standing there, paralysed by fright. Paul felt sluggish, unable to think clearly. He grabbed the end of the bed and began dragging it towards the door.

After a moment, Justin helped him. As soon as the bed was wedged against the door, the creatures started to batter against it. It began to open further and further with each thrust. Paul tried to force the door shut with his mind, but he could not get the talisman to work; he was groggy, thick-headed, and he realized that their food must have been drugged. They were meant to sleep heavily and succumb without a struggle to the slavering pack.

The door behind them opened, and Kate stood woozily in the doorway. At this point the creatures surged again, and Justin's nerve cracked. He bolted past Kate.

Paul scrambled back into Kate's cell. She helped him drag the bed into the doorway, while staring with horror as the creatures bounded into Paul's room. Paul snatched a candle from the wall and lit the end of a blanket. The dry bedding took fire quickly, and the wolf-creatures reared back on sight of the flames. The mattress was filled with straw and the wall of fire provided an effective, if temporary, barrier.

They retreated into Teresa's room; Teresa herself had already fled into Willie's cell with Justin. Kate looked as drugged as Paul himself felt, but as the wolf-creatures began to scramble over the dying wall of fire, she lifted both hands and used all her energies to raise a wall of ice in the doorway.

Again they fled into Willie's cell. Willie was sitting on his bed, staring as Justin cowered against the far wall. Willie had already glimpsed the creatures, and the threat they presented was made far worse by the terror they had instilled into Justin. Teresa, meanwhile, stood trembling beside the bed, the savagery of the pack having overwhelmed her mind with revulsion; drugged and terrified, she was feebly striking her bracelets together, but without effect, her mind too fraught to work the transformation she desired.

Paul desperately began trying to summon Therion. Justin suddenly raised his hammer and swung it against the wall. The stones cracked under the blow but were not dislodged. The creatures were baying and clawing madly at Kate's ice-wall, their outlines distorted by the uneven planes of the candle-lit ice. Justin swung his hammer once more, desperate to batter a hole through the wall so that they could escape. But the drugged food had weakened him, and again the stones held. Once more he swung.

The wall gave way under the blow, two large stones being punched out of it to create a hole big enough for a person to leap through. But the stones vanished abruptly from sight, and beyond the hole was a yawning emptiness: Willie's cell abutted the sheer edge of the crag. The only way out was straight down.

Teresa would have fled, flown away, had she been able, but she still could not summon the will-power to work the magic of her bracelets. There was a cracking of ice, and suddenly one of the creatures burst into the cell, leaping on Kate.

It dragged her down, and its mouth lunged for the top of her head. A wave of panic and disgust burst from Paul, and even as he thought of it, the creature

196

was hurled off Kate and slammed so hard against the wall that the impact killed it instantly. As the body crumpled to the floor, Paul had a moment of lucidity in which he saw that it was wearing a peach-coloured robe.

Then more of the creatures came snarling and raging into the cell. Paul's mind was suddenly clear, filled with a revitalizing energy, and he knew that Therion had finally stirred and used his sorcery to banish the effects of the drugged food. Paul reacted instantly, sending the creatures hurtling forward so that they plunged through the hole which Justin had punched in the wall.

On and on the creatures came, like mad, ferocious lemmings with no instincts save those for the kill. Their delicately coloured robes contrasted utterly with their savage faces and blood-red eyes, but they were unmistakably the nuns and monks of the monastery transformed into beings like werewolves. One after another Paul impelled them straight across the cell and out through the hole in the wall, sending them snarling and spitting to their deaths on the rocks below, until finally no more came.

There was a silence. No one moved for long seconds. Kate was still lying on the floor, unmoving, her eyes closed. Paul was at her side in an instant.

As he put his arm around her to lift her up, her cold body made him think that she was already dead, until he remembered that it was just the effect of her frost-cloak. At that moment her eyes opened.

'Are you all right?' he asked.

For a second she stared at him without recognition; then she nodded.

Her silvery hair was stained with small patches of blood where the creature had clawed at her scalp. But the wound proved to be minor, a mere scratching of the skin. Paul was profoundly relieved; he did not like to think what might have happened had Therion not come to his aid.

Suddenly Justin stepped forward and wrenched him away from her.

'Leave,' he said. 'Mine.'

Anger filled his thick face, an anger matched by Paul's own. Paul braced himself for a blow, braced himself to use the power of the talisman to hurl the blow back at him.

'Hey,' said Willie, stepping gingerly between them. 'Let's be sure we've mopped up the enemy before we start fighting among ourselves.'

# 13
## *Awful Truths*

Even the blood-red dawn was welcome after the night of horrors just past. They found no more of the creatures in the monastery, nor any trace of the nuns and monks. Therion confirmed they must have been beings, unknown to him, who were transformed from humans into devouring animals after dark. But what they did find was grisly confirmation of how the creatures killed – and fed.

On ground level the monastery was to all appearances normal, the chambers of the nuns and monks filled with the ordinary trappings of civilized life – furniture, tapestries, clothing, soap, towels, and much else. The garden was cultivated as normal, and there were pens housing Xhandarrean goats, pigs and chickens. But it was only when they came upon a stairway leading underground that they discovered the repellent truth about the inhabitants of the monastery.

The stench – masked by incense while they had been upstairs – reached their nostrils even before they arrived at the bottom of the stone flight of stairs. It was the smell of putrefying flesh. The stairs gave out into a cavernous chamber littered with skeletons.

Human skeletons. That was bad enough, but not all of them were mere bones: in one corner lay several corpses, and at the sight of these both Teresa and Willie fled upstairs.

Paul, Kate and Justin forced themselves to approach the decaying bodies. They were ordinary Xhandarreans, united in death by the fact that they had been disembowelled and had the tops of their heads removed. All the internal organs, including the brain, were gone.

They fled the chamber immediately, both Paul and Justin feeling their gorge rising. As he departed, Paul saw in the far corner of the chamber an elaborate contraption which the watching Therion was quick to suggest had been used for the grinding down of bones. Paul recalled the pale, ashy colour of the soil in the garden, and suddenly he was vomiting on the stairway.

When his stomach was finally empty, he stumbled up the stairs. The others were out in the garden, gulping in fresh air. Paul decided to say nothing of his suspicion that the soil had been fertilized with human bone.

Lutlenl's wolf-body had been dragged from the cell, and Kate was examining its muzzle.

'The teeth look powerful enough to crush bone,' she told them. 'They must bite straight through the skull to the—'

'Kate,' Paul said, 'not now.' Her detachment dismayed him after what had happened to them, the more so because she was the one who had come closest to becoming the creatures' victim. Paul gulped in lungfuls of fresh air and tried to forget the miasma of the cellar.

'We should ride straight back to Pholvenx and root

out the poisonous dwarf,' Willie was saying. 'I'd cheerfully slit his throat.'

Paul said nothing; he was thinking of the bearded man's taunt as they had made their escape from the town: 'May the night-fiends suck your skulls dry.' It had been no colourful curse; the local people knew the true nature of the monks and nuns, and Quisp had made sure that he got away from the monastery before sunset, abandoning them to their fate. More than betrayal, Paul felt a sense of disappointment.

'We haven't got time for petty revenge,' he said. 'I think we should get out of here and press on to Madrimar.'

Everyone was agreeable to this except Teresa, who suddenly slumped against a low wall and started to cry.

'I can't go on,' she sobbed. 'I can't.'

Grinding days of sleeping rough and the horrors of the past night had taken a greater toll on her fragile constitution. She felt sickened, bled dry by the constant privations and threats which they had faced; the urge to escape from it all, to fly away to somewhere placid and beautiful, was stronger than ever.

The others did their best to comfort her and persuade her that they had to continue. But in the end it was the memory of her old, indomitable self which made her determined to press on. In her former guise she wouldn't have given up so easily; and she wasn't going to let herself down.

'At least we can take plenty of food with us,' said Willie. 'The larders are stocked with goodies.'

'No,' said Paul.

Willie glared at him. 'Why not?'

'I think we should try to put everything about this

place behind us. We should even shake the dust from our feet.'

'It'll only go to waste. What's the point of leaving it?'

Paul could see that Justin was also determined to raid the larder.

'I think they fertilized the soil with ground-up bones from their victims,' he said.

Willie hesitated, then shrugged. 'It still tastes like ordinary food.'

'It's the principle.'

'We eat stuff that's fertilized from cow dung. This is a lot nastier, I'll grant you, but in the end it's the same thing. We all rot.' He glanced at Justin for moral support. 'Look at it this way – if we survive and kill the sorcerer, those people won't have died in vain.'

Paul was too repulsed by the idea to argue further, even though he sensed that both Kate and Teresa shared his distaste. But when they finally made to leave, neither Willie nor Justin took any food from the larders.

The horses were unharmed in the corral. As they led them out, a gust of wind threw up white dust. Was the dust also human bones? Paul wondered. How long had the monastery stood on the crag? And how many humans had fallen victim to its inhabitants?

These questions were half-addressed to Therion before it dawned on Paul that the old sorcerer had left him.

They led the horses down the hillside path. The corpses of the wolf-creatures littered the rocks at the base of the crag, and scavenger birds like mottled magpies were already picking at their corpses. On a tall rock sat an animal resembling a brownish-yellow rabbit. It regarded them as they approached, then suddenly skittered away, vanishing in leaps and bounds over a low hill.

Paul and the others gave the corpses of the wolf-creatures as wide a berth as possible. Then they inadvertently passed close by one of the corpses and saw that it had begun to deliquesce into a dark, viscous mass as though melted by the gloomy red light of the sun.

There was no sign of Quisp or of their mules. Once more Willie began to curse and berate the dwarf.

'At least he left us the horses,' Kate remarked.

Yes, thought Paul; if the dwarf had departed knowing that they would be killed, why take the mule and leave the more valuable horses behind?


They rode on for most of the day over gentle, treeless hills which gradually became moorland the higher they went. Their pace was slow, their conversation once more limited, each one of them still numbed by what they had experienced and seen at the monastery. More than ever they all realized that being actual warriors undertaking a dangerous quest in a world of sorcery and strange creatures was quite different from the vicarious experience of their role-playing games or the books which they read. Paul had a large collection of fantasy books, and in them the heroes usually shrugged off hardship and danger and were constantly strong, courageous and noble. But in reality each battle for their lives drained them and made their courage more fragile, while nobility was a luxury that none of them could afford. There was friendship, loyalty and even affection, but Paul recognized that all of these were being increasingly tested and strained by the rigours of their journey.

Justin rode ahead of them, alert for any danger. Paul knew he was hoping for the chance to use his hammer and redeem himself after the fear he had displayed when faced with the wolf-creatures. Justin had never liked to show weakness, and in this respect he was just like his old self. Yet all of them had changed to a greater or lesser degree, consolidating the personalities which had been exemplified in the figurines. No doubt they were better equipped to survive the perils of their journey as a result, but the blessings were very mixed. Justin was becoming increasingly tempestuous, in Willie there was a growing streak of callous self-interest, while Teresa had lost much of her pluckiness and was turning into a being of very limited courage and motivation. And then there was Kate – Kate who in her new identity was at times so aloof and imperturbable that it seemed as if nothing could touch her.

He knew that he, too, had changed. He had been forced to take on the mantle of leadership, forced to make decisions and persuade others to follow him in a way that he had never done before. He felt that he had discovered a certain kind of courage in being prepared to face death when destroying the birdbats. Perhaps it had been a foolish sort of courage, prompted by the instincts of martyrdom, but it had nevertheless gone some way towards banishing his conviction that he was a coward.

And yet he remained dissatisfied. Courage was not always marked by grand, life-saving gestures; there was a quieter sort which sprang out of a fundamental confidence in oneself and was expressed in a more personal and intimate context. He was thinking of Kate in this last respect, thinking of how he still baulked at the idea of telling her how he had always been attracted to her. He had a strong feeling that she was finished with Justin, yet he could not bring himself to approach her; he feared an aloof dismissal, a rejection that would be the more crushing because it was careless and dispassionate.

Shortly after midday they stopped and ate a spare, silent meal before riding on. Though they were now in high moorlands, the afternoon proved hot, the bloated sun dominating a cloudless sky of pale purple. There was a springy dark-green heather dotted with lime-coloured flowers beneath their horses' hoofs, and rocks the colour of blue slate jutted from the earth, encrusted with gold and orange lichen; in sheltered cracks thorn-bushes blossomed like magnetized clusters of iron filings. A steady, refreshing wind blew. Even under the gloomy sky the moorlands possessed a rugged beauty which was very calming.

They rode on throughout the afternoon, undisturbed by sorcerous apparitions or wild animals which might have presented a threat. It was as if they were deliberately being given some respite, though they remained alert for danger. The sun sank towards the horizon. Gradually all of them became possessed with the feeling that this was the last lap in their quest, that soon they would reach their destination.

Night fell, and there was no moon. They continued riding. Overhead the expanse of stars was brilliant, the familiar constellations a great comfort to Paul. For the first time since they had been on Xhandarre, all five of them felt a sense of tranquillity, of being temporarily at peace with nature.

Presently the red-veined moon rose, less than half-full now. The heathery smells of the moorland air gave way to a more salty tang. Willie was at the head of the group, slowly urging his horse along a difficult surface of boulders and loose flakes of rock, when suddenly his horse started and veered to the left. Willie had a glimpse of a wide expanse of moonlit water far below him as the frightened animal backtracked.

Moments later, when he had calmed the horse, he was able to establish that he had almost ridden over the edge of a precipice. The land along which they had been riding abruptly terminated in a sharp drop, which went down perhaps half a mile to the thin strip of flat coastline. Beyond that, extending to the horizon, was the rippled sea.

The five of them stood on the edge of the precipice, filled with a profound sense of space and vastness; for the first time they had a true impression of Xhandarre as a world as large as their own Earth. The cliffline stretched away on either side of them until it was lost in a tangle of foliage. Several miles to the north, over a hump in the shoreline, there was a hint of light in the sky, as if a city lay beyond the hill.

They decided to spend the night on their lofty vantage-point, finding a grassy patch sheltered by broad-leaved trees and shrubs not far from the cliff's edge. The sound of rushing water came from close by, and pushing their way through the vegetation they came upon a V-shaped fault in the coastline, down which a frothy stream tumbled towards the sea.

They lit a fire and attended to their rations. All of them were aware that this might be the last quiet moment they would have to themselves, that soon they would be fighting the ultimate battle for their lives. No one actually said as much, but there was a silent drawing-together as they sat around the fire, even Kate braving its heat.

After they had eaten, Teresa wandered away to refresh herself at the stream, while Justin went to check the horses, who had been tethered to a rotting tree-trunk near the stream. He had grown to enjoy the company of these mute creatures, whose eyes seemed sometimes to gleam with intelligence; they reflected his own Xhandarrean character, in which the sophisticate was locked inside the barbarian. He was conscious that he had played little part in the decision-making during their long journey, but in Xhandarre he could lead by action, by sheer physical prowess. He despised himself for the panic he had shown in the face of the wolf-creatures; but when they finally met the dark sorcerer he was determined to be fearless.

He heard voices from further down the stream. Peering through a bush, he saw that Willie had joined Teresa. The rushing water prevented him from overhearing what they were saying, but it was clear that Willie had deliberately chosen his moment to be alone with her.

Teresa had been splashing water on her face, and she was startled when she heard a rustling behind her.

'It's only me,' Willie said, emerging from the foliage. He grinned and leapt up on a rock by the waterside.

Teresa wiped her face with the sleeve of her tunic. The water was cold and pure, and very refreshing after the long ride. But she felt tired and bedraggled.

To Willie, however, she looked beautiful. The pale pinkish moonlight lit up the droplets of water which still beaded her face, and the whole scene was like something out of a clichéd romance. And yet his appreciation of her beauty was real and profound.

'I wish I had a camera,' he said.

Teresa turned and stared down at the stream-drenched ravine. 'It's beautiful, isn't it?'

'I wasn't thinking of the scenery. I meant you.'

He stepped down off the rock and approached her, touching her arm. She flinched at the contact, as though taken by surprise.

'What do you think we'll do when this is over?' he asked.

'I've been trying not to think of it. I just hope we survive.'

She seemed to shiver at the thought, and Willie took the opportunity to put his arm around her shoulder.

'Don't worry,' he said. 'We've managed to fight off everything from serpents to human wolves, and we've come through with no more than a few scratches. I think we're pretty well prepared now for the grand finale.'

Willie actually felt less confident than he sounded, but he was trying to put her mind at ease. He sat her down on a large rock covered with a blue-green moss.

'Listen,' he said, 'when this is all over I'd like you and me to spend some time together.'

She simply stared at him as if innocent of his meaning.

'Alone. Just the two of us. I want you, Teresa.'

Then he drew her face to his and began kissing her.

As before, she did not immediately resist, even though she had been hoping that he would not attempt to force himself on her. She was flattered by his desire, but she had not wanted him to make a physical demonstration of it because she remembered what had happened the last time he had kissed her: she had felt as if she couldn't breathe, and she had been profoundly relieved when Justin had interrupted them. Though she did not like to admit it to herself, she had actually been somewhat repulsed by what had happened. Not because she didn't like Willie – in their former lives she had always been fond of him – but because to be held and kissed made her feel as if she was trapped and being devoured.

The moment Willie's mouth was on hers, these feelings surfaced once more, accompanied by an anxiety at the way he had said 'I want you', as if she was some kind of object or creature whom he could possess. Willie had changed, and she wasn't sure she liked the person he had become. She was also aware that he was attracted to the graceful new her rather than the plain and dowdy person she had been. All her life she had longed for someone to tell her that she was beautiful, but now she felt as if she was a fraud, a toad inhabiting the body of a princess.

All these emotions combined to make Willie's embrace insufferable. His mouth was suffocating her, his arms were hemming her in, crushing her . . .

She began to struggle, and twisted her head aside. 'No, Willie,' she said. 'Please stop.'

Willie paused and she wrenched herself free of him, standing up. She had to do everything in her power to resist the urge to strike her bracelets together and fly away from him.

He stood up slowly. 'What is it?'

'I just can't.'

He stared at her. 'Can't or won't?'

There was an aggrieved note in his voice, and she knew she could not possibly explain.

'Is it me?' he demanded. 'Do you find me repulsive?'

'No. It's not that.'

'Then what is it?'

She shook her head helplessly, fearful of the way he was glaring at her.

Willie himself wanted to slap her across the face at that moment. She had encouraged his attentions, only to snub him just as he had been snubbed so many times as his old self.

'You're just like all the rest of them,' he said bitterly. 'Look but don't touch. You make me sick.'

Then he stormed away through the bushes, his anger hot on his face. He found a secluded clearing near the cliff's edge and sat down, almost surprised by his own bitterness. But he could deny it no longer.

Until he came to Xhandarre he had always felt that his life had been a placid and contented one overall, but that had been a wilful illusion. As an only child, he had been doted on by his parents until his father died when he was thirteen. Then everything had changed for the worse. His mother had become a professional invalid, taking to her bed with a series of undiagnosed ailments and Willie had started to grow.

Until his father's death he had been a boy of normal size, but afterwards it was as if he was physically trying to fill his father's shoes. Within a year he had passed six feet and he had also begun to broaden. His growing size made him self-conscious with everyone, but in particular the opposite sex. While all the boys around him were acquiring girlfriends, he felt too awkward and cumbersome to interest them, and soon he became the butt of endless jokes about his size and clumsiness.

From that time on his life had been a catalogue of minor humiliations. Even his mother had become ever more demanding, calling him a 'lump' and treating him like a household slave whom she expected to wait on her every whim. Paradoxically his very size had made him suppress his anger in favour of a tolerant fatalism; he didn't want anybody to think he was a bully. But the resentment and bitterness had been there, hidden from himself until he came to Xhandarre and became a character who no longer had to worry about intimidating people by his sheer size; then the long-suffering mask had fallen away, and the self-effacement was replaced by a determination to give as good as he got.

Thinking about it now, he realized that he blamed his mother most of all. Far from giving him support, she had made his life a quiet misery with her endless and unreasonable demands. And if he tried to refuse her she would call him selfish, cling to him, make him promise that he would never leave her. He was almost glad that she had been left on her own for days and didn't have him to hang on to, to clutch at, to fill his nostrils with the sickly perfume which she always wore.

This line of thought was making Willie feel uneasy, for it was accompanied by a vivid memory of grappling with the crone in the forest and finally plunging the knife into her belly. But suddenly he heard the sound of raised voices. Heading back through the undergrowth towards the campsite, he encountered Teresa. They did not look one another in the eye.

After Willie had left Paul and Kate alone beside the fire, Paul stared into the flames for long minutes, trying to think of some way in which to initiate a conversation with Kate that would lead up to telling her that he had always found her attractive. Kate was sitting some distance from the fire, her cloak wrapped about her shoulders. Her expression was remote, and Paul felt helpless, not knowing what to say.

'Do you think we'll make it?' she asked abruptly. 'Back to Earth.'

He met her gaze. 'I don't know.'

'Sometimes this all seems like a dream. Sometimes I wish it was.'

'Do you want to go back?'

'Of course. Don't you?'

'Yes, but it's not a foregone conclusion that we'll be able to, even if we manage to overcome Avron Kromar.'

'Do you think we will overcome him?'

'We have to hope we can.'

'But do you think so?'

'No.'

When she did not react to this, he went on: 'I think we're just being toyed with. We're innocents here, pawns in some mysterious game, made to think that we can control our destinies, but without real power. It's like being in one of Justin's games, with an invisible hand throwing the dice. And when our number comes up, there'll be nothing we can do about it.'

He had moved closer to her. She continued to stare at him without expression, the paleness of her face and the silver-white sheen of her hair making her seem like a statue. But he was determined not to be daunted.

'Are you afraid of dying?' she asked him.

'Yes,' he said. 'If you're young, I think you have to be mad not to be.'

'I wish I was.'

He waited for her to explain. She stared away. 'I feel that I should be afraid, and yet I'm not. I know that the odds are against us – like you, I have the impression that we could be snuffed out at any time. I should be petrified, but all I feel is a sense of inevitability, as if there's no point in getting worked up about it.'

Both her lifeless tone and her absence of expression only made Paul more eager to rekindle something of the old Kate, not only for his sake but for hers.

'Perhaps you are petrified,' he said, 'but in the sense of having had your feelings desensitized.'

This sounded trite and pat, and he immediately regretted it. But she was staring at him in a questioning way.

'It's the characters we've become, Kate.' He was sitting right next to her now, and could feel the chill of her cloak. 'We've taken on not only their powers but their personalities. And yours is aloof, with its feelings under tight control. But I think it's dangerous for us to let them take over too completely. We've got to hang on to something of our old selves or bring them back to life again. If we lose them, perhaps we really will have no hope of ever returning to Earth.'

'I don't think I want to be what I was,' she said.

'I'm not saying we don't have to change, to adapt to circumstances and learn from our mistakes. But there's a balance.'

Paul felt as if he was talking as much to persuade himself as her. And Kate did not look entirely swayed.

'The way you are now scares me a little,' he said. 'I remember the old Kate, emotions all up front.'

'Like an open book.'

'It had its attractions, you know. I'm not sure I like the new version as much.'

He was trying to stir some response in her, and he succeeded in raising the faintest of smiles.

'I take that back,' he said. 'I've always been a secret admirer.'

The words were out before he knew it, sounding like smooth patter whereas they had in fact emerged quite naturally. The ghost of a smile lingered on her pale lips, and Paul reached up and took her by the shoulders. They were cold, her whole body was cold, but he was prepared for that and he did not hesitate in planting a kiss on her mouth.

There was a cracking of branches, and Justin surged into the clearing, brandishing his hammer.

'Leave her,' he shouted to Paul, and advanced on them.

Paul broke their clinch. 'Wait a minute, Justin,' he began, but Justin did not halt in his angry stride, and the hammer was raised. His face was dark with rage. Paul pushed Kate away, before flinging himself aside as the hammer came plunging down into the earth where he had been sitting.

Paul scrambled to his feet. 'Justin, stop—'

But Justin was already charging again.

'Traitor!' he bellowed.

The hammerhead had begun to glow a dull red, and Paul leapt away as Justin swung it again. The hammer came down on an outcrop of rock, which promptly shattered.

They circled one another. Justin could not contain his anger; on seeing Willie and Teresa together he had realized that Kate and Paul were alone at the fire, so he had immediately gone back to the campsite to make sure that they weren't getting up to anything behind his back. But his worst suspicions had been confirmed when he had seen Paul and Kate kissing. A

214

tremendous rage had flooded through him, and now he simply wanted to smash Paul.

Paul backed away, not wanting to use the power of the talisman if he could avoid it. His foot came down on a loose rock and he stumbled, fell backwards. Justin advanced, the hammerhead still glowing.

'Justin!' Kate shouted, running forward and trying to stop him.

'Bitch!' he yelled, and with a sweep of his forearm he hit her across the chest, sending her reeling back. She slumped to the ground.

This finally galvanized Paul. As Justin made to bring down the hammer Paul concentrated, feeling the talisman beginning to pulse, and exerted his will to immobilize Justin.

The hammer was poised in mid-air, and Justin was paralysed. He began to strain against the invisible force which held him like an enveloping strait-jacket. His jaw went rigid and veins stood out like ropes in his neck as he gritted his teeth and tried to overwhelm the power of Paul's mind by sheer brute force.

To Paul, who was still lying on the floor, it was a frightening sight, as if the barbarian warrior in Justin had taken over completely. And he could feel Justin's tremendous physical strength like a pressure against his mind, threatening to burst through his defences. Kate had been stunned by Justin's blow, but Paul concentrated harder, trying not to be distracted by the sight of her.

For long seconds they were locked in stasis. Then Willie and Teresa burst into the clearing.

'What's going on?' Willie shouted, and Paul immediately felt Justin cease his struggling. He dropped his mental guard and scrambled over to Kate, who was lying on her elbows, looking groggy.

'I'm all right,' she told him, shrugging off his helping hand and climbing to her feet. There was something in her manner which told Paul to keep his distance at that moment.

Justin stalked up to the two of them. He had dropped his hammer, as if to indicate that he no longer intended physical violence. But he still looked very angry.

'You,' he said to Kate. 'Mine.'

Kate stared back at him.

'You don't own me,' she said with perfect calm. 'You never have. It's time you got it into that thick head of yours that we're finished, there's nothing between us any more. You have no claims on me.'

Justin was rooted with fury. He was struggling to speak, doubly infuriated by his inability to express himself with his old venom.

'Two-timer,' he finally said. 'Slut.'

Kate felt calm inside, but Justin's insult made her want to wound him. She reached up her sleeve and removed the photograph which she had carefully preserved there throughout all their travels. Though it was crumpled and stained, the young woman's face was still clearly recognizable. Kate brandished it in front of Justin.

'This fell out of your pocket when we were going down to Paul's cellar. Who's been two-timing who, Justin?'

She allowed him to study the photograph for only a second before she tossed it on the fire.

Justin reacted instantly, rushing forward and trying to snatch it from the flames. But it buckled and blackened and flared up before he could reach it.

For a moment no one moved. Kate prepared to defend herself against her former boyfriend, but Justin's face was empty of emotion. He turned and strode off through the trees.

Only Paul understood what had happened, for he had recognized the person in the photograph. Kate had the expression of someone who knew she had miscalculated but did not understand how. Paul wondered if perhaps it would be better to say nothing; but he knew he would have to do the decent thing and tell her who the young woman in the photograph was.

'I think we'd better talk,' he told her quietly, then led her away through the trees until they came to a hillock near the edge of the precipice. There was no sign of Justin, and Paul told Kate to sit down. She did so, gazing distantly out over the moonlit sea.

'Did you know that Justin's parents were divorced?' Paul began.

Kate nodded. 'He told me that his mother walked out on his father when he was small. He swore me to secrecy about it. I always thought that's why he had to have the upper hand with me. He didn't want history to repeat itself.'

'You may be right,' Paul said. 'But did you also know that his mother was pregnant when she walked out?'

Kate stared at him, then slowly shook her head.

'Well, she was. She gave birth to a daughter – Justin's sister. Justin only found out about it a year ago when he decided to track down his mother. He discovered where she was living but he couldn't pluck up the courage to go to see her on his own. So he asked me to go with him.'

Paul remembered it vividly. Up to that time,

Justin had always claimed that his father was a widower, but one day he had taken Paul aside and told him, very uncomfortably, about his mother's desertion when he was only three years old. For years he had hated her because of this, but finally he had decided that he wanted to find out what sort of person she was. He had tracked her down to an address on the Isle of Dogs in East London, and Paul had been persuaded to accompany him on an unannounced visit.

Justin's mother had turned out to be a brassy blonde who had not been pleased to be re-acquainted with her long-lost son. But there was a teenage girl named Lucy living with her, whom Justin had soon established was the sister he had never known about. To Paul's surprise, Justin and Lucy had struck up an immediate rapport despite their mother's hostility. Afterwards he had sworn Paul to secrecy and he had never mentioned his sister again. But a strong attachment had evidently formed between the two of them, for the photograph which Kate had burned was of Lucy.

Paul saw that Kate had realized what he was leading up to even before he had finished. She looked surprised, but she was holding back any stronger emotions. He ploughed on to the end.

Kate stared out over the dark, moonlit ocean.

'I see,' she said, and all she could think of was that Justin had trusted Paul with the secret of his sister but not her. If she had wounded him, it was his own fault for not having taken her into his confidence. It was as much a betrayal as anything else, evidence that he had never been completely honest with her. And she was never going to forgive him for knocking her down.

Paul was waiting. She wondered if he was expecting some display of emotion – remorse or self-pity, well lubricated with tears. She was determined that there would be none.

# 14
# *Madrimar*

Dawn.

They rode silently along a shoreline of ochre sand, having descended the cliffs along the cleft of the stream. The grey breakers swirled up the beach, carrying all the salty smells of the ocean. Seagulls with pink and gold plumage soared and swooped over the water, their raucous cries uncannily like those of seagulls on Earth. The sun hung low on the horizon, spreading a rippled band of redness over the waves.

There was a strained atmosphere between them, a product of what had happened the night before. Kate had insisted on taking first watch, while the rest of them had bedded down some distance from each other. Justin had not spoken since his return to the campsite, and Paul had sensed a tension between Willie and Teresa, as though they had had an argument. None of them had slept well, Paul being kept awake by thoughts of Kate and her ambiguous response to his overtures. He was also wondering how Justin was taking her rejection of him – and his own attempt to take Justin's place.

Kate rode through the shallows amongst driftwood

and wrack-like seaweed. Since rising she had seemed more aloof and glacial than ever, and Paul had kept his distance. All five of them were riding apart from one another, Justin spurring his horse ahead, Willie lagging some distance behind, and Teresa favouring the reed-fringed dunes further up the coastline. As a group they were hardly in the best of fettle for riding into Avron Kromar's capital city.

Paul tried to summon Therion, but there was no response from the old man. He wanted to know exactly how they should approach the city and what they should be guarded against. They had no idea what sort of reception might be waiting for them. An army? Hordes of demons? The sorcerer himself astride a fiery chariot? During their last conversation Therion had hinted that they should simply try to sneak into the city as inconspicuously as possible. Paul only hoped that news of their exploits in Pholvenx and Sharalidor had not travelled ahead of them.

After an hour of riding they began to climb the hill beyond which they had seen the glow the previous night. A fresh sea-breeze had sprung up, and it seemed to be urging them on. Again Paul tried to summon Therion, but the old man remained in-communicado.

Justin was the first to reach the top of the hill, and silhouetted against the red sky he looked more than ever the warrior as he raised his hammer to them, as if to indicate that they had finally reached their goal. The others spurred their horses and joined him on the hilltop.

Below them, nestled in a wide bay, was Madrimar.

All of them had expected it to resemble Sharalidor, but it did not. It was clustered at the centre of the wide arc of shoreline, hugging the coast at one end and extending inland at the other to a range of foothills. It looked far more spacious and sprawling than Sharalidor, and its buildings were decorated in predominantly bright colours, giving it a festival-like appearance even from afar.

'Look,' Teresa whispered.

She was pointing out to sea. A mile or two beyond the shore, a dark building like a circular ziggurat rose up out of the waters. It was a squat, brooding structure, built on a rocky island which seemed crushed by its massiveness. It commanded the entire bay, and radiated an awesome air of menace, everything in its immediate vicinity seeming darker and more sinister than elsewhere.

'Dremund Castle,' said a voice.

It was Therion, and Paul was quick to inform the others of his coming. He felt a great sense of relief that the old man was with them once more.

'What should we do?' he asked.

'Do?' said Therion.

'What strategy should we adopt?'

'Ride on to Madrimar. What else?'


About half an hour later they reached the outskirts of the city. They approached it from the landward side, coming upon isolated buildings set in spacious gardens which were without exception overgrown. The houses themselves looked as if they had once been mansions for rich folk, and while they still appeared to be inhabited, an air of dilapidation hung over them. Paul wondered: were they about to encounter the same squalor and neglect that they had found in Sharalidor?

'Wait and see,' Therion told him briskly. 'I will tell you everything you need to know.'

They were riding along a pebbled track, and gradually the density of buildings began to increase. They were mostly squat, ornate structures, painted in bright pastels, with arched doorways and tiled roofs like umbrellas. Chimneys of all shapes and sizes sprouted from them, and in many of the courtyards Xhandarrean chickens or geese could be seen strutting around; the chickens had peacock-like plumage, while the geese were as yellow as custard.

Their arrival in the city was greeted with neither hostility nor acclaim; they were simply ignored. Draped in their oilskins with their weapons hidden, they rode slowly down the streets. People passed them by without giving them more than a glance, as if they were accustomed to travellers entering the city on horseback and saw nothing remarkable in them. There was about the average citizen nothing of the furtiveness and weary poverty which had marked practically everyone in Sharalidor; Madrimarans seemed, if not exactly blithe, then workmanlike, hurrying about their business without fuss or anxiety; and yet the sorcerer's citadel lay only a few miles across the bay. Paul was puzzled.

'If you live on the slopes of a volcano,' said Therion, 'you are content each day that it does not erupt.'

The streets were now fully urban, a clutter of tall, terraced houses interspersed with larger buildings decorated with domes and towers and spires. There were open-fronted shops selling food and household goods and clothing, barbers' stalls where men were being shaved at the side of the road, tinkers peddling bright scarves and leather belts, women dressed in skimpy clothing soliciting custom from attic windows several storeys above the street. Crowds milled about on either side of them, jabbering and laughing and arguing and bartering. It was like market-day in some joyous metropolis.

'Don't be fooled,' said Therion. 'They love Avron Kromar no more than anyone else.'

'There are no soldiers,' Paul said, having failed to spot any purple-robed figures.

'Why should the sorcerer need soldiers when the people live in his very backyard?'

Paul took the point. Evidently the citizens of Madrimar had decided that there was nothing for it but to get on with the ordinary business of their lives and forget about the terrible threat under which they constantly lived.

The streets were broader than in Sharalidor, many of them planted with flowering trees like green candy-floss which had been strewn with pale confetti. Carts and hansoms and rickshaws passed them on either side, and there was the occasional man or woman on horseback, somewhat more richly dressed than those on foot. Had an aristocracy or a rich merchant class been preserved even in the shadow of the sorcerer?

'Avron Kromar likes this city,' said Therion. 'He tries to do as little damage to it as possible.'

This sounded infinitely sinister in its very casualness. Did the sorcerer know that they had already arrived, and was he simply biding his time before he attacked?

'He is powerful but not omnipotent,' Therion told him. 'All you can do is to remain on your guard.'

They rode on, and presently Therion said, 'Turn left here.'

Paul conveyed this instruction to the others, and they rode down a broad but short street which gave out into a great cobbled plaza. Beyond was an imposing building of milky marble which resembled an ancient Greek temple. It was half-ruined, fragments of stone and rubble spilling down a broad flight of steps.

'King Qhoron's palace,' Therion told Paul. 'It was destroyed by Avron Kromar during his final offensive. The king himself was torn apart by the sorcerer's demon familiars. It's said that his entrails were spread from one end of the square to the other, then eaten by the city's dogs.'

The plaza itself now showed no signs of this climactic battle: stalls had been set up around its periphery, and people milled around them, buying and selling and bartering; the king's plaza had become a market square where commonplace goods were sold and the ordinary citizens of Madrimar gave vent to their entrepreneurial instincts. Barrows and drays were being hauled across the cobbles, and mules laboured under heavy loads of linen or grain. Only one part of the square remained free of the restless ebb and flow of commerce: near the foot of the broad stairway leading down from the palace was a strange-looking conical sculpture, to which all the Madrimarans gave a wide berth.

Paul and the others pushed their way through the crowd. As they drew close, they saw that it was no sculpture at all: it was an ornate stone pedestal supporting the figure of a young man encased in a transparent cone.

He wore a tunic of blue and white, with a long gold cloak hanging from his shoulders. There was an angry, defiant gesture on his handsome face, and yet he looked like a museum display sealed in glass, all his strength and determination abruptly frozen in. He was fair-haired, with a thin beard, and there was an undeniable nobility about him.

'King Qhoron's son,' Therion said. 'Prince Jarmassad.'

The pedestal supporting the glass cone was equally bizarre: it comprised a circular slab supported on the broad back of a stone man who was on his hands and knees, his head bowed, his thickly bearded face caught in an expression between anger and despair. His hair was long and bushy, and his body was draped in a loose-fitting robe.

'That is Meldorion,' Therion said. 'He was Qhoron's sorcerer, and for a while he succeeded in holding Avron Kromar at bay. But in the end the dark sorcerer defeated him and turned him to stone to provide the base for a living statue. Jarmassad had been taken alive during the final battle, and Avron Kromar wanted to make an example of him without turning him into a martyr. So he encased him in a crystal cone and put him on display here in the plaza to discourage any thoughts of rebellion.'

'You mean Jarmassad is still alive?' Paul asked.

'Indeed, though he will remain in a deep trance until the cone about him has been shattered.'

'Has anyone tried to free him?'

'I believe that several attempts have been made over the years. But the cone was forged with magic, and it is not easily disintegrated. Those who have tried and failed did not live long to tell the tale.'

Paul conveyed what Therion had told him to the others. The trapped prince seemed to be staring directly down at them. Suddenly Justin flung off his oilskin and leapt up on to the pedestal. Raising his hammer in both hands, he smashed it hard against the cone.

The resounding echo, like steel hitting unyielding ice, was sufficient to make every Madrimaran in the plaza stop what they were doing and turn to stare. Paul had been hoping to make an unobtrusive entry into the city, but now Justin had signalled their arrival in the most dramatic manner.

And the crystal cone still held, its flawless surface bearing not a mark of the hammer-blow. Justin swung again, the hammerhead glowing redder, and this time the crack of the impact was even louder than before. Still the cone did not yield. More furiously, Justin began to pummel it with blows, the hammer-head becoming a blur of red-hot metal. But the cone was adamantine, and it was as if the force of every blow was deflected outwards rather than inwards, the shattering sound reverberating across the plaza so that each time it seemed the prince's prison must break. But it did not, and in the end Justin slumped against its curving surface, defeated.

Everyone in the plaza was standing silent and still, waiting to see what would happen next. Paul knew that they could not back down now; they had to do everything in their power to try to free the prince.

Realizing that there was no further point in pretending to be ordinary travellers, they discarded their oilskins, baring themselves as warriors to the crowd. Willie stepped forward and plunged the sharp point of a dagger against the cone. It made no mark. He tried scraping it with the blade, tried twisting the point against its surface in the hope of boring into it. But the cone was as hard as diamond.

Kate raised both hands, and needles of ice raced from her fingertips at the cone. The ice shattered on impact with it, and again the cone was unscathed. Now Teresa struck her bracelets together and took to the air. She tried to penetrate the cone, but some mystic aura made it impervious even to her wraith-like form.

Paul was the last to try to crack it. He concentrated hard, staring intently at the cone, willing it to shatter. Nothing happened. He squeezed his eyes shut, conjuring up a vivid image of the cone bursting into fragments. The talisman pulsed on his chest and his brow was knit tight with the intensity of his mental effort. But the cone would not break, and finally Paul could sustain his mental pressure no longer. The stone stopped pulsing, and he opened his eyes. The prince was still trapped in his flawless prison.

They looked at one another while the crowd waited, silent and still expectant.

'The cone is likely to be weakest along its axis,' Therion told Paul. 'I would therefore suggest that you direct your efforts at its apex.'

Paul consulted with the others, and a plan was quickly agreed. Before the astonished eyes of the Madrimarans, Kate created a spiral staircase of ice which wound up and up until it towered directly over the tip of the cone. Then, taking great care, Paul and Willie began to mount the stairway. Kate had made the ice so cold that they had few problems in keeping their footing.

Reaching the top, Willie withdrew a stiletto, the sharpest and thinnest blade which he carried. The knife point would be aimed straight at the apex of the cone, and Paul would use all the power of the talisman to propel it with as much force as possible. If Willie's aim was true, the knife might penetrate the cone along its line of weakness, splitting it apart.

Willie took aim, relishing the opportunity to display his accuracy with the knife, aware that the eyes of everyone in the plaza were now on him.

'Ready?' he said to Paul.

Paul nodded, concentrating on the knife.

Willie threw. Immediately Paul put the whole power of his mind behind the flight of the knife, and he sensed some added sorcerous help from Therion. It was as if his entire consciousness was suddenly poured into the trajectory of the blade so that he saw the apex of the cone come flying towards him an instant before the knife bit deep into the crystal. There was a moment of resistance, then everything shattered.

Kate and Teresa, who stood watching, saw the knife flash down and heard the shattering sound. But the cone did not break like ordinary glass or crystal – it exploded outwards like a burst balloon, its fragments dissolving even as they sped through the air.

When the sound of the explosion had faded, no residue remained – no fragments of glass or rubble. The pedestal was intact, the crouched stone figure of Meldorion still supporting the slab. Jarmassad stayed motionless with his sword held high for long seconds. Then he stumbled forward and only barely stopped himself from falling over.

Paul and Willie were hurrying down the spiral stairway. Jarmassad was peering around him wonderingly, a man abruptly woken from his trance. There was a hushed moment, and then slowly, inexorably, a great cheering began to rise from the Madrimarans in the plaza before they surged forward to welcome back their prince.

# 15

# Consultations and Confrontations

'We must attack the sorcerer's citadel as soon as possible,' Jarmassad said.

'But how?' came the response from a short, dark-haired man. 'We have no fleet.'

'Perhaps we will not need one,' said the prince. 'Perhaps we can get there without boats.'

'But how?' the man persisted. 'We cannot walk on water.'

Jarmassad stared at him for a moment, then gave a deep sigh. 'It has been a long day, and I am tired. We can discuss strategies in the morning. I need to sleep.'

'What if the sorcerer attacks tonight?' asked another man.

Jarmassad gave a thin smile. 'Then we must defend ourselves the best we can. You will excuse me now.'

The men – there were eight of them in all – began to shuffle towards the door. Without exception they were elderly, with haggard faces, stoops and haunted eyes. When they were gone, Jarmassad turned to Paul and the others, who had been sitting in a corner silently watching the proceedings.

'What do you think of them?' he asked. And then, as if he had not really wanted a reply, he went on:

'They were all my father's advisers, though they are rather older than I remember them.'

He gave a humourless smile. Paul and the others said nothing; they did not know what to say. Jarmassad knew that he had been trapped inside the glass cone for twenty years and that the world he had known had changed irrevocably. He had accepted this fact with considerable courage, although Paul noticed that he continued to finger a large gold ring on his right hand. Earlier he had shown them that the ring contained a portrait of a young woman with blonde hair and an angelic face. He had told them that her name was Orial and that he had planned to marry her, before Avron Kromar launched his onslaught on Xhandarre. Now he had learned that after the sorcerer's victory she had been taken to Dremund Castle, where she was reputedly still held, a slave to Avron Kromar's passions. Paul reflected that this no doubt gave the prince added reason for wanting to attack the citadel as soon as possible. But Jarmassad must also have been aware that the woman he loved was now twenty years older, while he had not aged a day.

Jarmassad was young, and yet he looked capable of shouldering the great responsibilities which had been thrust upon him. He had a strong, forthright face and hazel eyes which commanded the attention. For half the day he had held audience to a stream of people who had come to welcome him back to the living and to pledge their allegiance to him in the attack on Dremund Castle. His abrupt liberation had galvanized the whole population of the city, and people were still chanting his name outside the large inn where he had been borne on the shoulders of his people, along with Paul and the others.

The inn faced the ruined palace on the far side of the plaza, and the landlord had swiftly provided the large room at its rear. Paul and the others had been hailed as heroes, and they had luxuriated in hot baths and filled their bellies with the best food the city had to offer, before being summoned by Jarmassad to answer questions about themselves.

From the outset Paul had decided that it would be better to tell the prince exactly what had happened to them. On hearing that they had come from another world, Jarmassad had shown remarkably little surprise.

'Meldorion often theorized that there were other worlds like ours lying on different planes,' he told them. 'I regret that he did not live to witness the truth of his speculations.'

Clearly the prince's familiarity with sorcery enabled him to accept that anything might be possible. Paul continued to speak frankly about their adventures, remaining silent only on one subject: he told the prince nothing about Therion and their link through his talisman. This was a precaution suggested by the old sorcerer himself; Therion feared that Avron Kromar might be watching and listening, and he had advised Paul to keep his existence secret. Paul had agreed, and he had also warned the others to keep silent; they would need every weapon in their armoury if they were going to triumph over the dark sorcerer.

Immeasurably grateful that they had freed him, Jarmassad was only too eager to have them with him in the vanguard of the assault on Dremund Castle. 'And when the sorcerer is dead,' he told them, 'if it proves impossible to return you to your own world, you will be richly rewarded here.' To this comment, both Willie and Justin showed considerable interest, a fact which left Paul feeling uneasy. Victory itself might present its own problems, should the attraction of great status on Xhandarre prove more powerful for any of them than returning home.

'When do you plan to attack the castle?' Paul asked.

'Tomorrow,' Jarmassad told him. 'As soon as I can muster a suitable force. We must hope that the sorcerer does not wrest the initiative from us before then.'

So far there had been no indication that Avron Kromar was aware of what had happened in Madrimar. Nothing had emerged from the dark citadel, even though the whole city was alive with rebellion. It was hard to believe that the all-powerful sorcerer did not know what was going on, and yet he had done nothing. It was almost as if he was waiting to be attacked.

There was a tap on the door, and the landlord entered with a large flask of the dark blue wine which was reputedly the finest in all Xhandarre. In the large public room beyond, everyone was still celebrating the return of the prince with much drunkenness and revelry.

'They will make a poor army if called up to fight in the morning,' the prince observed drily. 'But let them celebrate now, while they can.'

Jarmassad had no illusions about the task they faced, but he was hoping that they would be able to overwhelm Avron Kromar by sheer weight of numbers. Though he regretted his father's death, he spoke more fondly of Meldorion, whom he claimed had been the only person capable of neutralizing Avron Kromar's sorcery. He described Meldorion as a great bear of a man, with the gruff, cheerful mien of a farm labourer or forester rather than the student of the arcane.

'When Avron Kromar is dead,' Jarmassad said, 'I will have a new statue of Meldorion erected, with him standing upright and proud. And I will rebuild my father's palace and banish fear from Xhandarre.'

These were grandiose sentiments, and even Jarmassad seemed aware that they were more rhetoric than realistic possibilities. But the words were fitting to the occasion, and they all raised their glasses and drank a toast.

Then Jarmassad put down his glass and looked at each of them. Though he had told his advisers that he was tired, he looked quite alert, and Paul knew that he had dismissed them in order to talk further with the five of them. There was anticipation in his face, and his eyes reflected the glow of the candles around the hall as he leaned forward.

'Tell me about your Earth,' he said.


It was late before Paul, Kate and Teresa left the prince to go to the bedrooms which had been provided for each of them upstairs. Justin and Willie had slipped away earlier to join the revellers in the main room of the inn, while the prince had continued to listen with rapt attention as Paul and Kate and Teresa had done their best to describe what life was like on Earth and tried to explain such concepts as cars, computers, cosmetics and canned food. Jarmassad had listened like an innocent but intelligent young boy, his wonderment as profound as it was ungrudging. And whenever they had remarked on any

235

strangeness which they had encountered in Xhandarre, he would immediately retort that it was no stranger than tiny pellets which could be swallowed to banish a body's ills or huge metal wagons which could transport a person to the moon.

Eventually it was time to sleep; Jarmassad was to consult again with his advisers first thing in the morning, and all of them needed to get as much rest as possible, while they could. The inn was surrounded by a thick ring of men and women who had armed themselves with anything they could find from kitchen knives to pitchforks, determined to protect their prince should Avron Kromar launch an onslaught on the city. But even the mortal courage of thousands might not be proof against a sinister power that had subdued a whole world; every hour of respite was invaluable.

Teresa went to her room feeling a confusion of emotions, in which a sense of anticipation predominated. From the moment she had caught sight of Jarmassad, trapped in the crystal cone, she had thought how handsome he looked, and when he had been freed and brought back to life, she had found his eyes hypnotic and his whole manner so . . . so *princely* that she was entranced. She had relished every moment of the long evening which she had spent in his company, relished every glance and every word which he had addressed to her, felt self-conscious and tongue-tied when he asked her a direct question. By the end of the evening she had come to the inevitable conclusion that she was in love with him.

Closing the door to her room, she lay down and luxuriated in the feeling. *Jarmassad, Jarmassad*, people were still chanting outside, and it was like an invocation to the memory of his face as he had sat at

236

the table, drinking blue wine and listening as they told him of the wonders of Earth. Teresa knew that he had been in love with Orial, and perhaps was still in love with her memory; but Orial, if she was still alive, was no longer a young woman, and Teresa knew herself to be beautiful. She had done nothing overt to try to attract the prince's attention, but she thought that he had favoured her with more lingering glances than the rest of them. She could hardly wait until he saw her in all her glory, in flight. . .

Kate felt few emotions beyond a sense that events were moving inexorably towards the kind of climax to their journey which she had imagined from the outset. Paul accompanied her to the door of her room, but they did not speak; he seemed nervous, distracted. As she made to open her door, he put a hand on hers and said, 'Kate, can we talk for a moment.'

'Not now, Paul.'

'It won't take long.'

'I'm tired, Paul.' She took out the key which the landlord had given her.

'I just wanted to tell you that I meant what I said the other night. About how I feel towards you.'

She stared at him, and summoned a smile. 'I appreciate it. But all I want to do at the moment is get this over with.'

Then she turned the key in the lock and went inside, closing the door behind her without another word.

She locked the door, and after a moment heard Paul's footsteps recede along the corridor. She sat down on the bed, relieved that Paul hadn't lingered. If they survived this adventure, she was going to get away from everyone for a while, find somewhere isolated to escape from people's emotional demands on her. Turn herself into an island, wanting nothing from anyone and expecting nothing of them in return. What bliss that would be. . .

She lay back on the bed, drawing her frost-cloak around her. As ever, its coldness was comforting. In her old life she had always had difficulty sleeping on her own, trivial worries and apprehensions tending to press in on her during the small hours when she was alone and isolated. On Xhandarre she had welcomed her solitude, and found that she was able to banish all worries from her mind so that sleep would quickly claim her. This alone made her new identity a thing to be cherished.

She closed her eyes, and slept.

Paul entered his own room feeling that he had failed, finally and utterly, with Kate. It had been their last chance to talk, but she had withdrawn inside herself and it had been impossible to gauge what she was feeling. Tomorrow they might all be dead, and he would never know.

Outside the chant of *Jarmassad, Jarmassad* went on. Paul closed the shutters on his window, considerably reducing the noise. His room faced out on to the plaza, and the not quite familiar smells of trodden fruit and vegetables filled the room along with other, unidentifiable aromas. The smells of another world. Even now he had to keep reminding himself of that fact.

On the table beside his bed an oil-lamp shaped like an hour-glass provided a mellow light. He left it burning, and lay down on the bed hoping that sleep would come quickly. It did not. At length he heard voices in the corridor outside – the voices of men and women talking and laughing flirtatiously.

The men's voices sounded familiar. Opening his door he saw Justin and Willie coming down the corridor, each with a woman under his arm; they were also carrying flasks of wine. Seeing him, they halted outside his door; but there was no nod or gesture of recognition, merely a sneer from Willie.

'What are you looking at?' he murmured drunkenly. In his bleary eyes Paul saw only a dull resentment. Justin gave a grunt which seemed to indicate a similar lack of goodwill. One of the women giggled.

Both women were attractive, but in a blowzy, opportunistic way. Justin and Willie must have selected them from the revellers in the front room of the inn, and the women were clearly enjoying their attachment to two heroes of the moment and looked as drunk as them. Paul had a feeling that they would similarly welcome a general of Avron Kromar's army, should the sorcerer prove victorious.

'You got someone in there?' asked Willie.

'No,' said Paul.

But both Willie and Justin pushed past him to peer into the room.

'What's the matter?' said Willie. 'Couldn't you find any action? Or did Kate give you the cold shoulder?'

He gave a ribald laugh, though Justin glowered at the mention of Kate's name. Then all four of them sauntered off down the corridor.

Paul watched them go, then returned to his room, closing the door. Their laughter continued in the corridor, and he was sure that it was directed at him. A sense of foreboding filled him, and he twisted the key, locking himself in for the night.

\*

Some hours later, Paul awoke from a muddled and disturbing dream in which he was being chased across a bleak, dark landscape by a hulking figure of stone. He jerked upright in bed, unnerved and disorientated.

The oil-lamp was flickering beside his bed, making shadows shift on the walls. All was silent around him, but Paul was possessed with the conviction that there was someone else in the room. Then a figure seemed to materialize out of the shadows at the foot of his bed.

It was the yellow-clad dwarf, Quisp.

There was a twisted smile on his face which immediately made Paul want to harness the power of his talisman to defend himself. But even as he thought of it, he realized that the talisman was gone from his neck.

The dwarf's crooked smile broadened, and he raised his hand to reveal the talisman dangling from its chain; he had stolen it from Paul's neck while he slept. And now his eyes began to glow like red-hot coals.

# 16

## *The Road to the Shore*

Willie awoke with a pounding head and a dry mouth. He rolled over in the tousled bed, blinking at the harsh red light which filtered through his window. A woman's aroma filled the room, but there was no one beside him in the bed. It was morning, and he was alone.

He sat up, and his head began to pound even more violently. He could remember very little of what had happened the night before, beyond the fact that he and Justin had drunk their fill of wine and ale, then taken two willing women back to their rooms. But whatever passion he had spent on his bed was now lost to him, snatched away by an alcoholic oblivion.

It was painfully ironic. He knew that he had only taken the woman as a reaction to his disappointment at being rejected by Teresa, just as he knew that Justin had been similarly motivated after losing Kate. They both needed to prove themselves, to grasp some comfort and physical gratification from whatever women had been prepared to offer it them. And there had been plenty, for they were heroes and everyone was keen to enjoy their favours; they were plied with drinks, with conversation, with beguiling looks from the many women in the crowd. They had taken their pick of them, but all that remained now was the blurred and hazy aftermath. It was even possible that he had immediately lapsed into sleep the moment he had got the woman into bed.

Willie felt wretched; in the mirror beside the washbasin he saw that his eyes were red-rimmed and his tongue was coated. There was a pitcher of water next to the bed, and Willie lifted it to his lips and drank freely. Then he poured the rest of the water into a basin and splashed his face, before drying it on the rough towel which had been provided.

He was naked, his clothes lying scattered about the floor. But he saw that he had hung his whip and belt of daggers from the bedpost, and this pleased him: though drunk, he had made sure that his weapons were close at hand during the night.

He dressed, and began to feel more himself immediately he had buckled on his daggers and slipped his whip into his belt. He was a fighter once more, and the confusions of the night no longer seemed to matter.

Leaving his room, he crossed the corridor and opened Justin's door. Justin was still fast asleep on the bed, soft snores issuing from his mouth. He was naked, but the bedclothes were coiled about his waist and his arms were wrapped around his hammer as if he was embracing it. His woman had also left him.

Justin was dreaming of laughter when Willie shook him awake. The laughter was directed at himself, and he surged upright, grasping his hammer and wanting to strike out at something, anything.

'Easy. It's only me.'

Justin blinked, and registered Willie.

'How did it go?' Willie asked with a grin. 'Have a good time?'

Justin shook the grogginess from his head, and gave a grunt to indicate that he had been well satisfied. Willie's grin broadened.

'Me, too,' he said. 'I think I'm going to like being a hero.'

Justin reached for his clothes. There was a dull ache in the back of his head, but his hangover was less pronounced than Willie's and he remembered practically everything of what had happened during the night – much to his profound embarrassment. For, in fact, he had proved utterly unable to satisfy his urges with the woman, the combination of too much drink and quite a bit of nervousness making him impotent.

He turned away from Willie as he dressed, feeling his face grow hot with shame at the memory. The woman had purred and petted him and told him what a big, powerful man he was and how much she wanted him; but it had all been to no avail, and eventually he heard a note of disdain creep into her voice, as if she could not believe that someone who looked so masculine could prove so inept a lover. His prolonged embarrassment had finally flared into anger, and he had thrown her from the bed and told her to get out. Then, in a turmoil of frustration and rage, he had surprisingly succumbed to sleep.

Dressed, Justin hefted his hammer and stared out of the window. The plaza was still thronged with people, many of them now armed with makeshift weapons such as rakes and kitchen knives tied to long poles, others properly armed with bows and arrows, axes and swords. Morning was well advanced.

Justin felt ready for action himself. He wanted to

243

smash a few heads, to release all his frustration in battle. Willie had begun to wax lyrically about how good a lover his woman had been. Justin made for the door.

Downstairs they were greeted by the innkeeper, who led them to a small back room where Kate and Teresa were sitting over the remains of their breakfast, a kind of brown gruel, with fruits like pink avocados and fluffy bread the colour of granite. The innkeeper returned with platters of the same fare for Justin and Willie, but neither of them felt like eating anything.

'Coffee,' Willie said to the innkeeper. 'I don't suppose you have any coffee?'

The word sounded foreign, and the innkeeper shook his head with incomprehension. The absence of tea and coffee in Xhandarre had been a persistent complaint amongst all five of them ever since they began their journey. Xhandarre had its own equivalents, but they tended to taste of mud or treacle.

The innkeeper hovered, wanting to please his honoured guests.

'Forget it,' Willie said.

He and Justin sat down at the table opposite Kate and Teresa.

'You know what I miss?' Teresa said. 'Cream cakes. I'd give anything for a doughnut or a chocolate eclair.'

It was a lie: she didn't miss them at all, but had hoped to relieve the tension between her and Willie by referring back to her old self. Willie, however, did not react. Both he and Justin studied the food on their plates without enthusiasm. Xhandarrean forks were two-pronged affairs made of wood, with a sharpened edge for cutting; but Willie preferred to use one of his knives on anything tough.

At this point a door opened and Jarmassad entered. After greeting them, he said, 'Eat a good breakfast. At noon we ride on the sorcerer's citadel.'

Then he was gone as abruptly as he had come. Willie caught a glimpse of his various advisers clustered around a table in the room beyond, before the door closed. He also noticed the expression on Teresa's face as Jarmassad departed, and a wave of resentment washed over him. She fancies the prince, he thought, and felt only contempt. I'm not good enough for her, haven't got blue blood in my veins. She wants only the best, and what could be better than royalty itself?

'Have you seen Paul?' Kate asked.

Justin glowered at her but said nothing.

'Isn't he up yet?' Willie asked.

Kate shook her head.

It was then that Willie remembered his encounter with Paul in the corridor when he and Justin had been taking the women back to their rooms. He remembered, too, that he had spent much of the evening complaining about Paul to Justin, who seemed to share all his grievances. They were both suspicious of his supposed link with Therion and the way he kept trying to give them orders. They only had his word that he was in touch with the old man, and they weren't happy with the way he was running things. In particular they were no longer so sure that they wanted to hurry back to Earth if they managed to defeat Avron Kromar. Jarmassad would probably shower them with riches and honours, and they were determined to hang around to enjoy the fruits of their success. And if Paul insisted otherwise, they would have to do something about him.

Shortly afterwards Paul himself appeared. He looked as if he had slept heavily and was still not fully awake; he sat down at the table like a sleep-walker.

'We're marching on Dremund Castle at noon,' Teresa told him.

Paul looked up, blinking at her.

'The prince says we should all eat a hearty breakfast,' Teresa continued, eager to pass on his words.

'Like condemned men,' Paul said quietly.

The assembled army filled the plaza. It comprised a medley of Xhandarreans from the outlands as well as Madrimar. They were armed with sharpened poles, mallets, chisels, carving knives and anything else that could be made into a weapon; they ranged in age from young boys to white-haired women, all eager to fight; they were dressed in everything from rich robes to rags. And at the head of them, mounted on a silver-grey horse, was Jarmassad, dressed in his royal colours of blue, white and gold.

The colours of a summer sky, Teresa thought, as the prince marshalled his forces to begin the advance. She and the others would ride alongside him, with perhaps thirty other men mounted on horses – the remnant of King Qhoron's cavalry.

It was a raggle-taggle army, but its willingness to fight compensated for the deficiencies of its weapon-ry. The citizens of Madrimar had lived as best they could under the sway of the dark sorcerer, but now their prince had returned and they were ready to make one last bid for freedom. Jarmassad himself wore no obvious accoutrements of his royal status, but his presence was commanding. He had already vowed that he would only don his father's crown when Avron Kromar was dead.

Teresa and the others drew their horses up behind the prince as he turned to give a final word to his army.

'We march on the sorcerer's citadel,' he said. 'Let no one doubt the dangers we will face, but let no one lack for courage.' He swept his arm back to indicate the five of them. 'With us we have five warriors whose rare powers have already been displayed for you. They freed me from the crystal cone, and now they have joined us in our determination to destroy the tyranny of Avron Kromar and make Xhandarre a land of peace and freedom once more. With every effort, we can succeed. Onward!'

He wheeled his horse, turning it into the broad avenue which ran down the centre of the city to the shore. Teresa thought that the speech had been perfectly judged, neither too long nor overblown with bombast, and containing a reminder that the five of them were no ordinary warriors but had special powers like the sorcerer himself. It had been sufficient to fire the army's enthusiasm, and with a great roar of acclamation and defiance they surged after their prince.

Teresa felt immensely proud to be riding alongside him. Cheering crowds were clustered on either side of the avenue, throwing ribbons and flowers and lucky charms at them. They were crouched in the boughs of trees, or hanging from windows and rooftops and towers. Most looked either too old or infirm to fight, but they were sufficiently demonstrative in their goodwill as to whet the appetite for battle of every person in the prince's army.

Teresa glanced at the others as they rode along the tree-lined avenue. Willie and Justin both looked as if they were enjoying being at the forefront of the parade, and Kate was an imposing figure on her green horse. Only Paul looked somewhat detached from the proceedings, as if he was preoccupied with something else. Since rising he had been rather withdrawn, and she could sense a vague anxiety. But there was no opportunity to talk to him now.

They rode on down the crowded avenue until finally they came in sight of the coast. Madrimar was no great port, and the small harbour lay some distance to the north of the bay. Jarmassad led them to a promenade which gave out on to a beach of white sand. Beyond that, the waters of the bay stretched to the sorcerer's dark citadel.

Still Avron Kromar had made no move to prevent the rebellion; look-outs had been posted all around the bay, but they had reported nothing untoward: the castle remained dark, with no hint of any activity inside it. And yet no one believed that the sorcerer was not aware of their coming.

The swollen sun filled the dusky sky overhead, colouring the water of the bay so that it seemed as if Dremund Castle rose up out of an ocean of fire. The small Xhandarrean navy had been destroyed by Avron Kromar after the defeat of King Qhoron, and since then the sorcerer had permitted only merchant vessels to sail the waters of the bay. Perhaps thirty of these had been mustered in the shallows, along with a host of smaller boats and rafts. It was no armada, and many of the craft looked only marginally seaworthy. There was a contingency plan, by which Kate would attempt to freeze the waters of the bay so that they could make some sort of progress to the citadel on horsback and foot. But even with Paul's help, that would require a mental effort which they were not sure they could muster. And, as it turned out, there was to be no need for either boats or ice.

Paul had been trying to summon Therion ever since awakening, but the old man had not responded to his calls, and Paul's distracted mood stemmed partly from this. But as they reached the shores of the bay Paul finally sensed the old sorcerer stirring in his mind.

'Where have you been?' he said.

'Attending to my own business,' Therion said tartly, though in a whisper. 'Do you think I am a dog who will come running whenever you call? I was not needed until now, and it was better that I remain hidden.'

'I'm glad you're here,' Paul whispered back, though at the same time he was aware of a nagging feeling that he had something important to tell the old man but had forgotten what.

'Something is troubling you,' Therion said.

Paul did his best to recall what he wanted to say, but it was no use. Therion made him recount everything that had happened following Jarmassad's release from the crystal cone, he himself having departed from Paul's mind when they were carried in triumph from the plaza. Paul gave him a resumé of their various conversations with the prince, and he even mentioned his brief nocturnal encounter with Willie, Justin and their two women outside his door.

'What then?' Therion urged.

'Then I slept.' Suddenly it seemed to him that there was nothing he had to remember.

'And that's all?'

Paul could think of nothing else. 'That's all.'

'Perhaps you had a dream you've forgotten.'

Again Paul considered, but there were no dreams. 'I slept heavily,' he told Therion, 'and woke late. I think I'm concerned about Justin and Willie. I'm afraid of what they might do.'

Therion gave a sceptical snort. 'You're worried about *them* when you're about to face the dark sorcerer? Have I chosen to roost in the mind of an imbecile?'

Therion's familiar grumpiness brought Paul back to his senses.

'What do you want me to do?' he asked.

'Do nothing except fight as bravely as you can. I will be poised in your mind, awaiting my moment. Try not to summon me unless it is absolutely necessary. Perhaps then the sorcerer will not be aware of me until I strike.'

'What do you plan to do?'

'Do you think I am going to tell you that? It would be like writing it on a piece of parchment which the sorcerer could pick up at any time and read. Better that you do not know until it is done.'

Paul was about to speak further, but he heard someone cry, 'Look!'

Several hands were pointing to the east. Far out over the horizon, a great dark mass of cloud was rolling towards them. It poured rapidly across the sky, quickly blotting out the sun.

A few horses whinnied, and Jarmassad's army stood immobile, staring skywards in wonderment as the clouds enveloped the entire sky. They were slate-black, and where a twilight noon had prevailed only moments before, now the landscape was as dark as night.

Paul and the others, remembering the rain of fire, braced themselves for some attack from the heavens. But this did not happen. Instead another strange transformation began to take place.

The sea started to glow.

A pale light filtered up from the depths of the water, gradually building in strength until the waters took on a pearly hue. The faint breeze of the afternoon accentuated the effect, creating rippled shadows in the waves. And then, without warning or drama, the entire sea went flat.

It did so in the blink of an eye, so that what had been restless waters were now like the surface of a phosphorescent mirror – fluid instantly transformed into a solid surface like plate glass. The boats in the bay were immobilized as though frozen in shining ice. But Kate could not have wrought such perfection of the surface with her powers, such a levelness and clarity, such an awe-inspiring effect.

It was at once beautiful and frightening, manifest evidence of the effortless power which Avron Kromar could command. Every one of Jarmassad's army stared in silence, every one of them knowing that the surface could now support the weight of an army. The sorcerer had created the dramatic arena on which the battle would be fought.

Jarmassad spurred his silver horse forward, descending to the beach, then riding out on the shining surface. His horse's hoofs resounded on it as though it was marble. Justin rode after the prince, and the other four followed him. The rest of the prince's army hung back, still too awestruck to move. Then there came a distant, booming laugh from the citadel, and a horde of black shapes began to spew out of its lowermost tier. They made a chorus of obscene squeals and screeches as they came surging forward across the bright plain, rapaciously eager to engage the enemy.

# 17

# The Dark Army

Jarmassad raised his sword high, then drove his horse
forward across the bright plain. Paul and the others
rode after him. Behind them, the prince's army
hesitated for a second, then rushed forward *en masse*.

The dark creatures pouring out of Dremund Castle
were clearly the products of sorcery, and they had
obviously been designed to strike as much fear into
their opponents as possible. They looked like giant
spiders, huge millipedes, armour-plated lizards and
flying scorpions. It was said that, except for Orial,
Avron Kromar craved no human companionship in
his citadel, but surrounded himself with his four
demon familiars and countless other abominations
created through his sorcery; and these abominations
had now become the army which would fight for him.

Riding forward to confront them, Paul was aware
that the rest of Jarmassad's army was following close
behind. But some of their courage had already been
drained by the sheer sight of the dark army, and Paul
decided on a dramatic opening onslaught in the hope
of stiffening their resolve. In the vanguard of the dark
army was a small group of creatures resembling huge
black cockroaches; summoning all the power of his

talisman, Paul directed a burst of mental energy at them.

The entire group exploded in a mass of yellow-green gore. A great cheer erupted from the foot-soldiers, and they surged forward with greater purpose; the creatures might not be ordinary animals, but they could be killed like any living thing.

Battles are seldom ordered affairs, least of all for their participants; each soldier is soon engaged in the immediate cut and thrust of the fray, so that larger issues and higher principles quickly fade into the background as mortality is tested on the most basic and individual level. For each participant the battle contracts to a narrow sphere of attack and defence, so that a human being is never more alone than while facing such ruthless onslaughts on his life.

Fear frequently passes away under such circumstances to be replaced by the rawer, more furious instincts of survival. It is in the final minutes or seconds before combat is fully engaged that fear is paramount, when the enemy looms and his mettle has not yet been tested. And as Paul and the others rode across the plain to do battle with the dark army, they each experienced their own kind of fear. Paul's early attack on the creatures was a convenient means of translating his dread into forceful action. Kate, too, reacted similarly by sending out bursts of ice from both hands, in which several squealing beetle-like creatures were immediately encased. Willie felt a more profound terror at the sight of the creatures, for he knew that he would have to engage them in closer combat; had he been able to, he might have fled, but the tide of the attack was already carrying him irresistibly forward and there was nothing for it but to plunge headlong into the battle and defend himself with all the fierceness and skill which he could muster. Even Justin, though filled with battle-lust, experienced a tremor of dismay at the hideous sight of their foe; but as soon as Paul had destroyed the advance group of creatures he felt a complete resurgence of his bravado and was resolved to kill as many of the creatures as possible.

Teresa was the only one of them who quailed. Her delicate sensibility was repulsed not only by the sight of the creatures but also at the touch of their rudimentary consciousness, in which a raw instinct to destroy combined with a positive hatred for life, which she knew had been instilled into them by Avron Kromar. It overwhelmed her mind in a disgusting wave, and before she knew it she had struck her bracelets together and soared into the sky.

The instant she became immaterial, the creatures' minds were shut out of her own, and as she flew higher her panic and disgust gradually ebbed away. Far below she could see the two armies engaging on the bright battleground like two hordes of ants, and she told herself that if she had remained material her illusions would almost certainly have proved ineffectual against such a great and multifarious horde. But then she thought of Jarmassad battling in the middle of the host, and she knew she could not remain aloof from the conflict. Mustering all the resources of her courage, she swooped down towards the seething mass.


Warped creatures continued to pour out of Dremund Castle as quickly as they were killed. Both Paul and Kate possessed powers which could act on several foes at once, Paul exploding them with the raw power of his mind, Kate expelling clusters of ice spears which impaled creatures of every description. In death, they all exuded a bile-coloured ichor. Paul and Kate destroyed as many at a time as they were able, but they were limited by their own mental stamina and powers of concentration, and could not dispatch huge numbers of the creatures at once. Paul sensed Therion peering out through his eyes, but the old man continued to keep himself in reserve for the confrontation with Avron Kromar himself. But that was contingent on them destroying the sorcerer's army.

All five of them had now dismounted from their horses so that they would be less conspicuous targets for the flying creatures which swooped low over the battlefield. Justin was flailing with his hammer at every creature who came near him, mostly with devastating effect. A battle frenzy gripped him and his hammerhead glowed white-hot as he engaged the enemy, heedless of their claws and mandibles and talons. Willie, too, flashed with his whip, bringing flying creatures to ground and plunging his knives between their armour-plating. They squealed like frenzied pigs as they died.

Meanwhile Jarmassad, still astride his horse, flashed with his sword at bloated black wasps, which swooped at him, and scuttling locust-like creatures, which tried to pull him from his saddle. Teresa flitted close by, fighting down her repulsion and trying to distract the enemy by flying about their heads. And all around them the ordinary folk of Jarmassad's army, men, women and children, were defending themselves to the death with whatever weapons they possessed.

Avron Kromar's creatures were vicious and dangerous, but they were also stupid, reacting out of instinct rather than intelligence. They were killed by the score, but still they came. Jarmassad's army hacked and bludgeoned and stabbed and flailed until every fighter was coated with yellow-green gore and the shining battlefield was dimmed with a litter of bodies. Most of the corpses were Avron Kromar's creatures, but there were many dead humans as well.

Paul, Jarmassad and the others fought on, pushing towards Dremund Castle and gradually gaining ground until they were within striking distance of the citadel. Then there abruptly followed one of the still moments which sometimes occur at the heart of the battle, when immediate threats cease momentarily. As Paul stumbled around, free for the first time in over an hour from the need to defend himself, he suddenly saw a familiar face.

It was Maric, the young boy they had met in the farmlands. His youthful face broke into a smile when he saw Paul, and he came running forward. He was holding a mattock and was covered with livid gore like all the rest of them.

'I followed you to Madrimar,' he told Paul breathlessly, the light of battle in his eyes. 'I joined the prince's army, to fight for our freedom. I've already killed—'

Suddenly he slumped against Paul. At the same instant a dark creature like a praying mantis had come swooping out of the sky and plunged against his back. The creature squawked and hissed furiously, its leathery wings flapping as it tried to lift the boy into the air.

Aghast, Paul wrenched it free with his mind, then exploded it.

Kneeling beside the fallen boy, he saw that he had

acted too late: the creature's mandibles had torn into his back, and when Paul put his arms around him to lift him up, they were wet with blood. Maric opened his mouth to say something, but then both his mouth and his eyes closed forever as he slumped lifelessly in Paul's arms.

Paul had no time to mourn his passing, for already more creatures were advancing on him. With a scream of rage, he disintegrated them with his mind, the talisman pulsing furiously on his chest. Paul surged forward, immersing himself in the heart of the fighting once more. But he felt responsible for Maric's death; he had originally told the boy that they were warriors, thus encouraging a reckless bravery which had proved fatal.

Minutes later, Paul and Kate were engaged in a dual assault on a group of creatures like huge black lice; they continued scuttling forward, dying under a hail of ice spears and blasts of talismanic energy, until finally none remained. Paul and Kate braced themselves for a further attack from another quarter, but none was forthcoming. Suddenly they realized that everything had fallen silent on the battlefield, and that no more creatures were pouring out of the citadel.

They stared around them. Justin, Willie, Teresa and Jarmassad stood nearby, all looking relatively unscathed. The shining plain was covered with dark bodies, and only a third of Jarmassad's army was still standing. But all their foes were dead.

They had won; they had defeated the sorcerer's army.

Out of the dimness, their five horses cantered towards them, as though eager to carry their riders the final stretch of the way to the citadel. But as Paul and the others moved forward to reclaim them, they abruptly shimmered and twisted, before becoming huge white-eyed snakes which reared at them.

Paul reacted instantly, blasting the head of the cream-coloured serpent which had once been his mount. Justin was also quick to dispatch the dark blue snake with a tremendous blow of his hammer between its eyes. Kate hesitated momentarily before shearing the head off the green serpent with a thick blade of ice, while Willie leapt on to the neck of the tawny snake and plunged a long knife into the top of its head.

It was left to Jarmassad to kill the roan snake, Teresa being immobilized with shock. The prince darted forward and hacked off its snout below the eyes with a two-handed swipe of his sword.

The dead serpents bled yellow-green. They were the sorcerer's creatures, and it was as if Avron Kromar was telling them that the horses could have been turned against them at any time.

Once more there came laughter from the citadel.

It was the harsh, heedless laughter of someone who had just enjoyed an entertaining spectator sport and was entirely uncaring of the lives which had been spent in battle. It was the laughter of a schemer and manipulator, of someone wholly unconcerned that his forces had been defeated in battle. It filled the air, filled the ears of everyone who still lived.

Then Paul and the others felt the ground ripple beneath their feet, as though an earthquake was beginning. But it was not earthquake: in an instant, and without a sound, the solid surface on which they stood returned to water.

# 18

# *The Sorcerer's Citadel*

The sea was warm, and as salty as any on Earth. Paul's immediate thought on plunging into the water was how refreshing the sudden immersion was after the rigours of battle. It was an incongruous reaction, and one that swiftly vanished as he rose to the surface.

He peered about him, and saw that they were less than fifty yards from the rocky shore of Dremund Island, a distance he could manage to swim without too much difficulty. But what about the others?

Of Paul's four companions, only Kate was also able to swim. Teresa had managed to take flight, but Justin and Willie were both floundering in the water. Justin was in the greatest danger, for he was obstinately clinging to his hammer, and its weight was dragging him down. Luckily Kate had spotted him. Though hampered by her long cloak, she managed to swim down and grasp him by the shoulders before pulling him towards the surface. Justin did not resist her.

Willie was also continuing to clutch his whip, but his panicky attempts to swim were to no avail. He went under, water pouring into his mouth, then surfaced again, coughing and spluttering, convinced that he was going to die. Then suddenly he was lifted abruptly from the water and raised into the air.

It was Paul, supporting him with the power of the talisman. Then Kate stretched out a hand. A patch of water froze, before bobbing up as a flat ice floe on to which she clambered with Justin. Paul lowered Willie on to it, then began to swim towards Dremund Island.

He was the first to arrive on dry land. The dark rocks were covered with a slippery grey seaweed, but he managed to find a purchase and clamber ashore. Turning, he saw that Jarmassad was swimming towards him, his sword still held in his hand. Beyond, and all around the ice floe on which Kate, Justin and Willie were clustered, the sea was a flailing mass of bodies.

Paul propelled the ice floe towards the island with the power of his talisman. Teresa flew overhead and materialized as Jarmassad hauled himself from the water; she was quick to offer the prince a helping hand. The others clambered ashore from the ice floe, stepping on to the island, where a stillness and a gloom hung over everything like a portent.

Within ten minutes most of the survivors of Jarmassad's army had reached the rocks. Bedraggled and exhausted, they slumped amongst slimy boulders, coughing water from their lungs and not daring to look upwards.

The citadel loomed above them like the blackest and most daunting of castles. All of them were close to collapse after the long battle and their near-drowning, but Paul and the others knew that their severest test was yet to come. Avron Kromar had not deigned to appear with his host during the battle, but they had heard his laughter and they knew that he was inside the citadel, waiting for them.

It was Jarmassad himself who provided the lead. The prince looked as determined as ever to confront the sorcerer, and without warning he suddenly began clambering up the rocky incline, his sword at the ready. Hauling themselves up, Paul and the others went after him.

As they climbed, the air around them seemed to grow darker and more oppressive. None of Jarmassad's army were following them.

'Courage,' Therion whispered to Paul.

It was the first time he had spoken since the battle. Paul had no strength to respond; all his energies were focused on the climb.

The air continued to grow thicker and even more still. No one spoke, and the rasp of their breath was muffled. Then suddenly the curving obsidian wall of the citadel's lower tier was before them, mere yards away. As they stared, a dim red portal opened in it like a cat's eye.

'It's a trap,' Willie said. And even Justin looked hesitant.

'We must enter,' Therion urged Paul. 'There's no turning back now.'

But again it was Jarmassad who decided the matter for them by striding forward. The red light grew stronger and more orange as they advanced, so that it was as if they were approaching the open door of a welcoming house inside which they would find a blazing fire for their comfort: a dangerous illusion.

Without panic, Jarmassad strode straight through the portal. He was closely followed by Justin, Teresa, Kate and a reluctant Willie. Paul was the last to enter, and he was strongly reminded of their passage through the mirror in his uncle's cellar at the outset of their bizarre adventure. The threshold they were now crossing was sure to prove equally momentous, one way or another. At the same time he felt a recurrence of the conviction that he had something important to remember, something which remained obstinately out of reach of his memory. He wondered if Therion sensed this too, but the old sorcerer was coiled like a cat in his mind, focused outward and prepared to spring at the slightest sign of danger.

Paul stepped through the portal. It was like entering a great hall filled with a pale fire which did not burn. They could make out nothing except their own vague shapes, and they all drew close together, moving forward like blind people in the enveloping light.

It was very warm, and the sea-water began to evaporate from their bodies, shrouding them in steam. Time seemed halted in the heat and the light as they crept forward, waiting for the attack to begin. But nothing happened. Their clothing dried out, and salt crusted their faces. Suddenly a sinuous stairway loomed in front of them.

Slowly they began their climb, their weapons at the ready. The heat and light began to fade, and when they reached the second tier they could see clearly once more – see the warped geometries which confronted them.

They were standing in a long room whose walls and ceiling and floor were buckled. The walls sprouted tendrils and polyps, and there were mangled parodies of chairs, tables and the ordinary accoutrements of any household. Everything looked as if it had been made from black tar which had been warped and deformed under heat into unnatural shapes. As they stared, a smell began to permeate the air – the smell of rotting fish and animal dung, strong enough to revolt all of them.

Ahead was another twisting stairway. They climbed again, the miasma following them. It was as if Avron Kromar was still toying with them, trying to unnerve them with his travesties of human architecture and the stench of corrupt flesh. But the smells gradually faded as they climbed higher into the deepening gloom, and suddenly they emerged into an ordinary stone chamber lit by the pallid red sunlight which bled through a broad window. In front of the window stood a woman dressed in white.

'Orial!' Jarmassad said with a gasp of amazement.

The women smiled and beckoned to him. It was indeed Jarmassad's betrothed, dressed in a flowing gossamer gown. She looked radiant – and not a day older than her portrait of twenty years before.

The prince rushed forward and took her in his arms.

'Orial, Orial,' he murmured, covering her face with kisses. 'I can scarcely believe that you are alive.' He cupped her face in his hands. 'I will free you from this place, and when Avron Kromar is dead I will make you my queen.'

'*Your* queen?' she said disdainfully, and something flashed in her hand. Jarmassad slumped to his knees, still clinging to her waist with his hands.

'Why should I want to be your queen,' Orial told him, 'when I am already queen of another far more powerful than you?'

'The sorcerer,' Jarmassad gasped. A black dagger protruded from his side.

'I am no prisoner here,' Orial said. 'When Avron Kromar brought me to his citadel he offered me lasting youth and powers like his own in exchange for my unswerving devotion to him. It was a bargain I gladly accepted.'

Only now did Jarmassad seem to realize that she had not aged. Without a word, he pitched forward at her feet.

Orial laughed. The rest of them had been rooted by the tableau, but now they hurried forward. Orial gestured with her hand, and a wall of white fire flared up in front of them.

Everyone but Teresa recoiled instinctively. Teresa, seeing Jarmassad betrayed and brutally stabbed, surged through the flames in a frenzy of rage and conjured up a vision of an enormous putrefying monster looming over Orial. It was an illusion made more potent by her fury, and Orial staggered back in surprise. Teresa made her think that the floor was pitching under her feet. She teetered back, then went plunging through the open window. There was a scream, then an abrupt silence.

Teresa rushed to Jarmassad's side. She had been singed by the flames, but she thought only of the prince. She raised him up and his eyes flickered open. A profound relief filled her: he had been wounded, not killed.

Mocking laughter filled the chamber, as if Avron Kromar cared nothing that his mistress had been destroyed, as if it had been just another diversion for him. The laughter came from a narrow stone stairway which led upwards.

'I'll be all right,' Jarmassad told Teresa as the others moved to the foot of the stairway.

Teresa hesitated, still concerned for him.

'You must go with them,' Jarmassad said. 'They are your friends.'

For a moment she did not move. Then she hurried after them.

Paul and Justin were advancing abreast of one another up the stairs, Justin's hammer glowing a dull red, Paul's courage stiffened by the thought that Therion was with him. As they climbed, the stairway grew darker until they could see nothing ahead of them. Willie and Kate followed close behind, with Teresa coming after them. They trod slowly, lightly, on each step, making no sound apart from the hiss of air in their nostrils. In the ruddy glow of the hammerhead, Paul saw that Justin's muscular face was taut with apprehension. And suddenly Paul was aware that Therion was gone from his mind.

It was not simply that the old man was refusing to respond to his mental overtures and was lying hidden; he had left Paul, abandoned him. Paul scarcely had time to register this fact before the stairway gave out.

'Do come in,' said a familiar voice.

A blood-red light banished the darkness to reveal a circular hall of stone.

Sitting on a tall, twisted black throne was Therion.

'Welcome,' he said. 'I am pleased you were able to attend me.'

The throne was mounted on a black dais, and at the sorcerer's feet crawled the four cats who had been with him in his house in the mountains near the Glazed Plain. He was dressed just as they remembered him, in his frayed green robes. They had been duped. Far from being their ally, Therion was the very person they had to destroy.

No one felt the betrayal more profoundly than Paul, and yet he also felt that he had failed to heed some inner voice which had been trying to warn him of the old man's duplicity. The others were simply dumbfounded. But it was Kate who first recovered her composure.

'Your mistress is dead,' she announced.

Therion merely laughed. 'She was of no account. She thought she was a sorceress and that some day she could rival me. But she never tested her mettle in battle until today, and I took care to ensure that her powers were limited. It is no surprise that you overcame her easily. She was a pawn, nothing more.'

The cats had lined up around his feet and were staring at them with their egg-yolk eyes.

'It has been an entertaining game,' Therion said, 'but I think we need prolong it little further.'

He was holding his wooden staff in his hand, and he struck it hard on the dais. In an instant he was transformed from a doddering old man in threadbare green robes into a tall, lean figure of middle years in a voluminous purple robe so dark that it was almost black. His flowing hair and beard were pepper-and-salt, his face cadaverous, his greenish eyes bright. He was Avron Kromar, the dark sorcerer.

His staff had turned into a long black wand. He swept it over his four cats, and they were instantly transformed into man-sized creatures like gargoyles with black, leathery skin. His demon familiars.

Their eyes gleamed yellow as they crouched like predators, ready to spring at their human foes. Paul and the others spread out, giving themselves room. The stone hall was bare apart from the throne and a tall, black-rimmed mirror which stood behind it. All five of them were knotted up with fear, but they had no thought of fleeing or trying to bargain for their lives; they knew that they could do nothing but fight.

The demons leapt.

They transformed themselves as they bounded forward, each one choosing a specific target. Kate's demon erupted into flame, becoming a creature of fire. She immediately raised a wall of ice in front of her, but the demon began to melt through it, dissolving the wall as fast as Kate could re-form it. Willie flashed with his whip and unsheathed a knife, only to see his demon shimmer and become a crystal being on whom his blade scraped ineffectually. Justin swung his hammer at his opponent, but it liquefied under the blow, then re-formed itself into a fluid creature which poured over him. Teresa's demon became a huge spider which spurted sticky white filaments that ensnared her before she could strike her bracelets together.

Paul was left to contend with the sorcerer himself. Avron Kromar raised his black wand: blood-red lightning bolts burst from it and sped at Paul. Paul surrounded himself with a barrier of mental energy, the talisman pulsing on his chest. The sorcerer flourished his wand, redoubling the energy of the bolts and forcing Paul to strain harder to maintain the shield. There was a smile on Avron Kromar's pale lips. He had been with them all the time on their journey, watching them and toying with them, creating dangers whenever he wished. Again Paul felt that this was a realization which should have come to him earlier.

The lurid red bolts crackled and writhed about him, and Paul gradually found himself weakening under the onslaught. He saw that the others were also in trouble. Kate was succumbing to the unquenchable advance of the fire-demon, Willie was being battered by the crystal creature, Justin was enveloped by the water-being, and Teresa was hopelessly trapped in the white web of the spider-thing. They were all valiantly trying to defend themselves, but it was hopeless: the demons had taken on characteristics expressly designed to counter their particular abilities.

Paul realized that they were being defeated because they were fighting as individuals rather than an interlocking unit. They could overcome the demons if he led by example. If he put his life on the line.

Concentrating hard, he repelled the sorcerer's bolts with all his might, then immediately turned his attention to the fire-demon. Kate was cornered, and the demon was about to break through her ice-wall, when Paul lifted the creature with his mind and flung it so hard across the hall that it plunged straight through the wall, bursting into fiery fragments which plummeted down towards the sea.

Kate had the presence of mind to react immediately. Justin was closest to her, and she instantly froze the water-creature which was drowning him. Suddenly encased in ice, Justin gave a great wrench of his powerful muscles, and the creature shattered into pieces.

Justin spun round, hefting his hammer. Racing forwards, he kicked the crystal creature off Willie, then smashed his hammer down on it. A tracery of fine cracks clouded the creature's body. Justin brought the hammer down again, and it disintegrated into dust.

Willie surged forward and plunged a long knife into the spider's back. The creature began quivering, and its legs twitched. Willie plunged a second knife into it, and it slumped dead beneath him. Justin was already wrenching the white filaments from Teresa's body, and she was quickly freed.

But Paul himself had fallen. In lowering his guard to dispatch the fire-demon, he had been unable to resist a further onslaught from the dark sorcerer. The red bolts had enveloped his body like a powerful electric shock, and he had slumped to the floor, only barely conscious.

But as the others made to advance on the sorcerer, Avron Kromar suddenly lowered his wand in a gesture of truce.

'You have fought well,' the sorcerer said. 'You have proved yourselves better warriors than I had anticipated. I confess that I did not expect you to show such resilience and adaptability in battle. Perhaps you are now thinking that you can destroy me; but before you attempt to do so, pause and listen to what I have to say. I am sure you have many questions, so allow me a few moments to answer them.'

The sorcerer sat down on his black throne, his sudden polite and obliging manner making him no less sinister. Paul, too weak to stand, raised himself on his elbows.

'No doubt you are most eager to know why you were brought here,' Avron Kromar said. 'Well, it is simply explained. I will be as brief as possible.'

He drew his robes together and leaned forward, his manner that of a parent about to tell a group of young children a fascinating story.

'Much of what I told you as Therion was true,' he began. 'I did indeed discover a portal between this world and your own – a portal which was centered on the very room where you meet each week to play your games. While I could not cross physically to your world, I nevertheless found myself able to infiltrate my mind into the body of a gullible host, whose will I could usurp temporarily. I need hardly add that that host was Ivor Kinnersley.' Avron Kromar did not look at Paul. 'I came to him during his seances, pretending to be his dead wife so that he would allow me into his consciousness. It was then a simple matter to seize control of him.

'I was fascinated by what I saw through his eyes. Your Earth is an interesting place, so like yet unlike Xhandarre. I soon became eager to explore it with my four familiars. But alas, it transpired that in order to make a physical transition to Earth we would require host-bodies – human beings from that world whose forms we could inhabit. Naturally the five of you presented yourselves as the perfect candidates. It was an irony that while I could not cross to Earth myself, I discovered that it would be possible to lure humans from Earth to Xhandarre, fashioning them in any shape I wished. A useful irony, for it enabled me to contrive the plan by which you were brought here.'

He studied them, as if awaiting some response. But no one said anything.

'The figurines,' he continued, 'were, of course, designed to appeal to each of you. I had probed your minds and I knew what qualities and strengths you secretly admired. It was a simple matter to embody them in statues, which I carved while in control of Ivor Kinnersley's mind.'

Paul did not like the way the sorcerer seemed to be ignoring his presence. He had the feeling that Avron Kromar was working his way towards some sort of bargain or proposition, and that he had already been excluded from it.

'I made them heroes with special powers,' the sorcerer went on, 'because I knew they would appeal to you, and I contrived a quest because I knew you would readily undertake it. Needless to say, most of the dangers which you faced on your journey here were either created or contrived by me, but I took care to intervene whenever you were in serious danger of death or even imprisonment. It was important that you reached Madrimar, that you came here for our final confrontation.

'My purpose? Simply to wear you down physically and mentally so that when you were finally defeated your minds could be easily overwhelmed, thus enabling myself and my familiars to take possession of your bodies and return to Earth. Fit and rested, you might have been able to resist our attempts to usurp your minds. But after a long and perilous journey through a strange land, I could bring you to breaking-point.'

He settled back in his throne and regarded them almost wistfully. 'Such was my intention, but circumstances have changed. I did not anticipate that you would destroy my familiars, but it means that I now require only one body.' At last he glanced at Paul, before returning his gaze to the others. 'There is no need for the rest of you to die.'

Throughout all this, Paul had a vague feeling of *déjà vu*, as if much of the story had been presented to him before. But this was impossible. He felt like a whipped dog at Avron Kromar's feet, wanting to leap up and bite him, but too weak to move. There was a long silence.

'Why should we believe any of this?' Willie said. 'I think you're just playing for time. You didn't expect us to destroy your demons, and now you're trying to wriggle out of a tight spot. What's to stop us from putting paid to *you*?'

Justin gave a grunt of agreement, but before either of them could move, the sorcerer rose slowly from his throne. There was a vexed, condescending smile on his face.

'You do not seem to understand,' he said softly, 'that while your wills might be your own, in this realm you are warriors of my creation.'

He waved a hand at them, and suddenly they were in agony.

Justin's hammer had instantly increased its weight tenfold, dragging his arm to the stone floor. He was incapable of letting go, and all the strength in his body was flooding out of him and into the hammer-head. Kate's cape had wrapped itself around her like a strait-jacket, squeezing the breath from her, and Willie was being choked by his whip, which had coiled itself around his neck. Teresa's bracelets had slammed together like two magnets, forming mana-cles which radiated a burning heat. And Paul was being strangled by the chain of his talisman.

Avron Kromar watched impassively, allowing the torture to continue for perhaps a minute before he freed them with another wave of his hand. Kate and the others were on their knees by this time, while Paul was on the brink of unconsciousness once more. He knew that he had no hope of using the power of the talisman on its creator.

It was a display of power that was profound in its implications. All five of them realized that they had not merely been toys of the sorcerer ever since their arrival in Xhandarre but his puppets, whom he could have crushed the life from at any moment.

'Why?' Kate gasped in both anger and despair. 'Why was all this necessary? If our weapons and our powers could be turned against us at any moment, why didn't you just bring us here in the first place?'

Avron Kromar smiled again. 'It's true that it would have been a simpler matter altogether. I could have imprisoned you, tortured you until your minds were ripe for annihilation. But there would have been far less amusement in that.'

They stared at him uncomprehendingly.

'Can you understand what it must be like to be the absolute master of a world?' he asked. 'Can you really understand? To have no rivals or enemies of any substance, to have no one who can stand against me. I can reshape the world according to my whims, do anything I wish without the least fear of resistance. An attractive prospect, you might think. And so it is, for a time. But absolute power breeds its own tedium when it can only be wielded against insignificant opponents. So I decided to make you formidable enemies, to give you a sporting chance, while remaining secure in the knowledge of my inevitable victory.'

Again there was a silence. No one moved.

'And now I am offering you a reprieve,' the sorcerer told them. He gestured at the mirror behind the throne with his wand. The mirror began to shimmer and glow, and its surface went dark. There was a sense of space beyond it, of a world opening up.

Earth. It was the portal back to Earth.

'You can enable me to cross to your world,' Avron Kromar said, 'and I will allow you to stay here as warriors and heroes. You can tell the people of Xhandarre that you destroyed me, tell them whatever you wish. I am sure they will be profuse in their gratitude. You will retain all your powers here and live in luxury for the rest of your lives.'

He paused, studying them. 'It is a generous offer. I

could snuff out your lives, if I wished, with a wave of my hand. But imagine the alternative. You need only sacrifice one of your number—'

'No,' said Kate.

'Wait a minute,' said Willie. 'What happens if we refuse?'

'You die,' the sorcerer said simply.

He sat back and waited, while Paul continued to lie helpless on the floor.

The others did not look at him, and their thoughts were racing. None of them had any desire to sacrifice Paul's life, and there was no reason to suppose that the sorcerer could be trusted in his bargain. But what alternative were they being offered? If they did not accept, they would all die. And what would be the point of them all becoming martyrs?

Justin and Willie were both taken by the idea of remaining on Xhandarre as warriors and famous heroes. Justin wondered if the sorcerer could restore his powers of speech as part of the bargain, and it occurred to Willie that Avron Kromar might be persuaded to work a spell on Teresa so that she would be unable to resist his charms. Teresa herself was drawn by the thought of remaining beautiful, of being able to fly anywhere she wished. And if Jarmassad survived, she would have him, too.

Only Kate was more cautious. She knew that it would be foolish to enter into any bargain with the devious sorcerer; by doing so, they would not only be sacrificing Paul but also putting the whole of Earth in danger. Avron Kromar would clearly be bent on conquering it as he had done Xhandarre, and his prodigious magical powers might prove more than a match for all the paraphernalia of modern military technology. Yet in a pragmatic sense it was hard to see what else they could do.

Paul watched the play of emotions on his friends' faces, and he did not know how they would decide. He felt utterly abandoned, fearing that his friends would sacrifice him, while also wondering what he would have done in their position. Whatever happened, he was resigned to dying.

But at that moment the talisman began to throb. Paul felt something stirring within him as the stone pulsed more and more rapidly. Then a stream of yellow-coloured smoke started to pour from it, and suddenly his memory of what had happened the night before came flooding back.

# 19

## *An Adventitious Apparition*

The others were engrossed in their dilemma, while Avron Kromar looked like Mephistopheles urging them to sell their souls to him. Paul was now nothing more to him than the instrument of their damnation, and he did not immediately notice the smoke billowing from the pulsing stone. Paul felt the weight of his exhaustion evaporate as the smoke coalesced into the yellow-clad figure of the dwarf, Quisp.

Only then did Avron Kromar and the others realize what was happening. But no sooner had they registered the sight of the dwarf than his whole body flickered and transformed itself into that of a tall, thickset man dressed in tawny robes. His long hair and beard were a rich brown, and he radiated a great air of both physical and moral vitality.

'Meldorion!' said the startled Avron Kromar. 'It cannot be you!'

But Paul knew that it was; and he remembered everything.

When he had awoken during the night to find the dwarf standing at the foot of his bed with his talisman, he had immediately assumed evil intent. And when Quisp's eyes had started to glow, he was sure that he was doomed. But Paul had found himself being calmed rather than attacked by the fiery gaze, and he had heard Quisp say, 'I mean you no harm.'

There was something in his voice that made Paul want to believe him, and in any case he knew that he could do nothing to defend himself.

'You are a sorcerer,' he whispered.

The dwarf smiled, then dropped Paul's talisman into a chest beside the door, closing the lid firmly.

'Yes,' he said, 'I am a sorcerer. But more than that: I am Avron Kromar's mortal enemy.' He tapped the lid of the chest. 'It is important that we are not overheard.'

Paul waited while the dwarf sat down cross-legged on the chest. Then he confirmed that he was none other than King Qhoron's former sorcerer, Meldorion.

Paul sat in silence while the dwarf told him of how, during the final battle against Avron Kromar, he had gradually found himself being overwhelmed by the dark sorcerer's power. Knowing that all hope was lost, he had saved himself at the last moment by transferring his spirit into the body of a dwarf who had fallen in the gutter nearby during the battle for Madrimar. The dwarf was all but dead, and Meldorion had taken possession of his body scant seconds before his own physical form was turned to stone by Avron Kromar. Suspecting nothing, the dark sorcerer had bellowed with triumph, while Meldorion had slunk away from the plaza, knowing that he would have to hide away, to recoup his energies, to watch and wait until the time was ripe for him to strike back.

So he had become Quisp, travelling about Xhandarre and supporting himself by his wits or by taking whatever menial jobs were offered him. He never used his magical powers, told no one who he secretly was, and even guarded his thoughts against memories of his past life, aware that Avron Kromar had rapidly established an absolute dominion over Xhandarre and would be alert to the merest hint of sorcery. Eventually he had come to Pholvenx, where the inhabitants were preyed upon by a pack of wolf-people who roamed the mountains and attacked humans by night to feed off their internal organs. They were creations of the dark sorcerer himself, creatures who required no sleep and who by day became humans of normal intelligence and guile, hiding in the mountains and forests so that they could not be tracked down.

Everyone in the surrounding area was terrified of them, and out of desperation a grisly compromise was suggested in the hope of making both species' lives somewhat easier. It was the custom in Pholvenx to execute criminals by boiling them in vats of water, but now a body of opinion formed that they be offered up as sacrifices to the wolf-people in the hope of appeasing their appetites.

This idea was enthusiastically taken up, and it quickly proved more successful than anyone had hoped. Condemned criminals were taken up to a crag several miles from Pholvenx and tied to stakes before being left overnight. The creatures had an unerring instinct for humans, and they quickly found their victims. Soon the wolf-people came nightly to the crag to feed on their victims, and there was a corresponding reduction in attacks on people elsewhere.

The citizens of Pholvenx then resolved to try to formalize this arrangement so that attacks on innocent people could be eliminated entirely. The task of delivering the criminals to the crag had already fallen to Quisp, and now he was ordered to approach the wolf-people direct and offer them the opportunity of a permanent settlement on the crag in exchange for a regular supply of human meat.

Meldorion disapproved of this callous compromise from the outset, but as the dwarf he was aware that he was only accepted on sufferance by the insular Pholvenxans, and he knew that he had no choice but to do as they instructed if he wanted to remain in safe seclusion far away from Avron Kromar. So he duly waited one evening on the crag with his victims for the wolf-people to come.

It was a frightening moment, even for a sorcerer, as they emerged out of the darkness. But, though feral, they were still half-human at dusk when they came, and they allowed him to speak. To his surprise, they immediately accepted the proffered arrangement and he returned to Pholvenx to inform the townsfolk, abandoning the criminals to their fate. Thus the wolf-people gained a permanent home in the shape of a 'monastery' built on the crag. They were quick to acquire all the trappings of civilization, adopting the role of monks and nuns who cherished life and whose hospitality was impeccable by day. And Quisp the dwarf continued to function as the district executioner who delivered up criminals for their larder, many of them unsuspecting of their fate.

'It was a role under which I always chafed,' he told Paul, 'but I accepted it as a form of penance. The criminals would die horribly in any event, and at least this way many innocent lives would be saved. Many times I was sorely tempted to use my magic to eradicate the creatures, but I knew that if I did so

Avron Kromar would be alerted. I was still not strong enough to challenge the dark sorcerer and I knew that I had to preserve myself if there was to be any hope of freeing Xhandarre from his rule. Sometimes we are faced with choices not between good and evil, but between a lesser evil and a greater one. Avron Kromar himself could have scarcely contrived a more invidious existence for me, but I was determined to bear it and remain outwardly the brash and cheerful dwarf whom everyone knew.'

He displayed his lop-sided grin for Paul, but there was nothing of his old manner about him: he was a different man entirely.

'Then news of your exploits in Sharalidor reached us,' he went on. 'Pholvenx is a large town, and frequently visited by boatmen travelling downriver from the city who like to bring gossip with their provisions. They were all alive with the story of how five strangers with remarkable powers had dispatched the city guard and escaped through the north gate. They called you sorcerers who were surely bound for Madrimar to destroy Avron Kromar. I was intrigued, for to my knowledge no other sorcerer except for myself had survived Avron Kromar's accession to power. I knew that if you were bound for Madrimar you would pass through Pholvenx. So, at great personal risk, I kept myself alert for your coming, and when I sensed your approach I worked subtly to ensure that you would enter the inn in which I was performing so that I could inspect you. I even helped to contrive the fight so that you would be forced to display your powers. And when I saw that you were indeed possessed with special powers, I determined to take you to the monastery.'

He assured Paul that his intention had been for

them to destroy the wolf-creatures once and for all. He had said nothing to them about the true nature of the monks and nuns because he feared that they might continue on their way without accepting the challenge. He had even allowed them to eat the drugged food, confident that they could dispatch the creatures. He had sensed the presence of another sorcerer, working through Paul's talisman, whom he was convinced would not allow them to be killed.

'Another sorcerer?' Paul said guardedly. 'I don't know what you mean.'

'He calls himself Therion, but that is not his real name. And that is why I came here tonight while you were both asleep and slipped the talisman from your shoulders. I put it in the chest so that he would not be able to overhear us.'

There was no point in pretending. Paul said, 'He's promised to help us fight Avron Kromar.'

The dwarf gave a humourless smile.

'Therion *is* Avron Kromar,' he said.

While Paul sat there, dumbfounded, the dwarf told him that by judicious probing of their minds whenever he knew that Therion was not awake in Paul he had discovered how they had been brought to Xhandarre and had learned everything about their quest to date. In particular he knew of their encounter with the old man who lived alone with his four cats. He assured Paul that there had never been any sorcerer in all Xhandarre by the name of Therion, and that the old man and his cats were undoubtedly Avron Kromar and his demon familiars, who were guiding and manipulating them in practically every step of their journey. For what ultimate purpose, he could not say, but that was why he had come to Paul by night and revealed his true identity at considerable risk.

Paul stared at him, and for long moments there was a silence.

'How do I know,' he said, 'that this is not just another trick? How do I know that *you* are not Avron Kromar trying to deceive me? Why should I trust you?'

'I left your horses at the corral,' the dwarf retorted. 'Why would I do that if I was not confident that you would destroy the creatures?'

'Perhaps they were part of the arrangement you had with them,' Paul said; he was not going to be so easily convinced.

'All they wanted from me was human meat.'

'You didn't honour your promise to meet us at the foot of the crag the next morning and show us the best route east.'

'Ah, but I was there. I was the small brown creature you saw bounding away. It would hardly have gone well for me had I appeared as the dwarf.'

Paul considered. 'That may be true. But it hardly constitutes proof of your good intentions towards us.'

The dwarf shrugged. 'I could show you my true self – become Meldorion for you – but that would not constitute proof either. Where sorcery is concerned there are illusions within illusions, and what your eyes see and your ears hear cannot always be trusted. The only answer is to look within yourself for the truth. Consider my words and actions, and consider those of the man you call Therion. And if you consider carefully enough, the truth will make itself plain to you.'

But Paul was, in fact, already half-convinced. He had had his own vague doubts about Therion ever

...nce Sharalidor: somehow the whole episode of locating his lost friends and contriving their escape had been too convenient, and he realized that some unrecognized instinct of doubt had made him demur from summoning the old man again until they had been cornered by the wolf-creatures. His relief at Therion's intervention had suspended his doubt since then. Until now. It was true that the old man had saved his life on more than one occasion, and yet he had a convenient knack of being absent until the very last moment or of not giving them advice or information along the way which might have prevented them from getting into scrapes in the first place. On the contrary, they had seemed constantly to walk into danger, been forced to endure as many difficulties as possible. And yet the idea that the gruff old man could actually be the dark sorcerer himself, hiding at the very heart of them, was not one that Paul could could easily accept.

The dwarf was waiting.

'What do you propose?' Paul asked.

'While he is asleep,' the dwarf said, 'it would be possible for me to transfer myself into the stone of your talisman and hide there, unknown to him until the last moment. In that way I might be able to help you in your final confrontation.'

'Just as Therion himself has promised,' Paul said; he was still cautious.

'No doubt,' said the dwarf. 'But in order for me to remain hidden from his awareness it would be necessary for me to suppress your memory of this whole encounter once I have entered your talisman so that Avron Kromar could not discover the truth from your thoughts.'

'Wait a minute. You want me to let you into my

stone, then make me forget that I've done so?'

The dwarf nodded.

'That's asking a lot,' Paul said.

'I agree. But I can assure you that if you do not, the dark sorcerer will certainly destroy you.'

Again there was a silence as they stared at one another. Paul knew that this was perhaps the most important decision he would ever make in his life.

The dwarf stepped down off the chest and came to the foot of the bed.

'Well?' he said.

'I'll do as you say. Give me the talisman.'

'I think it would be wiser for you to fetch it yourself. I'll hide myself and wait until you're sure that the sorcerer is not awake. Then I'll be able to hide in your stone.'

'And then I'll forget everything about what happened tonight?'

'It's the only way,' came the reply, the dwarf's voice growing faint as he seemed to melt into the shadows. Paul peered into the gloom, thinking that perhaps he was hiding behind a curtain or an item of furniture. But it was as if he had truly disappeared.

Paul got out of bed and took the talisman from the chest. The pearly stone was as opaque as a blind eye. He hesitated, then draped the chain over his shoulders.

The stone nestled against his bare chest as if it had always belonged there. He listened, feeling as if he was doing the mental equivalent of putting his ear to a keyhole. There was nothing; Therion was absent.

'It's all right,' he said in a faint voice.

'Get into bed,' came the whispered reply, from a direction he could not identify.

Paul did so. Suddenly he saw a yellowish fog

drifting up from a corner of the room. It formed itself into a cone-shaped cloud, which sped towards him, sped towards the stone on his chest, pouring into it like a gas being sucked into a nozzle. Paul was entranced by the effect. Then all the mist was gone and a huge weariness overwhelmed him. He slumped back on his pillow, and slept.

Only now, with Meldorion materialized from his stone, did Paul remember all this. Clearly the plan had succeeded insofar as Avron Kromar had remained unsuspecting of his arch-foe's existence; the dark sorcerer was rigid with surprise. Meldorion raised both his hands, and golden forked lightning flashed from his fingertips.

The blasts were directed at Avron Kromar, but the dark sorcerer raised a web-like shield of deep crimson around him which the golden lightning could not penetrate.

The others backed away in sheer surprise at the attack, Paul stumbling to his feet and joining the rest of them. Avron Kromar stood astride his black throne, while Meldorion faced him at the base of the dais, his arms raised high above his head. Jagged bolts of mystic energy crackled around them, gold wrestling with red and filling the stone hall with an unearthly light.

At first it seemed as if Avron Kromar must succumb to the ferocity and suddenness of Meldorion's onslaught. But Avron Kromar was no ordinary sorcerer, and his defensive screen held. Both the sorcerers' faces were bulging with the strain of pouring forth their magical energies, and radiant under the interplay of light. Meldorion had the advantage of surprise, but Avron Kromar had defeated him once before and managed to resist his initial attack. Now the crimson tendrils of his power began to push out, forcing back the golden bolts of his opponent.

The initiative was passing to the dark sorcerer.

'We have to help!' Paul shouted to the others.

They stared at him, as if not knowing what they could do. But Paul sensed that he was still able to use the talisman; although it was the creation of Avron Kromar, the dark sorcerer was too distracted to control it. It could be turned against him, as could the weapons and the abilities of the others.

Racing forward, Paul hurled a bolt of mental energy against Avron Kromar's defences. The crimson web buckled, but held. He hurled another bolt, and saw Avron Kromar become aware of this new danger. But all the sorcerer's energies were taken up with staving off Meldorion's attack, and he could do nothing. Suddenly a battering ram of ice hit the shield, a hammer was being pounded against it, knives were being plunged into it as Kate and Justin and Willie joined the attack. Meanwhile Teresa was straining hard, concentrating on conjuring in the sorcerer's mind a vision of his shield disintegrating around him.

Surrounded, attacked on all sides, the sorcerer could do nothing except hold his defences for a few seconds, the determination on his gaunt face giving way to impotence and finally despair as the six-pronged attack overwhelmed him.

He screamed, then Meldorion's golden bolts punctured his blood-red web. There was an implosion of light and sound, which hurled the rest of them back.

Half-stunned, they lay on the stone floor, only gradually coming to their senses. Finally they were able to look up. Meldorion was on his hands and knees, his head raised. His beard and hair had been singed by the blast, but he looked otherwise unhurt. They saw that Avron Kromar's throne had melted into a black sludge, which was solidifying even as it drooled down the dais. But of the dark sorcerer himself no trace remained.

# 20
# *Departures*

'Meldorion!' cried a voice from the back of the hall. 'I can't believe it's you!'

It was Jarmassad. The prince had managed to stagger up the stairway and was leaning against the entrance to the hall. The wound in his side was bloody, but the flow had ceased. He supported himself on his sword.

Teresa was the first to rush to him. She helped him to stand upright while Meldorion climbed to his feet. Then all seven of them came together at the centre of the hall, embracing one another. There were cries of joy and profound relief. They could scarcely credit that they had survived. And triumphed.

While Meldorion and Jarmassad renewed their old acquaintance, Paul told the others what had happened the previous night and how the king's sorcerer had plotted to save them. Only when he had finished did they become aware that a mellow light was shining into the hall through the hole in the wall made by the fire-demon. Meldorion and Jarmassad were already standing in the breach, staring out.

Paul and the others hurried forward. The hole faced out over the bay, and they saw a summer evening at once familiar and startling.

sunlight. Golden sunlight. And an expanse of pure
blue sky. It was as if a bloody veil had fallen from the
sun, restoring vividness and colour to the landscape.
They stared in silence at the deep blue of the sea in the
bay, the mottled green and brown of the coastal hills,
the bright buildings of Madrimar and the dark dots of
people who crowded its shore. A pale crescent moon
hung in the sky to the north, no different from Earth's
moon as seen by day; and everywhere the land and
sea spread out before them in a richness and profusion
of colours which they had not seen in all their time in
Xhandarre. Avron Kromar had made the world a
twilight realm during his dominion, a place of gloom
and lurking shadows where his evil could flourish; but
with his passing it had been restored to its former
glory.

No one moved for a long time. Finally it was
Meldorion who stepped back into the hall. Reluctantly the others turned after him. Avron Kromar's
throne was now just a shapeless black mass, but
behind it the mirror was still shining, while through
and beyond it lay cavernous darkness.

The portal to Earth was still open.

'I do not know how long the doorway will hold,'
Meldorion told them in his rich voice. 'Perhaps I will
be able to master the opening and closing of it some
day, as Avron Kromar did, but for the moment it is
beyond my control. If you step through it now, you
will be returned to your own realm; but if you delay
you may forfeit the chance to return home.'

They stared at the shimmering doorway, at one
another, at Meldorion and Jarmassad. They were
victorious, the conquering heroes who had saved a
world – perhaps two worlds. And yet if they lingered
to enjoy the fruits of their triumph they might be

condemned to remain in what was, in the end, an alien realm.

Paul could feel the talisman still warm against his chest, still capable of translating his willed thoughts into mental energy. Somehow their powers had survived the sorcerer who had created them; and so, too, had the personality traits which they had acquired. If they stayed in Xhandarre they would remain warriors with unique abilities, and Jarmassad would reward them for their achievements. They would be celebrated, renowned – and no longer the people they had once been. Although they had finally turned the tables on the dark sorcerer, if they relinquished Earth they would have to live with the knowledge that they remained his creations to a considerable degree.

Yet to return home was to condemn themselves to forgetting heroism and adventure, to put behind them all the romance and mystique of a sorcerous realm. They would never be able to tell anyone their story and expect to be believed; they would be dragged back into a mundane existence, their lives becoming grey and ordinary once more. But how could they live a normal life again after all they had experienced here?

'You would be welcome to stay,' Jarmassad told them. 'The people of Xhandarre are eternally in your debt.'

'I would be intrigued to learn of your world,' Meldorion added, 'as I'm sure you would be eager to learn more of this one. But the choice must be yours.'

Paul studied the others. He had made his choice, but he still did not know what they would do. They all had good reasons for wanting to remain in Xhandarre, but the possibility that they might be shut off from Earth forever made their dilemma more acute.

At that moment the mirror began to flicker.

'The portal is fading,' Meldorion said. 'You must make your decision.'

Kate was the first to move. Without a word or a glance at anyone else, she walked forward and stepped through the mirror, into the darkness.

Paul hesitated for only a second, he too having decided that there was nothing for it but to return to Earth.

'Goodbye,' he said to Jarmassad and Meldorion, then offered his hand.

They stared at it, and Paul realized that hand-shaking was not a social gesture to them. He smiled awkwardly, embraced them both, then hurried after Kate.

Justin watched him as he stepped into the shining frame and was enveloped by the blackness beyond. The instant he had disappeared, Justin knew that he would have to go too. Giving a grunt of farewell, he strode forward, not daring to look back.

Willie, suddenly feeling that he was being abandoned, was quick to follow, eager to keep Justin in his sights. As the darkness closed around his friend, Willie plunged after him, afraid of being left behind.

Only Teresa lingered, not wishing to give up her beauty, her powers of flight, her prince. But with the departure of the others her place in Xhandarre seemed unreal, even her longing for Jarmassad a fairy-tale thing which couldn't possibly have the happy outcome she desired. Yet she knew that she would be making terrible sacrifices.

'I must go,' she said to Jarmassad.

He nodded slowly. 'Farewell, then.'

Teresa lingered. The prince smiled, then reached forward and kissed her on the forehead and both cheeks. She broke free, fled towards the mirror, towards darkness and the end of all romance.

# *Epilogue*

As she stepped through the mirror, feeling the dark air thicken around her, Kate was possessed with the urge to turn back. She quashed it, pressing forward, and suddenly stumbled out into the cellar.

The room looked just as it had done when they had left it, and Kate immediately knew that she was her old self again, even down to the colour of her hair. Her frost-cloak was gone, and in its place she was holding the figurine of her Xhandarrean character. She was wearing her yellow dress and all the make-up she had put on to meet Justin. It was as if she had returned to the starting point of their adventure in time as well as space; as if she had never really left the room.

Then Paul emerged through the mirror. He, too, was his old self again, dressed in Levis and a navy-blue shirt, his figurine grasped in his right hand. He blinked at her, but she looked away, feeling a blush of shame.

She hoped he would never ask her why she had decided to return to Earth. It was because of him – because of her guilt over him. When Avron Kromar had offered the rest of them a reprieve in exchange for

Paul's life, she had come to the conclusion that there was no option but to sacrifice him; only Meldorion's intervention had prevented her from making this expedient choice, and afterwards she had realized that she would have to return to Earth if she was not to risk losing all her humanity.

The mirror shimmered, and Justin stepped through. He had been compelled to follow them out of a jealous instinct: even at the last, he couldn't bear the thought of Kate escaping him, especially if she was accompanied by Paul. He, too, was his old self again, the muscle-bound barbarian gone, and replaced by the slender blond in the leather jacket; his iron hammer had become his figurine.

Justin was closely followed by Willie, who found himself once more the tall, hulking Willie of old; he instinctively stooped as he emerged through the mirror. He stared at the figurine in his hand and immediately began to wonder if the whole adventure had really happened. Then he thought of Teresa, and realized that he had left her behind in Xhandarre.

But Teresa stepped out of the mirror only seconds later. She stepped out as the squat, plump Teresa in her khaki shirt and denim dungarees.

Behind her the mirror flickered a final time, then went silver. The cellar was plunged into darkness. Paul opened the door and turned on the stairway light. Teresa did not dare look at herself in the mirror: she knew only too well that she was her old self again. But the figurine which she held was a graphic reminder of what she had been; she immediately slipped it into one of her deep hip pockets.

No one moved or spoke. They stared at one another as if they were strangers.

Then Paul saw his uncle lying on the floor. He put

his figurine down on the table and crouched beside him, thinking that he would surely be dead. But his body was warm, and he seemed to be breathing normally. Immmediately Kate was kneeling beside him, checking his pulse and putting a hand to his forehead.

After a moment she announced: 'He'll be all right. I think it's just a faint. But we ought to get him to bed.'

Paul looked at her, still not quite able to absorb the fact that she was her old self again. He nodded.

At this point Ivor Kinnersley's eyes fluttered open. 'What happened?' he murmured groggily, staring around him. 'What am I doing here?'

'You fainted,' Paul said. 'It's all right. We're going to get you to bed.'

His eyes closed again. Without prompting, Justin and Willie came forward to lend a hand. Justin had slipped his figurine inside his leather jacket, while Willie's had gone into one of the deep pockets of his coat. Neither of them looked Paul in the eye.

Paul took his uncle's shoulders. He was unconscious once more, but they carried him up the stairs from the cellar without difficulty. Late evening sunlight shone through the shop window, and people were passing by on the street outside. Laboriously they climbed the second flight of stairs, Willie stumbling once as they reached the landing but managing to right himself. Kate opened the door to the bedroom, a cluttered place of old furniture and musty smells. Teresa pulled back the bedclothes, and Paul put his uncle's head down on the pillow. When he was covered, Kate checked his pulse once more before assuring Paul that he would be fine if left to sleep. Paul wondered if he would remember what had happened in the cellar. Somehow he doubted it.

On the bedside table was a digital clock, incongruous in its modernity amongst the antique furniture of the room. Its red numerals indicated the date as well as the time. It told them that they had been away no more than an hour.

'I don't understand,' Paul said, and had it not been for the figurines he might have been inclined to believe that he had experienced a particularly vivid hallucination. But despite the fact that none of them seemed to be suffering from exhaustion after their climatic battle in Xhandarre, he knew they had spent twelve days there.

'It happened,' Teresa said: her voice was gruff again. 'I know it happened.'

Paul nodded vaguely. But if Xhandarre was a counterpart of Earth, the time-scales should be equivalent. Then he remembered that they had left Earth during evening but had arrived in Xhandarre at night. Was it so remarkable that a sorcerer who could alter the appearance of a sun and a moon could also manipulate time?

'It's a mystery,' he said. 'But we've just got to accept it. At least it means we won't have to account for a lengthy absence.'

His uncle began to snore peacefully. Again they looked at one another.

It was a moment for reaffirming what they had been through together, a moment for telling themselves that what had happened was almost too incredible, and that they wouldn't have believed it if they hadn't all been in it together. It was a moment for nervous, relieved laughter, for hugs and back-slaps, for congratulating themselves that they had actually survived an amazing adventure, had not only survived but come out of it as heroes whose names would always be remembered in the world they had just left.

And yet none of this happened. Everyone one of them was conscious that things had changed profoundly and irrevocably between them. Their old relationships were a thing of the past. In Xhandarre they had become the characters of their most secret desires, but they had not always behaved honourably or honestly or humanely or bravely. Far from encouraging a greater intimacy between them, their adventure had left all of them feeling to varying degrees as if their dirty linen had been revealed, their personal privacy violated so that the others knew far more about their innermost cravings than they would ever have wished. It was as if they had been caught red-handed in a crime.

Only Paul was filled with more positive emotions. He stared at his uncle, and thought of Brian. For the first time his memory of his cousin was not accompanied by the terrible guilt which had warped his life for so long. He did not believe in the idea of courage as something that was permanently embodied in an individual, but he knew that there had been moments during their adventure in Xhandarre when he had displayed both courage and resolution. He still accepted that by hesitating he had allowed Brian to drown, but he had in the end attempted to save him at great personal risk, and he could not let a moment of cowardice mark his whole life.

Teresa, meanwhile, was preoccupied with more physical considerations. She had inadvertently glimpsed herself in the spotted mirror of the dressing-table, and at the sight of her plain, freckled face and dumpy body she had felt crushed. In Xhandarre she had been beautiful, but it was all gone, all gone. She thought of Jarmassad, of herself in delirious flight, and she wanted to weep. A gritty part of herself was telling her that she would get over it in time, get used to being her plain old self again; but for now she just had to get away from the others. Without a word she turned and fled, tears brimming in her eyes as she hurried down the stairs.

The others, all wrestling with their own problems of identity, made no attempt to stop her; but Willie was consumed with shame. Seeing her as her old self, he felt as if he had tried to exploit her in Xhandarre, felt that he had exhibited a general disregard for the finer feelings of the others. He knew that they would never see him again as a gentle giant after the character he had become in Xhandarre, a character of very questionable virtue. Now he was the big lummox once more, and he just wanted to crawl away and lick his wounds. He realized that his mother would be waiting for him when he returned, waiting with her incessant demands for cups of tea, aspirins and all the rest of it. He despaired at the prospect. But there was nowhere else to go. He determined that he was going to be firmer with her and more independent from now on.

He waited until he was sure that Teresa was gone before saying, 'I'd better be on my way, too.'

He sounded, and felt, awkward. The others said nothing. He turned and shambled out of the room, wanting to kick something, anything, as he stumbled down the stairs.

Justin studied the other two. He had not spoken since their return but had been waiting, biding his time. Seeing both Kate and Paul as their old selves again gave him added confidence. He regretted the loss of his warrior's impressive physique and the hammer, which had almost become an extra limb to him; but that only made him more determined to compensate for it.

'It's time we were going as well,' he said to Kate.

Kate stared at him, apprehension beginning to fill her. Justin was giving her his best, most casual and confident smile. She forced herself to remain calm, forced herself to shake her head.

'I meant what I said,' she told him.

'What's the matter?' said Justin. 'Didn't Paul tell you that the photograph was of my sister?'

He evidently thought that that was the only reason she had turned against him.

'Yes,' she said. 'But that doesn't alter the way I feel.'

His gaze became hard. 'What the hell is that supposed to mean?'

She could feel herself becoming agitated, but she was determined to hang on to something of the aplomb of her Xhandarrean character.

'Things have changed,' she said. 'I'm not the person I was.'

'Listen,' he said, 'in a few days the whole thing'll seem like a dream.'

She said nothing, even though she had an urge to accept the olive branch he was offering her, if only to avoid an argument. But she knew that it would be foolish to return to her old relationship with him, to become the dependent young woman once more. In Xhandarre she had been too aloof, but she needed to cultivate a degree of emotional toughness to prevent people like Justin from exploiting her.

'This is the last time I'm asking you, Kate,' he said. 'Are you coming, or not?'

'I'm leaving in my own good time. Not when you say so.'

Justin stared at her for long seconds without speaking, and anger began to burn inside him. But he managed to translate it into contempt: contempt for both Kate and Paul.

'You can have her,' he said to Paul. 'I don't think she's worth the trouble any more. To hell with the lot of you!'

Then he stormed off down the stairs. His rage was something he could almost relish; it had been his source of strength in Xhandarre and there was no reason why it couldn't be on Earth. Even as he slammed the shop door behind him he was determined to forget Kate, to find fresh challenges, fresh conquests. He had been a warrior in Xhandarre and he was going to continue to be a warrior of a different sort here, letting no one get the better of him.

Upstairs Kate said, 'I don't think he's learned anything.'

'Maybe,' Paul replied. 'Though maybe the lessons will just take a while to filter through. You know what Justin's like.'

'Do I? After all we've been through, can we take anything for granted?'

Paul stared at her, and his longing was as acute as ever.

'How about a cup of tea?' he said.

She smiled. 'The British answer to everything. A nice strong cup of tea.'

They went into the kitchen, and Paul put the kettle on the gas ring. It was an old, battered whistler, which his uncle refused to throw out.

Kate watched him as he spooned tea into the pot. He had certainly changed, but she could not sort out

301

her feelings towards him; she still felt guilty that she had been prepared to sacrifice him in the sorcerer's citadel.

'Paul,' she said suddenly. 'I have to go. Now.'

He looked at her, and she expected him to protest. But he simply nodded.

They went down the stairs together, and he opened the door for her. She lingered.

'Will I see you again?' he asked.

'Of course. Next week at least.'

He shook his head. 'I don't think there are going to be any more of our gatherings here. I think all that's finished.'

She looked thoughtful. 'We should be feeling victorious. But there's just this incredible sense of anticlimax.'

'It's inevitable,' he said. 'We haven't got any evil sorcerers to fight here. Everything's greyer, more ambiguous. It always is when the heroics are over. Can I see you in a few days, Kate?'

She was staring up the street. People walked past, dressed up for a Friday night out in the West End. She felt like a visitor from another planet.

'All right,' she said, looking at him. 'But Paul – don't expect too much of me.'

'I don't expect anything. I only hope.'

She smiled, then reached up and kissed him on the corner of the mouth before hurrying away.

Paul watched her until she was suddenly hidden by a knot of people who emerged from a pub. It was as if the real world had absorbed her once more. He went inside and closed the door behind him.

All around him on the shelves there were brightly coloured boxes showing goblins and ghouls, warriors and warlocks, beasts and barbarians. There were vampires, aliens, trolls, starship captains – a gamut of larger-than-life characters, the products of human imagination. To him they looked as flat and two-dimensional as they were; he had lived through the real thing, and the paradox was that for the time being at least it gave him a greater appreciation of everything that was ordinary and quotidian in the world he knew. They were heroes no longer, but there were other challenges to be faced in their real lives; more subtle, less dramatic challenges perhaps, decisions on which a single friendship rather than the fate of a world might depend. But that was only as it should be: everyone had to come down to Earth in the end.

He thought of Kate again. At that moment the kettle started to whistle. With a lightness in his stride, he bounded up the stairs to switch it off.

## Bestselling science fiction from Arrow

All these books are available from your bookshop or newsagent or you can order them direct. Just tick the titles you want and complete the form below.

| | | | |
|---|---|---|---|
| ☐ | THE JAGGED ORBIT | John Brunner | £1.25 |
| ☐ | 2001: A SPACE ODYSSEY | Arthur C. Clarke | £1.75 |
| ☐ | VULCAN'S HAMMER | Philip K. Dick | £1.25 |
| ☐ | IN OUR HANDS THE STARS | Harry Harrison | £1.50 |
| ☐ | ELRIC OF MELNIBONE | Michael Moorcock | £1.50 |
| ☐ | THE QUILLIAN SECTOR | E. C. Tubb | £1.25 |
| ☐ | THE SHADOW OF THE TORTURER | Gene Wolfe | £1.95 |
| ☐ | GOLDEN WITCHBREED | Marx Gentle | £2.25 |
| ☐ | SHARRA'S EXILE | Marion Zimmer Bradley | £1.95 |

Postage _____

Total _____

ARROW BOOKS, BOOKSERVICE BY POST, PO BOX 29, DOUGLAS, ISLE OF MAN, BRITISH ISLES

Please enclose a cheque or postal order made out to Arrow Books Limited for the amount due including 15p per book for postage and packing for orders both within the UK and overseas orders.

*Please print clearly*

NAME .................................................

ADDRESS .................................................

.................................................

Whilst every effort is made to keep prices down and to keep popular books in print, Arrow Books cannot guarantee that prices will be the same as those advertised here or that the books will be available.